THE MURDER OF TOBIAS WHEAT

by Michael A. Durney

ISBN: 9798379339241

Also by Michael A. Durney

Clifford Wendell, Daydreamer Extraordinaire

The Red Canoe

Pearls for an Infidel

The Adventures of Mary Winston

Crimes of a Secret Nature (Coming Soon)

Dedication

Thank you to my wife, my favorite proof reader. I will be glad when my dear readers have had their turn. A bottle of wine that I have saved for the occasion called TOBIAS awaits your good reviews.

Acknowledgment

"Execution is the Chariot of Genius" by William Blake

Table of Contents

CHAPTER 1

Chaff Lundergan's Story

Chicago. Chi-Town. The Windy City. Whatever you call it, it's big. Plenty of room for suits and dresses, bankers and salesmen, politicians and teachers, good neighborhoods and forgotten ones, good people—and thieves and murderers.

On Jimmy Scariff's sixteenth birthday, the kiddy gang—young miscreants living and thieving in the dark niches of the Southside—brought him a bag of watches, wallets, and necklaces. Blake Elliston told him it was a week's worth of snatches that he didn't have to split with nobody. Chaff Lundergan pushed Blake out of the way and said, "Most of it was from me. We've been doing extra pockets uptown."

"It don't matter who snatched it," Jimmy said through throaty damaged cords from numerous street fights, knife attacks, and cigarettes. He opened the bag and jutted his head out in disbelief. "It's a meaningful bag, that's for sure. We's brothers, equals, and as brothers, we're gonna celebrate together." He held the bag up above his head and smiled gleamlessly through dull-yellow teeth. "Let's fence this shit and party, brothers."

The gang was pleased that Jimmy was going to share the take. It was true leadership, which the others gave him not because he was older, but because he displayed the loyalty of a brother.

Like so many others captured by the undertow of poverty and dereliction, malevolent currents ripped them from nurturing hands and sent them out to sea. Disoriented survivors swam back to filthy shores and filthy habits. Jimmy Scariff, Blake Elliston, and Chaff Lundergan were among those that survived, bonding like a flock of hungry gulls.

Chaff Lundergan was the youngest, at twelve, and looked up to Jimmy as though he were a surrogate parent: dependable, caring, and always available. Nothing like the home life he had experienced till now. His father was in jail for a flawed bank robbery, his mother whoring for food and money. Chaff became a liability and an intrusion in his mother's self-preservation. He and his mother lived like a mischief of rats shoving at each other for life-sustaining morsels. Where food didn't exist, he found it on the street. Where love was nonexistent, the street provided.

The three of them, Jimmy, Blake, and Chaff, were the kiddy gang. Band of brothers.

It was a name given to them by Johnny Willow, a man of dubious intentions and notorious intellect for exotic criminal schemes. No one but Jimmy ever saw him or spoke to him. When he needed a diversion for one of his jobs, he would contact Jimmy, promising a small take, but there was always a catch, always a payoff tomorrow. Johnny's charisma held sway over Jimmy for months, but eventually, it got old. The next time Johnny demanded the help of the kiddy gang, Jimmy had his own ideas for payment.

Moral codes at street level are very shallow, the depth proportional to those you answered to. Willow had his code and Jimmy had his. Johnny Willow would do anything to enrich himself, forsaking any and all that got in his way. Jimmy fed his family and kept them safe. The spoils of the street were to be brought back to the nest and shared with the baby chicks.

The day came. Another request for diversion. The kiddy gang was to ride their bikes and skateboards through a crowd outside the Sears Tower at a precise moment. Exaggerate the scene, drawing all eyes to the center, steal an aluminum Halliburton case filled with something valuable in mid-handoff, and rendezvous at Lincoln Park four miles away. It was a simple plan. Jimmy didn't care what was in the silver case. He just wanted this time to be different—object for payment.

But after Johnny Willow requested Scariff's help, Jimmy overheard a conversation Willow was having with a man he had not seen before. Good fortune or bad, destiny would decide, but at that moment, it changed Jimmy Scariff's plans dramatically.

"The Africans have been using us for months to wash their little gems. We're taking all the risk, and they're getting rich. It's time we took our cut," the man said.

"We get a cut after every job. They're not the kind of people you double-cross," Willow said. "Besides, you don't have to do any of the dirty work sitting behind that detective's desk sucking up accommodations. We screw up and Tejan Cole comes after us. He'll come after you as well."

"I do plenty, asshole. Your operation—their operation—would have come crashing down if it wasn't for me." The man's anger creviced inside contorted cheeks. There was no mistaking his threatening tone. "It's not nice to be so unappreciative, Johnny." The man closed the proximity between them to an uncomfortable distance, breathing each other's air. Then he put his arm around Johnny's shoulders, forced a menacing smile, and walked slowly down the alley where they had been meeting.

"I'm not saying we double-cross them. Let your little leash rats steal it. They take the blame. We find the jewels, kill the rats, and the Africans take the loss while we come out heroes and rich. Don't forget being rich."

"And if Tejan sees through your plan?"

"Willow, I've never seen you this timid about stealing anything from anyone. What's got you spooked?"

"They're kids! You're not dealing with world-class thieves. Too much can go wrong."

"Don't you get it? That's the beauty of it. If your kids screw this up, it's all on them, not us. We bury them either way."

Jimmy was not religious, never set a foot inside a church; but he had to look up into the night and wonder if some god was protecting him.

The next day, he accepted Willow's offer; he even showed enthusiasm for the genius of the idea. Although he did not know what he was about to steal, he planned his strategy with deft skill. He did not share what he knew with Blake or Chaff. Scaring them about Willow's plan to have them killed would interfere with their assigned parts. This was no purse snatch. Precise timing and seamless coordination were paramount.

Jimmy figured that two could play the game. Secretly, he called his own plan the SS Reverse Play: Swindle the swindler. He smiled at his own clever thought: steal the case, then return it to the Africans directly, letting them in on Willow's plan and the unknown dirty cop trying to rip them off. Jimmy figured a small reward and living to see another day was better than being Johnny Willow's little rats on a leash. Johnny would live to regret his betrayal.

***

"All you gotta do is make noise, get their attention. Lots of it, just like always." Jimmy laid out a drawing he had made of the courtyard where the hand-off was going down. "This is where they will be standing. I watched them several times. They always stand here," he said, pointing to the two Xs on the drawing. He pointed out two others. "This is you." He pointed to Blake Elliston. "And this is me." He pointed to a second X. "Timing is everything, so stay close to the marks. You ride your bike into the center of the courtyard and start doing tricks. When the mark looks up to see what's going on, I'll board in and do the snatch, slide the rail, then drop my board and grab my bike parked at the bottom of the stairs, then the three of us— "

"Wait! What about me?" Chaff asked, alerted to the fact he was not an X on the paper.

"You're sitting this one out. Too dangerous." Jimmy put his hand on Chaff's shoulder like a loving father. "I can't coordinate three of us. Too risky."

"I call bullshit!" Chaff pushed his hand away. "I'm in! I'm going, like it or not. I'm not your baby brother. I'm your *brother*. You said so. We're brothers—equals." Chaff looked over at Blake for support. Blake was only two years older and could see it both ways. He looked at Jimmy and shrugged his approval.

Reluctantly, Jimmy agreed. "Strictly distraction then, just like Blake. After it goes down, we crisscross the city like we've done a thousand times before and make the switches all the way here." He pointed to the favorite meetup spot like a general with military precision. "If anyone gets caught?"

They all yelled out at once, "Tongues in a knot!" Then they slapped high fives and laughed at their chant. The three of them drank beer, then skated on the smooth cement for an hour before finding their chosen corners to fall asleep. Tomorrow would change their lives forever.

CHAPTER 2

Nine Years Later, Tobias Wheat's Story

Today, at the age of twenty-two, mortally wounded by a bullet lodged in the lower chamber of my heart, I was allowed—so the Lord insisted—to rise from my deathbed. I do not know if the glory of the moment is my soul's first flight without gravity, the embrace of heaven handing me my new glorified body, or a remedy the doctors concocted releasing all the body's self-healing antibodies at once. No doubt I had come alive by God's instruction: *Tobias, come out!* I had my Lazarus moment, although not as encumbered by bandages wrapped head-to-foot to delay the inevitable stench to come. A stiff, white sheet and a white knit blanket pretended to hold me in place while all in attendance looked upon me as I was prepared for my sendoff.

Father Romano blessed me and apportioned the sacraments as prescribed. Friends and family paid respects, dampening all the paper products on the hospital's third floor, promising every sort of change in behavior, forgiveness to all, and proper care for my loved ones and my few possessions. With all the hand-holding, lovely affirmations, and dreadful tears, in my unconscious fog, I could only think (or dream) of my friend Chaff Lundergan.

Our lives were so intertwined and dependent on one another that at the moment of my death, I hope he is there to welcome me home. Should I live, I trust my prayers saved him from frightful judgments. Chaff was my friend—my truest friend. So, I should begin once again to pray for mercy to grace his soul. Yes, I have come alive so that I might tell you a story of an improbable friendship, the beauty of its promise, the horror of its infidelity, and the Lord's promise to harvest souls: first the Chaff and then the Wheat.

***

The doctors rushed me into surgery at four in the afternoon. The bullet and pieces of bone were extracted at five ten in the evening, to the shocked surprise and relief of the surgeon in attendance, as I found out later.

Post-surgery, it would not be customary for an attending surgeon to visit the recovery suite, but standing at my bedside two hours later, he spoke when my eyes first fluttered. The voice sounded ethereal, emanating from profound darkness.

"How are you feeling?" came from the man with a clinical voice.

"Floating, groggy—weirdly happy," I replied. That's what I think I said; intended to say. My tongue felt two sizes larger, making my words garbled. "I can't thee you."

"To be expected. The medicine will wear off soon," the voice said.

Slits of light entered my eyes in strobes. A ghost image. *Is he part of my dream*?

"I'm the surgeon."

"The surrrrg'n—not annngel."

“Depends on your understanding of an angel,” he said. I heard him chuckle.

The surgeon watched as two nurses went about post-op care. They checked my ID bracelet, noted my blood pressure, and made some notes. One of the nurses turned to the doctor.

“God must have wanted him to live.”

“You think God saved him?” The man’s tone was arrogant and the nurse demurred. “Mr. Wheat was dealt a death stroke, no coming back from that kind of wound.” He held up his hands to her as if on display.

“Congratulations,” she said with subtle sarcasm, adding, “Never seen a surgeon visit recovery patients.” The nurse lifted the safety rail to my bed.

The surgeon ignored the comment.

I was unable to keep my eyes open. Even my thoughts were defective, lacking complete narration. The drug-induced stupor lifted in slow motion and I still couldn’t move. The world spun in surreal fluctuations.

“Surrrg.”

“Yes, name is Doctor Comstock.” The doctor shook his head in disbelief. “I must admit, I was curious if you would wake up.”

“Steady hands,” I muttered. The nurse rolled her eyes and left the room.

“Yes, but that’s not what saved you. Your heart opened like a can opener. Bone fragments mostly. The metal hit broadside, exploding your rib cage, which means it went through something before it hit you. No one should be talking to you in light of the damage, even with steady hands.

"The bullet lodged sideways against your left ventricle. Lucky for you, it depressed and bruised your heart muscle—lodged, but didn't pierce. It took three hours to remove the fragments. You lost a lot of blood. If I didn't know my own skills, I would say you were saved by luck."

The curtain lifted a little more. I saw him in his blue scrubs, a surgical mask hanging from his neck along with a matching cap. An ID tag dangling from his waist.

"Thank you." Licking my lips. "So thirsty."

"Nurse." A command. "Get this patient some ice chips. No water yet."

"Yes, I'm aware," the remaining nurse said. "On the table next to his bed." She waited for an apology but none came.

"I don't visit my patients in recovery, but you are a unique case, my friend. There was no expectation your heart would restart. I expected you to die on my table, but…well, here you are." The surgeon finished with a disbelieving snort. "Get some rest now. Your primary will follow up and check on you this evening. You're not out of the woods yet."

I barely understood anything he said. Words hovered above me but grasping their meaning took time; but time didn't have meaning either.

"So, I'll live?" My question was sent into the hazy cloud.

"For now, yes." The doctor began to exit the room, reaching for the light switch to darken the recovery suite, then turned back. "The police will want to talk to you. The other guy didn't make it, you know."

I winced—but only in my mind. Like a shot of adrenaline, it awakened my senses for a moment. My friend, Chaff, was taken. In his last act upon this Earth, he gave his life for mine. For all that we'd been through together, it was not a time for sadness. No, it was a moment of great joy. The fleeting awareness rushed away as fast as it came. Everything went dark.

***

After the surgeon left, I was told the next day that I fell back into unconsciousness. As my mind awakened, coming out of my stupor, I heard voices surrounding me. One voice—a woman—pleasant, said, "I'll be leaving now, the Friday shift is here. I hope he comes out of it."

I wanted to say I'm okay. The words would not form and my lids would not lift. Minutes passed. I was wrapped like a pig in a blanket lying on a hospital bed.

Finally, my eyes narrowly opened and I absorbed in periphery, left to right, the few blurred faces in the room. I felt the same as when the surgeon visited, but now, new voices hovered. Someone sobbed. My mother. I recognized the technique: genuine, sniveling moans. Filmmakers could use her sobs as a soundtrack in a movie. Mom was holding my father's hand as he stood with a macabre expression.

A crucifix, placed on my chest, and a priest, Father Romano, in the midst of prayer. In Latin, I think. Fast, melodious chants rise in cadence, falling in quiet pleadings.

His hands clasped against a tilted, bald forehead, eyes squeezed shut.

My wife, Susan, was kneeling on my right side with pink and puffy bags below her watery eyes. Nurses filtered in and out of the room. A suited man I didn't recognize stood outside the door as it opened and closed. Just the flash of a person.

Another man entered the room. A nurse stepped in with him, smiling, and a constant beep somewhere above me. The man approached—a doctor. He checked my heart. Lifted my eyelids and a small penlight beamed a sliver of light into my eyes. I flinched. He flinched.

"He's awakening!"

I heard a collective gasp.

"Mr. Wheat, do you hear me?" the doctor asked. "Mr. Wheat?" He reached for my hand. "Squeeze my hand if you hear my voice."

"Wouldn't it be easier if I just said yes?" I spoke before fully opening my eyes, blinking against the wetness and the glare of light. "What's going on?"

The doctor paused and glanced around the room for a reaction other than his own, disbelieving eyes mirroring his own. He turned back to me. Stared.

"I'm Doctor Lantz."

Cheeks hung loosely on his face below round, heavy, black rims. Black and gray stringy strands of hair brushed back over a balding head. Intelligent, experienced eyes pressed closer together by the muscles centered between them. Concerned? Surprised? I couldn't tell. The lack of a pocket protector in his white smock made me curious. No stethoscope. No hanging name tag gadget. I thought it an odd observation on my part. Maybe he was on call and was interrupted by some event.

"You've been in an unconscious state for the last twenty-four hours," the doctor said. He glanced at the monitors and stepped back to face my wife and parents standing behind her. "Tobias's blood pressure is fine, his heart rate is good, his breathing is clear. All signs point to a hopeful turnaround." The doctor stood straight and clasped his hands in front of him. He stalked all the eyes around the room and smiled as if something he had done resulted in my recovery.

I looked down at the crucifix. "Last Rites?" I questioned Father Romano, managing a smile; one of the few parts of my body that did not hurt.

"As the doctor just pointed out, a miracle has occurred. Your family all thought we were losing you, Tobias. Your vitals declined. We needed God to intervene."

"He did. Thank you, Father, I'm sure the sacrament didn't hurt. Either you came a long way or am I in New Jersey?"

"I came as soon as I knew," Father said. "Eight hours praying."

"What time is it?"

"Friday, three in the afternoon."

"A special time of day on a Friday, Father. The hour of mercy."

"A sign indeed, my son." Father backed away to let the family gather like a membrane around a single-cell organism.

Still groggy from whatever was pouring through the needle hanging overhead and dripping into my left arm, I gave as much of a smile as I could around the room. "I'm happy you're all here." I tried to move but the pain was wrenching, even with the drip. The slightest movement felt like three hundred pounds on my chest, pinning me to the bed.

My mother's sobs continued, but with joy glistening through the tears as she approached me and held my hand. "We thought…" She couldn't finish her words. Instead, she ran her fingers through my hair, competing with my wife, Susan, for the closest position to the bed. Their hands bumped into each other as they combed through.

"Mr. Wheat." One of the two men from the hallway opened the door and stuck his head in, speaking my name. I turned a little toward him, a hulking shadow silhouetted by the hallway light behind him. "We need to talk."

Faces glowered in anger at the intrusion.

"I'm Detective Harrigan, Jack Harrigan—"

Doctor Lantz interrupted, "Detective. Not now. He just got awake. Tobias needs time."

"The man is awake—looks fine."

"Can't you give us some privacy with my husband?" Susan said impatiently. "I don't believe you have the right to interrogate him here, and certainly not now." She stood and faced the detective like a mother bear protecting her cub. "Leave us!"

"Besides," the doctor added, "With all the drugs, what kind of answers will you get?"

Eyes seemed to connect around the room and focused like a giant laser on Detective Harrigan, pushing back on his massive chest.

"Fine. I'll go have a coffee. My associate will need to remain posted outside the door—back in an hour." He looked over at Susan. "There's no pressure. Mr. Wheat doesn't have to talk to us—his choice, but it might be in his best interest."

The detective nodded and closed the door.

My family hovered around and over me until Doctor Lantz noticed my grimace and ordered an increase in pain medication. I fell back to sleep.

CHAPTER 3

The average bullet travels 2,500 feet per second, 1,700 miles per hour. To dodge a bullet traveling from five hundred feet away, I would need to be much faster than an Olympic runner. Chaff and I were only fifty feet from our shooter. The sound and the impact exploded as one. It traveled at the invisible speed of death. How many times in my life have I dodged it from a distance?

***

Waking the following morning, two days after my surgery, the detective was the only person in the room. He was sitting in the corner chair. I tried to lift my body but didn't have the strength. Grunting in pain, I fell back. My lips were chapped. A nurse I hadn't seen before today entered the room.

"Glad to see you awake," she said. "You look a little better. Pink in your cheeks."

"You must be measuring microscopically. Some water?" I asked.

The detective held up a hand to her and said, "I got this."

He stood and reached for a plastic cup sitting near my bed and placed the straw in my mouth. I turned my head toward him when I finished, and he returned the cup to the side table. The nurse took my pulse and blood pressure before withdrawing.

"How are you feeling?" he asked.

"That question gets asked a lot around here. How do I look?"

"Like you were run over by a truck."

"You're the detective from yesterday?"

"Guilty. Detective Jack Harrigan."

Detective Harrigan was shabby-looking, dressed in a wrinkled, gray suit that might have climbed out of bed with him. I'm sure he would never get it buttoned if a reason to do so ever arrived. Harrigan wasn't fat; his torso and chest were just indistinguishable and as thick as a good-sized tree trunk. A multi-striped tie, stained a bit on the end, hung loose around his neck two inches short of a fashionable length. The only obvious thing kept neat was his salt-and-pepper hair glazed and neatly combed straight back. A boxer's nose, probably no stranger to physical altercations.

"Can I assume…" I recoiled through a strained pause, releasing the air in my lungs to alleviate the pressure in my chest. Unfortunately, I had to breathe. "…You're looking for the truck?"

"I admire your humor, considering your condition," he said. "Managing the pain must be a challenge. To answer your question, the truck and the two men driving it got away. That's why I'm here. You up to talking?"

"Do I have a choice?

"We all have choices, Mr. Wheat. Your recent choices brought you here."

"Where is everyone? My wife—family?"

"I spoke to your wife this morning, explained that you might be in some danger, and she agreed to let me visit you. I'm here as a visitor—a friendly visitor." His head bobbed. The corner of his mouth pinned back, unmasking a façade of intent.

"Just a visitor then. Should we talk about family and friends? Play any golf lately? Should we play a couple hands of gin? Catch any crime movies we can talk about?"

Harrigan released a broad, forced smile. He had nothing to say for the moment. An awkward gaze dripped from his eyes. The little gear inside his head smoking from the friction, trying hard to size me up, no doubt saw me as damaged goods—vulnerable. I had never been put in this position before and I wasn't sure how to act—give in? Stall? Subterfuge? I had no idea how to behave.

That last thought fell out of some crime novel I read.

Finally, I said, "Why don't you relax in that chair and tell me what you want to know." He leaned into the chair as though told to stand at ease.

No one likes being questioned. The man had a job to do. I can respect that. Still, from the moment he made himself known yesterday, I felt like we were on opposing teams.

Harrigan's wide, six-foot frame filled the chair with no space to spare. He appeared to be about forty, with the body of a two-hundred-twenty-pound tackle, retired, with a camouflaged meanness that said, "You won't get through me, but it will make me happy if you try."

The pain made me see stars. A bulldozer rumbling over my chest. I tried again to lift to a sitting position but fell back, grunting loudly, more stars bursting all around. I inhaled in a slow, methodical draw as if placing each oxygen molecule in single file along the pathways of my bruised chest.

"I'm ready when you are, Mr. Harrigan."

His lips widened into a sarcastic grin like I was faking it. "First off, you don't have to talk to me. You may want to talk to your doctor first, or your attorney, whichever will make you more at ease."

"I thought you were here as a friendly visitor."

He bit his lower lip, then said, "Very well." He jumped right in. "Were you involved in the robbery of First Citizens Bank?"

"What robbery? Nothing that belonged to the bank was taken. Any detective could detect that fact yesterday."

"A robbery gone bad then," Harrigan said, eyes closed, nodding to my point. "An attempt is as much a crime. It still begs an answer to my question. Before you answer, I don't much care whether you say yes or no, but this will go a lot easier if you simply answer without all the confrontational swagger."

"Was I involved? Yes, I was there, but since no bank money was taken, my involvement is innocent." My eyes closed, deflecting the pain as I tried to shift my weight. "Hit the red button down there and lift me up."

Harrigan complied. The bed folded upward. “In my circles, you don’t find the words *involvement* and *innocence* in the same sentence, Mr. Wheat.”

“I was there at the request of a friend who needed me.”

“Chaff Lundergan?” the detective asked, knowing the answer.

“Yes…innocent as well.”

I knew the declaration of our innocence would not be accepted with ease. “Neither of us should have been at the bank. The circumstance was what it was.” I shifted my position and a sharp pain shot through my chest, causing me to let out a reflexive curse. As I reached for the water glass, Harrigan pushed it several inches closer.

“Thanks.”

“You should give that button you’re holding a little squeeze.”

“Trust me. If I squeeze this button, you might get one more question. Let me know when you have only one more question.”

Harrigan smirked.

“Will do. So, you decided to drive down to the center of town in Charlotte and join Mr. Lundergan at a bank rob—” correcting himself, “money exchange. A violent one. He gets killed. You almost die, and you’re both innocent. Very interesting. Are there any guilty parties in this version of the story?”

“Yes. You should try catching them. Look, Detective, Chaff and I had a complicated relationship. You would need to understand it to make any judgment. Was there guilt? Yes, plenty, but there was also repentance—a change of heart. Neither one of us went there to rob a bank. The others? They were there to rob us.”

“Are you telling me he changed his mind and got shot by his associates? Hard to believe.”

“They’re not his associates. Chaff’s involvement with them occurred from a distance and at the young age of twelve. His life changed afterwards. I met him when we were fourteen. He had a conversion—one hundred percent—religious experience and all.”

“Until yesterday, when the non-associates showed up.”

“He was involved through coercion. Chaff was given an ultimatum and he succumbed. That is his guilt. In the end, he made the right decision. The moral decision.”

“Whose morals?” Harrigan held his palm out. “Sorry. I withdraw the question.”

“Too late. Mind if I ask you a question, Mr. Harrigan?”

Harrigan jutted his jaw out an inch like he was daring me to take a punch. “Nah, shoot.”

“Your name sounds Irish. You are Catholic, Mr. Harrigan?”

Harrigan gave me a contemptuous smile and flashed at me like a defensive missile trying to knock an enemy rocket out of the sky. “I’m a renegade sheep. Who knows?

The Shepherd might catch me one of these days and drag me back from the briars." He snorted. "Why do you ask?"

"Makes it difficult to ask a question about morals."

"Mr. Wheat, Chaff Lundergan died with a bag full of money in his right hand with you lying next to him. Your portrayal of innocence sounds like a desperate concoction. His history and the bag of money he was gripping would not lead a reasonable man, or judge, to conclude that he is innocent."

"What do you understand of his history? We just met."

"We're not in the dark ages, Mr. Wheat. The precinct has computers."

"Well, he's dead, so I guess you can conclude anything you want at this point." I resented his tone. "You've already judged us both. Am I under arrest?"

"Nobody's arresting you. Not now, anyway. A few bad guys are still missing, and several bank customers are recovering from gun-whippings and hysteria. No one else died, so there's that. So far as I can make out, you are a key witness. No record. Model citizen. I haven't made the leap to suspect—yet." He smiled. "If you want to help keep that status, I'm listening. Though we need to clear the air about why you were there, and why here in Charlotte. The others involved hail from Chicago, a long way from home."

"How do you know that?" *Yeah, how does he know that?*

"We detected it." His head bounced again like a victory dance after a touchdown or a bully daring you to react.

"I told you, our relationship is complicated. Chaff's reason for being there has—had—a fourteen-year history. The truth is, Chaff never wanted to be there, but the threat to my life—my family's lives—made him a willing accomplice. Then a double dose of regret kicked in and he decided to give them what they wanted, which, as I said, was not the bank's money. Go investigate, the bank will tell you."

"Let me guess. That didn't go well with his crew."

I peered into Harrigan's eyes. This was the second time he didn't stop to ask whose money it was. My comment didn't bother him in the least. Something about his interrogation didn't add up. I kept trying to make my point.

"They weren't his crew."

"Yeah, so you said."

"I told you. Chaff was forced to work with them. I went to save him. In the end, he saved me."

I didn't want to let the money issue go.

"You knew nothing from the bank was taken," I said.

Harrigan bounced his fingertips together, giving thought to my assertion. I couldn't tell if he was developing some angle in his mind or if he thought I was playing him in some way. He knew these details but chose to hold back to get at some specific objective. I didn't know what that was.

Harrigan didn't seem to care as much about Chaff's murderer. I decided two could play the game of selective memory and selective answers.

I imagined him saying, *"Your turn."*

"My associates questioned the bank manager on scene. He said it wasn't the bank's money. It came from a safe deposit box. The bank wasn't aware of the contents. Records show it belonged to Tom Cruise. Care to explain?"

I had to laugh at Chaff's humor, made funnier because Harrigan didn't make the reference to Cruise's debut movie *Risky Business*.

"There's no simple explanation. It was years in the making and I'm not sure where to begin. Just telling you what happened on Thursday afternoon at the two o'clock hour wouldn't be fair to Chaff, or me for that matter. There would be no context. The truth is in the details of Chaff's childhood. I'm not trying to be misleading, but the story is complicated and it starts there."

I was trying to stall. My antennas tingled with questions of my own.

"Sounds like a sad story. Why don't you start with who was forcing him?" the detective said flippantly. "Will I eventually find out why either one of you were at the bank that day? Oh! Wait...for the money, right?" he grinned.

"Your sarcasm won't change the truth, Detective."

"Yes, that. That's what I'm waiting for. How did you come to meet Lundergan? Your story. I'm all ears."

"That would take quite a bit of time," I said in extreme discomfort. I pushed the button to summon a nurse. "I don't think I can do this now, and I'm sure my family will be coming back."

Harrigan stared at me like he was assessing whether I was stalling on purpose or not.

"Yeah, sorry for pressing so hard, but the details and the clues get fuzzy real fast in these situations. I'll leave you alone for now. You look pale. You want me to call the nurse?"

I shook my head no. "I already pushed the button."

He stood and started for the door. "By the way, I've posted a man outside your door."

"You think I'll escape?"

"Escape? No. He's there to protect you in case the not-so-friendly bank robbers return to eliminate a witness."

"He's not in uniform."

"He's from my unit—plain clothes."

"What unit is that?"

Harrigan gave me a closed-mouthed smile. "Get some rest, Mr. Wheat. I'll be back to listen to your story."

He walked out of my room and I felt the bad air go with him.

***

"He hasn't been forthcoming yet," Harrigan spoke into his phone.

Harrigan listened.

“No, Wheat is smart. Pushing will make him suspicious. Just give me time. He’s not going anywhere.”

The next communication made Harrigan pace. He stopped and leaned against a load-bearing beam next to his car. His coat swung wide. A woman walked by on the way to her car and stopped when she noticed his shoulder-holstered gun hanging free, exposed. He pulled his arm down and closed his coat, smiling and nodding to her. He pointed to his badge pinned to his belt. The woman looked away and quickly walked to her car several spaces away.

“Okay, I gotta go. We don’t want to scare him. I need him to trust me, so if he wants to tell me Lundergan’s story, I’m good at that. I’m half certain he knows, and it would be much easier if we just let him tell us. You waited this long. What’s a few more days?”

The call ended.

Harrigan muttered to himself. “Impatient asshole. I’m going to kill the son of a bitch if he ruins this.”

CHAPTER 4

Sunday, the fourth day since my surgery, I was anxious to go home. Recovery was slow. Dr. Lantz instructed me to limit my movement to allow my chest to heal. Pain is normal, he said, but would gradually draw down. He encouraged me to press for more medicine when needed.

Harrigan kept his word and stayed away for the next few days. It was hard to sleep. My thoughts continued to churn about the intermittent history of my relationship with Chaff Lundergan. Memories arrived like a strobe light, recoiling then soothing. My eyes closed but not for sleep. I rested inside the dark hallways of the mind, lucid at first, settling on the edge of sleep, taking that first step on the wing of a dream and hearing again the explosion that blasted us apart. My eyelids sprang open and I relived the terror.

Chaff Lundergan and I were fourteen when we met in the most unusual way and the most improbable of places. Our lives should not have been so connected. I was a young Catholic boy attending a Catholic boy's academy sent out from a middle-class family to be educated, sheltered from the heathen world and the random immorality sweeping through it like a malevolent wind. In my world I was to be trained in the classics, marinated for expected accomplishments, producer of honest dreams and multiple children. Most of all, I had to obey my God or be stricken by palsy because of my disbelief.

That is not how Chaff Lundergan's life began. He was an urchin, ragged and trained on the streets of Chicago where conquest trumps morality. No history and no future—eating, sleeping, and waking were accomplishments.

In the hospital, I lay staring at the starkness of my room; the rippling of sun through the vertical blinds, the only wall hanging—a temporary reflection. My thoughts ran the gambit from the early years of an improbable relationship to last Thursday—the last Thursday of Chaff's life. I smelled the hospital's antiseptic air. It triggered the memories of negative events I had no control over.

The squares in the drop ceiling were hypnotic, sending me foraging in the crevices of my brain for understanding—for answers. One vision stuck out, repeating: that we live in a maze of sin, to which all doors leading from it entice but do not open. Repentance is the only way out; but who can find its location?

I was disoriented and frustrated inside the maze by the false allure of being saved and helpless, and gave into the mystifying puzzle, picking a spot to encamp, learning how to survive beneath the thorny walls of my sins until a Savior came to my rescue. That is life. Waiting to be saved. Waiting for forgiveness—acceptance that avails on the other side of death.

Three more days into my recovery, in a sweat from circular thoughts, I tried to distinguish between memories and reality washing over me like waves crashing. My eyes popped open and I scanned the room. *Where am I*?

The pain seeped back into my nervous system, reminding me of my whereabouts and my condition.

Susan left me a note. She and my parents went home for a while to get something more than hospital food. She gave her approval for Detective Harrigan to visit again.

I attempted to sit up and slide my legs over the edge of the bed, squinting in excruciating distress, stuck between positions, unable to move in either direction, as if I had a giant charley horse in my chest.

"Nurse…"

Not loud enough to summon. The call button was awkwardly out of reach. My voice came out like a whisper. The man outside opened my door and glimpsed my distress. His deep voice echoed my murmur: "Nurse. Your patient needs help."

A young, beautiful nurse with smooth, black hair swept back and tucked into a bun, a stethoscope slung around her neck, came to the rescue, gliding across the room. "Mr. Wheat, let me help you. How did you get into this position?" she said with an urgent voice.

"Sleep walking?"

"Funny," she said, then she went to work grabbing me under each arm. "Are you trying to stand or sit up?"

"Stand," I said, holding my breath. I was trying to avoid the pain of inhaling and exhaling. "I can't lie there anymore." I noted her ID badge. Spriggs, Julie, LPN. "Lift me," I pleaded.

"Not recommended. You could tear your staples."

"Please, just for a minute. You can hold me."

Against her better judgment, she said, then she lifted me to my feet. We were chest to chest. I hung limp in her arms, close enough to smell the light wash of a perfume scent on her neck. She was small in stature, but stronger than she appeared. Probably no stranger to a gym.

My left arm was still attached to an IV, an oxygen tube fed into my nose, and various electrical leads sprang from my finger and my chest.

"I suppose dancing is out of the question," I said.

"I think you had better sit this one out," she responded.

Harrigan's familiar voice interrupted our co-mingling. "How cute. Does your wife know about this?"

The nurse lowered me to the edge of my bed and reached for the nurse's call button. "I need help in 213." Two other nurses arrived, helping to reacquaint me with my bed. One of them checked my wounds for any bleeding, another took my blood pressure. I was worn out from the three-minute escapade. Nurse Spriggs smiled at me and asked if I was comfortable. I said, "Yes. I hope we will see each other again."

She chuckled softly. "There's a good chance of that." Nurse Spriggs, Julie, gave Harrigan a quick glance as she stepped out of the room.

"She's pretty," Harrigan said. Not waiting for an invitation, he walked over and stared down at me. "You don't look so well."

"What do you want, Detective? You visit more than my wife."

"You can tell me how you and Lundergan hooked up and the names of the bank robbers."

"I told you the background is complicated . . . a long story, and I suspect you already have their names."

Harrigan rolled his eyes, but didn't argue the point. "Humor me. I have plenty of time. I like long, complicated stories. I'll stop you if it bores me. Hopefully, you can keep your finger off the morphine trigger till we get to the only part that interests me."

"You knew they were from Chicago. What do you really want?"

"True, but not why they were here in Charlotte, what they wanted, why they killed your friend. So, I guess I don't know much. I'm hoping you will educate me. What I want is to solve this case so I can go home, have a scotch, and watch the Hornets take on Miami. You a fan?"

"I'm an end-of-season fan. I like the playoffs, which means I don't watch the Hornets much."

My thoughts were drawn to the window. A light drizzle glistened on the pane. I experienced a moment of clarity; somebody had to know the truth. Only Detective Harrigan was available. He's police. Trust is one of the pillars of law enforcers. Why shouldn't I trust him?

"Are you serious about those guys coming back for me?"

"Yes. All possible. Whatever they're after, I don't think they got it. If your friend knew anything, they took that option out of the equation. That leaves you."

I was breathing like I had just run a twenty-six-mile marathon. He was right. I was now the prime suspect for what they wanted. I felt vulnerable lying in a hospital bed with nothing more than a gaggle of nurses and a faceless man outside my door to defend me. My body reflexively prepared for the coming assault as blood pooled to center mass, leaving my limbs cool. I squeezed the nurse's call button and requested another blanket.

"Is your man still outside the door?"

"He is."

"Is he any good?"

Harrigan chuckled. "I didn't mean to scare you, Mr. Wheat. Yes, he's very good. You can relax.

"I'll try."

Harrigan could see I was struggling more than he suspected. "Tobias, I have changed my mind. I'm pushing you too hard. Even though every day the case gets a little colder, it's obvious you need more time to convalesce." He put his note pad back in his jacket. "Let's pick this up later." He started toward the door.

"Detective."

Harrigan stopped and turned around.

"I want to continue. I need to continue. Call it therapy or call it guilt. I don't care, but I need to talk about it, if you're willing to listen."

"Are you sure?" There was perhaps a hint of empathy in his voice.

"Yes, I'm sure. I can give you two names, then you can leave . . . or, you can stay, and I can tell you how I met Chaff."

"Names first," he said.

"I don't know if it's their real names: Masters and Wallace, I think. I never saw them. Chaff and I were arguing. I didn't want him to go. The last thing he said to me was that he had to stop Masters and Wallace."

This wasn't exactly true. I had the unfortunate displeasure of their acquaintance in the past. A year ago, to be exact, when they showed up at Susan's apartment—Susan leading the way to the wrong end of a gun.

"Trevor Masters and Bruce Wallace. That's what we suspected. The Chicago PD tells us they were part of a diamond-smuggling operation. Enforcers. Found their way into the crosshairs of the FBI. On the run now. What does that have to do with you and your deceased friend?"

"Not sure. Chaff intended to fill me in, but we never got that far."

"It must be pretty important to motivate two thugs from Chicago to take a weekend getaway to our lovely city of Charlotte. You sure you don't know what they're after?"

"If I did, if I had it, I would give it to them."

"Where do you work again, Mr. Wheat?"

"Pike and Associates."

"Ah, yes. The big PR firm in the Hearst Tower. A big score of a job for a guy so young. Only a matter of time before your involvement in our little episode becomes unwanted headline material. Bad publicity leads to crisis management."

"What are you getting at?"

"I'm getting at how the story will be reported, how it goes down. You could be a hero, an unwitting victim of circumstances, or the lead suspect in a crime. Not good for business."

"The hole in my chest speaks to the victim," I said.

Detective Harrigan's shift in questioning made me hot again. I threw off the extra blanket. The detective seemed off, less friendly, like he had an agenda and I wasn't cooperating. But maybe this is how all detectives are, teasing at the truth through evasion and accusation, cynical of any answer.

Even still, I had a feeling; something telling me to be careful. I wondered why the FBI hadn't shown up. After all, that's who Chaff said he was working with. Given that premise, they would surmise we were connected. They must be aware I'm here. Maybe, unlike Harrigan, they're giving me time to recover. I decided to keep certain facts to myself for now, mulling over my concerns.

Harrigan smiled an odd, knowing smile. He tore off a piece from his notebook, pulled out his pen and stepped into the hallway. I heard him give instructions to someone about the names, then he returned. He sat down in the corner chair closest to me. "I'm all yours. Tell me your story, Mr. Wheat."

I began like I was narrating a movie script. Aside from a nurse check-in, a doctor visit, and several time-outs to manage my pain, for the next hour the story flowed from my consciousness like a parable without a punchline. It was therapeutic to put the last eight years into perspective.

Even as the words escaped my lips, I was still amazed by the improbability our souls had traveled in some quantum proximity to one another. Chaff and I were different in every way, yet inextricably connected. I didn't think anything I said would help Harrigan, but I felt sure it would help me. Harrigan took notes, never interrupting except for a few moments for clarification.

CHAPTER 5

The Academy Years

I began. The story flowed like a fairy tale once upon a time. Harrigan sat back holding his pen and notepad.

I explained the pertinent details of our lives, probably unnecessary, but a warming gift to myself.

Chaff Lundergan had a home for a short, unsettling time—*address* may be more accurate than home. A depraved mother treated him as an inconvenience.

His father, in name only, was Daniel Lundergan, an Irish immigrant. A broken man numbed by alcohol, hardened by a poverty of the spirit and convinced that his lot in life was to be full of bad luck and impossibilities. His imperfections would rot in jail for having decided to rob a small bank in Greenbrier Valley, West Virginia.

Chaff's mother fell into dysfunction, having lost her man; too uneducated to rise from the ashes, living on section 8 housing reimbursements and the occasional cash infusions from visiting male companions.

Chaff became a reprobate in training, brought up on the streets of Chicago's south side by other kids not but a few years older. Fractured by the collapse of the fragile promises of marriage, his would be a different path. The malevolent wind would have him for a time. To survive, Chaff found the street to be more accepting and accommodating—no more dysfunctional or toxic than his home. They called themselves the kiddy gang—ruffians for hire.

Of course, I would not know any of this until Chaff showed up at the academy. Our nascent friendship refused any personal information about his early life for the better part of our freshman year. Bits and pieces fell into our conversations like breadcrumbs left to see what I would do with them. He made building trust a gauntlet, which I survived and became a close—the closest—ally.

In 2009, at the age of fourteen, my father came home and stepped over the threshold with a widened smile detectable from Mars. He paused and scanned the room. My mother and I sat on the couch, she reading *Ladies Home Journal* and I reading Mark Twain's *Life on the Mississippi*, a homeschool assignment. Father's smile leaped across the room, first to Mother, then to me. My mother and I parroted his expression in dopey unison, waiting for the punchline.

"There must be a happy conclusion behind that smile," Mother said. "Care to share?"

Father reached into his vest pocket and removed a folded piece of paper. He snapped it open as if he were about to read from a scroll given to him by a king. "Hear ye, hear ye," he said comically. "Take notice all. It is hereby recorded that Tobias Wheat has been accepted for admittance to Saint Joseph Academy for Boys." At the end of the announcement, he took a proper bow, one foot behind the other and his right arm held at ease behind his back. Mother and I both released the muscles holding our faces properly and allowed our mouths to drop dutifully into the news that had drifted all-so-slowly to our side of the room. Seconds later, we were awash in the joy of a family hug.

"John, what great news," Mother said, all glassy-eyed. "Tobias, can you believe it?"

"Father. How?" I asked. "I thought we couldn't afford Saint Joe's."

He glanced at Mother with a knowing smile. "Father Romano has offered you a one-year scholarship, renewable each year with graded achievement."

"What grade?"

"Why would you even ask? You've been a straight-A student since you were six. Just do your best. Father Romano isn't looking for your genius. He wants conscientious students, successful students; students who will enrich the institution. I also think he wants talented soccer players." He turned and winked at his wife. "Father Romano saw you on the field this past summer."

"How do you know?"

"Because when he shook my hand after telling me the news, he said there's always room for intelligent athletes at Saint Joe's. I surmised the rest."

I glanced at Mother. "You knew?"

"Father mentioned it to us at Mass last Sunday, but we didn't want to say anything until it was official."

***

My parents surrendered me to my new school. Father Romano called me into his office. Before he closed the door, Mother and Father smiled at Sister Mary Catherine, the administrative assistant outside Father's office. Mother's face showed signs of nervousness. The sister assured them I would do well and offered a congratulatory hand to assuage any distress.

"You'll take care of him?"

It was my mother's final murmur for reassurance. She held her hands clasped in front. Her black purse dangled from her wrist like a single handcuff restraining her nerves and forming a counterweight against her joy at my acceptance to the Academy.

Sister Mary Catherine tried to make a joke to send them on their way. "I'm sure you will get him back in a slightly used condition. Today is only an interview. We'll send him out to you in a little while."

Father laughed at the conversation outside his door, closed it, and stared at me with grandfatherly pride. Through the glass window that formed the outer wall, I watched my parents as they walked arm in arm down the hallway toward the main doors and wondered if I could call them back.

Father Romano was intimidating. Up to this very moment, my encounter with him, or any priest, was from several pews back where I observed and prayed in the midst of his congregation. He gave Mass at the altar facing the tabernacle and spoke in perfect Latin with a Brooklynese-Italian accent. His speaking style was quite theatrical, making the various readings and the Gospel take on a certain melodramatic reality. The only Latin I knew was the memorized Latin prayer responses; not fluent otherwise.

His homilies were inspiring and instructive, if not, long, waging war with my memory and inclination for sleep. Now, I was but a handshake away. The power of the man standing in his black cassock hung over a pear-shaped body with a sizable girth, the only visible extremities: his head and polished, black leather shoes. His blue eyes were penetrating, as though I were an object of study. I didn't ask, but took him to be in his mid-sixties. His white hair grew on the sides of his otherwise bald head like ill-fitting muffs. But the thing I noticed the most was his broad smile, genuine in its glow and invitation. He appeared like a commander on the field of battle yet exuded a gentleness in nature.

He invited me to sit and repeated what Sister Mary Catherine had already told us. Father always interviews new students before giving his final blessing for acceptance. He wanted to be sure the student wanted to be at Saint Joe's and was not being forced to attend.

My parents would wait in the car for me. They were happy and so was I. Father welcomed me, asked me what I hoped to get out of the academy. He advised strenuous study and an immediate tryout for the school's soccer team. He gave me a quick tour of the school before releasing me back to my parents.

The empty hallways were daunting, lockers lining the walls interrupted by wooden doors leading to dimly lit and vacant classrooms. Father's voice echoed as we discussed the school's mission and expectations. Coming from the relaxed and secure environment of home, my classroom for the last eight years, the anticipation of merging with two hundred students caused my throat to swell.

My career at Saint Joseph's Academy for Boys in Edison, New Jersey, was fixed. Three weeks later, dressed in pleated khakis, white shirt, and blue blazer, I walked officially down the main corridor, entered the three combination numbers given to me, and opened my new locker. It was empty, like my stomach. I stared at the hollow space for a few seconds just as the other freshman did, standing nearby; doors opened en masse like wings ill-fitted upon pale, green, cement block walls.

Camaraderie had not been initiated. Too early. There was a recognition that we all shared a reverential awe for where we were—in an elite academy but at the bottom of the local totem pole as freshmen. We were apprehensive muttonheads, as the upper classmen would call us, a shepherdless herd waiting to be corralled and sheared.

Locker doors began to close as clashing cymbals, one after the other. No one dared to look at the others. It was an unwritten rule of awkward behavior. Once we allowed eye contact and posturing, the hierarchy would begin to take form: top, middle, bottom, popular, wanting, disregarded. We would allow chaos to manage us for the foreseeable days until orientation was absorbed and we were given our figurative walking sticks that would help us find our way.

Names? We would hear them for the first time repeated five times in the classes we attended. The freshman class consisted of forty boys. After three days of hearing the role calls, a large percentage of names stuck in our memory. Mostly last names, since the role was read last name first. Seats assigned in alphabetic order. Expectations spoken as though we were already being reprimanded.

One name stuck out: Lundergan, Chaff. Not because the name elicited the thought of worthless seed, but because it was announced fifteen times over the last three days, producing no answer. *Why did they keep calling that name?* It was obvious that this kid was not among us, and perhaps would never be among us.

After three days, an awkward glance would travel the room. An infectious snicker would rise when the name was called again. It was obvious to all but the staff that his sails were not set upon Saint Joe's. Sick? Scared? Whatever the reason, he was not coming. The name impacted upon all as a ghostly celebrity and created much comedy in the hallways and bathrooms:

"Hey, have you seen Lundergan?"

"You mean Lundergan, Chaff? No, not yet, but I think someone saw him over in E hall."

The conscript of Lundergan's presence awakened the fertile humor of boys who naturally hasten toward cheerful amusements to escape their inhibitions.

Having not met the upperclassmen, after the first week, the salient personalities of the forty boys beckoned leadership, followers, and shadow stalkers to make themselves known. It is an unconscious dance of confidence versus insecurity, one leading the other piteously. Cliques formed. Groupings, pairs, and single stand-outs coalesced. I stumbled through the many assemblages, leaving a vestige of neutrality behind so as not to be pinned wrongly to any donkey's ass. My permanent stake would be planted later. Society was a new feature in my life. I dipped my toe rather than splashing into the middle of the absurdity of boys attempting to become men.

The freshman class was well separated from the upper grades so we could acclimate to our new pubescent manhood. Our underarms perspired. Chin hair sprang to lonely lengths. Voices would not harmonize. All quintessential virtues displayed in naïve reflex and not as the natural adherence to personal grace. We were, in fact, fresh men in waiting. An equality of dress, age, and intelligence was not enough to eliminate the vanities of individuality, but enough to slow us down and humble us as lowly muttonheads.

CHAPTER 6

The second week set upon us. Our lockers were filled with notebooks, textbooks, photos, and assorted garments. The first assembly was called, whereupon Father Romano spoke in rapture about the need for good citizens and productive humanity. He bragged about the potential and hallmarks of Saint Joseph's students. He specified goals, missions, and dreams as pendants waiting for us at graduation. It was awe-inspiring.

Suddenly, a voice burst from the crowd like a harpoon thrown hastily into the sea. "Where is Lundergan?"

Eyes bulged. Cheeks bulged. Laughter blew up into the rafters like a geyser. To add to their surprise, a voice ending with its adolescent, high-pitched wailing answer barked out in a deep, resonating tone:

"Here!"

Our laughter shattered. Forty faces turned in unison to the epicenter of the spontaneous reply. The voice stood to be recognized.

"What's your problem?"

"Sit down, Mr. Lundergan," Father Romano said. "The rest of you, get hold of yourselves. Perhaps I should give another speech about behavior. I see you are still just little boys, and as such, we should treat you as little boys. Yes?" He slapped the podium with a three-foot-long rubber-tipped pointer.

All eyes and bodies snapped back to attention. Boys we were, but little boys, we were not. At least, we did not relish that designation. Our minds split in curiosity: first with the sudden awareness that Chaff Lundergan did, indeed, exist and was found among us, and then with the need to reassert ourselves as newly minted men. There were rules in the academy, three of which expelled you: recalcitrant behavior was one of them, fighting the most egregious, and lying, especially to staff, the third. A dozen other rules were punished in lesser ways.

Guilt did not rest in the outburst but in our collective response to it. The voice dared us and the mob responded, not with pitchforks and fire, but as bandits robbing each other of our senses. Certainly, a natural response for fourteen-year-olds on the street or sitting in public schools, but not ordinary in the least in Father Romano's academy.

"Dismissed," he said definitively. "Behave yourselves." Father turned to Mr. Moorefield, his vice principal, and quietly spoke some instructions that sent Moorefield on a secret mission.

Moorefield was the devil. Not specifically the fiend, but he was our devil. He would appear behind us, beside us, and ahead of us at times, making us think he could bilocate. He was massive, two hundred plus pounds of muscle wrapped around an expanded barrel chest. A crew cut rested above an elephant-sized forehead. A Roman nose hung prominently, needing only a helmet, spear, and red cape to finish the likeness of a Praetorian Guard.

For his size, he was deftly quiet. If you were unfortunate enough to catch his stare, a moment arrived when you were sure his eyes would burst into flame. All that said, Mr. Moorefield held the admiration of Father

Romano and was given great latitude for dealing with academy students. We attempted to remain sinless so we would not encounter his snare.

Several days passed without incident. The only change in our feeble freshman lives was the new corporal awareness of Chaff Lundergan in the halls we traveled. While he wore the same white shirt and blazer as required, Chaff appeared different in his uniform. In fact, nothing about him looked uniform. Proportionally larger than everyone else, his blazer sleeves were an inch too short, his shirt pulled up in awkward puffs around his beltless waist and his hair hung in dark, red Irish strands over his forehead in contrast to the combed sheen of conformity.

Lundergan kept to himself. In the two classes I shared with him, I observed little engagement in the subject matter or class discussions. On the few occasions the teacher tried to invite him into the matter at hand, his answers were short: Yes. No. I don't think so. Sounds right. It was obvious there was a layer of emotional rock under the surface, not ready to expose himself to the harsh elements of freshman society, one that appeared less than real. For Chaff, reality was in the street. The academy was somewhere in Middle Earth full of fairies and hobbits and little boys he was not familiar with.

On one occasion, I tried to engage him, to test his determination to remain separated as we were leaving Mr. Bonner's freshman English class. While we exited nearly side by side, I extended an elbow bump and said, "I'm not a fan of Ezra Pound. I don't really understand him. How about you?"

Chaff stopped and stared down at his arm where I tapped him. Without moving his head, his eyes rolled up at me, as though wondering what he was to do. The pause was uncomfortable and frightening. I felt the premonition of a violent wind that would sweep over me at any moment. That's not what happened. He spoke. "You're right. People don't understand him. That's why he spent twelve years in a psychiatric hospital." His posture straightened and he walked away.

I didn't move for several minutes. The wind struck me with anything but violence. It was the cold wind of indifference, but a subtle understanding was to linger. Beneath the sloppiness of his demeanor there rested a hidden intellect, protected, orderly, and breathing air through a reed.

The intriguing story surrounding Chaff Lundergan turned a new page. I was no longer interested because he didn't speak. He was no longer a zoo animal to be watched. I saw him more as an equation that needed to be solved.

CHAPTER 7

After second period, we rushed to the cafeteria where the amino acids of freshman life congealed into compound life-forms. Freshman society became a caste system, daring you to not escape your chosen lot. Friendships came to life: cliques, teams, and factions; the poets found other poets, athletes found their stars, math geniuses counted numerous, and the swordsman found his swordsmen. Mickey Sanders was the designated swordsman. I was not. I didn't know where I belonged, if anywhere, more pleased to be nothing more than an observer.

My imagination lifted me like a bird, circling above as I made my way among the many tribes. This one here. That one there. I knew at some point, I had to choose my pond. Neutrality would not survive the inquest. In a weak moment at lunch, caught unaware, Sanders attempted to vet me as one of his subjects.

"Wheat, what are you doing?"

My eyes bounced up from my third-period Principles in Math workbook, the last bite of my grilled cheese in my left hand. "I'm playing catch-up," I replied, lifting up the front cover of my book. "Not my easiest subject."

"Come sit with us," Mickey said.

I instantly wanted to take flight. His was not an invitation to visit, and most likely not a question. The certainty of the command was not to be mistaken. Mickey was recruiting, waiting to capture me, recruit me, and transform his group into a higher creature. Eventually, I made the decision to descend from my perch and squawk among his tribesmen. Bad decision.

"Yeah, sure." I meekly moved a few seats nearer.

"You have Bilsby for Math?" he asked. "The man's a ball-buster."

"No, I have, Miss Whalen. She's okay. It's me. Slow uptake, even slower to process."

"You processing that body? She's racked," Mickey Sanders said loud enough to make the whole table snicker in appreciation.

"Whalen? She must be thirty years old," I said in disbelief, appalled at his comment. "She could be your mother."

"In that case, I want to be adopted." His head bobbed and turned in each direction to catch the admiring sneers from his followers.

"Good luck," I said before getting up from the fire pit. "I have some math to solve."

Mickey could tell I didn't connect with him or his tribe, but he didn't want me to reject him. *He* would do the rejecting. "Wheat? What kind of name is that anyway? Is that some kind of Amish thing?"

"Yeah, Mickey. My horse and buggy are out back. I'll be trotting off now."

Somewhere between my arrival and departure, a conflict had begun. Friendship had melted down into its core elements of survival and conquest. With books underarm and my serving tray firmly in my right hand, I walked away cautiously. Legs jutted out from under the lunch table, as expected, in an attempt to trip me. The whole tribe demonstrated the drill. An observant smugness bloomed on my face.

"You boys studying to perform a dance routine?" an approaching voice said.

The voice was not loud, but the power of it swept over Mickey Sanders's table with a deafening effect. Legs withdrew. Heads snapped. The four freshman tribesman stared up at Mr. Moorefield. Arms hung robotically from his body, fingers relaxed, his figure obscuring a large swatch of sunlight. It was the ultimate power position.

"Tobias, you may continue on your way." He waved me away without looking at me.

If it were unsettled before, no mistaking now that Mickey and I were enemies. Now that Moorefield had rescued me, it will be noted I had a sizable piece of artillery in my arsenal. Apparently, my devil was showing his benevolent side.

I left, not privy to his reprimand, if there was one, but the penitent look on Mickey Sanders's face was apparent from across the room. I put my tray down and rose back up into the air in search of more fertile sites capable of sustaining friendship.

CHAPTER 8

The lunch period became a gauntlet. Finding a seat too far down the chain of communes projected an erudite aloofness sure to lock me into an unseen dimension. Too far up the chain and my mind would be sold into slavery. In the following days, I chose to be an early arrival, select an empty table, and wait for who populated it when the crowd assembled.

The first time I tried, I was amazed at how people avoided me like a polluted watering hole. One kid sat at the opposite end before being invited to join an assemblage of math prodigies. Without moving, I felt locked out of the room while all the vassals sat in their seats subordinate to their lords. I don't think I was being ignored but a victim of my own strategy. No one could figure out what I was about, where to peg me.

Ironically, I was also eager to answer that question. School society was an overgrown field of weeds compared to the microcosm of a homeschool. I would remain the observer staring at all possibilities.

Three pages into Harper Lee's *To Kill a Mockingbird,* the table shook through a minor seismic event. Reflex made me quickly grab my tray with one hand and my milk with the other. My book dropped to the floor.

"Interesting book," someone said.

My adrenalin calmed, leaving me to focus on the epicenter. Chaff Lundergan took a seat. His knees barely fit under the table.

"Sorry. I didn't mean to shake the table. My legs don't fit underneath these tiny excuses for fine dining."

"It's okay. No problem," I said. "Sacrificing the book for the food tested my priorities. Hunger trumps mind expansion." Our quick dialog hid my confusion about his visit to my table. I certainly had my curiosity about the guy, but never thought about forming an alliance with him. Chaff may have done better with Mickey's group.

"Have you read the book?" I asked.

"Yeah, a couple of times. I found Atticus Finch to be a very complex character. Subject of scorn, more or less because of his moral fortitude. People generally are not like him. The crowd mentality is usually what prevails." Lundergan motioned his head toward Mickey Sanders's group.

I didn't look. I was more fascinated by his take on Harper Lee's novel and with Chaff Lundergan himself. His intellect was like the sap of trees: not at all discernible through the ripples of bark. You had to trust it was there and could be tapped when necessary. Most curious, he was smart, in a casual way, not putting on or showing off.

"Uh-huh. Can I ask you a question?"

He motioned agreement with a lift of his head.

"Where were you before here? I mean, your education . . ."

His answer was short and incomplete: "I was tutored." He changed the subject. "Question for you. Have you noticed the upperclassmen sitting at oak tables with tablecloths?" He looked over his shoulder to scan the distant side of the dining hall. "Pitiful."

"Yeah," I said. "That's in our future, right?"

He ignored my comment. "Why do they let us see them?"

"What do you mean?"

"Doesn't it make you jealous? We're captured in some other world, fenced off, so we don't offend the masters. What is so special about them? They're just older, not smarter or better."

From my initial experience, I was surprised he was this talkative, let alone envious. His sudden obsession with upper-class privileges was curious.

"Chaff, right?" I inquired. "You may feel differently when you're a senior."

He turned around and began eating. No reply.

I understood his question, but I didn't share the resentment. My father once told me class struggle is not created by looking down. "Those at the bottom of the pit create the scaffolding for climbing out of rutted lives," he said in one of his philosophical diatribes. It made sense. Who would knowingly fall over the rail in hopes of reaching the bottom? The man in front of you, the story above, is the truer temptation to envy and ambition.

I twisted sideways to find where my book had landed, stretching as far as my torso would allow to retrieve it. A centimeter away from my grasp, a foot fell like a pendulum and launched my book across the floor. I pulled upright to find Mickey Sanders standing next to me with a menacing smile.

"Whoops! Sorry about your book, asshole."

I said nothing and got up to recover it, but his clan treated the book like an errant hockey puck. Table after table joined the field, keeping it in motion. Eventually, a game of three cup monte made me wonder under whose foot my book would be found. The humiliation of an ever-expanding weight held my legs in place. I stood there. Laughter rose around me into a wall of embarrassment. Why I even bothered to keep track was curiosity. These were the moments in life my father instructed me to walk away from. "Bad behavior is a contagion, son. Never try to intervene for fear of contracting the sickness." The book was a goner. I decided lunch was over.

When I turned back towards Lundergan, he was gone, leaving a tray of food. At first, I thought he didn't want to get involved, but then, an abrupt gasp sucked the attention of the crowd's jubilance at my belittling. A few tables over, Chaff Lundergan was pushing a freshman's face into his unrecognizable mashed food.

"You little twerp! You like that? You have something to laugh at now?"

Chaff held him by the back of his neck, moving his head like a ventriloquist's dummy.

"Now pick it up," he instructed. Chaff bent his head down to the floor. The freshman picked up the book. "Say you're sorry. Say it!" He turned his head toward me.

"I'm sorry," the freshman said, trembling, food particles dropping from his face like loose boulders.

Moorefield rushed from the shadows, raised his arm and guillotined Chaff Lundergan's hold on the boy. "To my office, now!" he commanded. There was no apparent smile on Chaff's face, but I suspected inside his mind he was smiling a contemptible, rebellious glee about his actions. Concern or fear were not present.

He communicated *mission complete* in a millisecond at a glance in my direction. I felt saved, but from what, I did not comprehend. Chaff Lundergan scared me. After the episode, I came to believe he was dangerous and I instantly wanted to distance myself from any further contact.

CHAPTER 9

With most disasters—earthquakes, tsunamis, hurricanes, war—populations cease to object to each other, overcoming their natural selfish natures and harmonizing to save their brethren. A flicker of a noble humanity scurries about to save the less fortunate.

The next day, the hallways of Saint Joe's buzzed with news of yesterday's events and unity of brotherhood. I received more than one pat on my back, shoulder grasp, and nod of sympathy. Jonathan Palitan came up to me at my locker and said he was sorry. This time without coercion.

"Are you the one Lundergan went gonzo on?" I asked, not actually sympathizing.

He simply nodded.

"Well, a lot of others to choose from that day."

Palitan hung his head and then slipped away into the nubbin flow of the academy.

No sign of Lundergan or Sanders in the hallways or in class. I thought it unusual until Moorefield approached me outside Mr. Bonner's class. He sauntered toward me through the hallway, an empty, dark void. Students bounced out of his way like unseen photons of energy. Moorefield stopped a few feet away and pointed at me, then waved an invitation to follow him. The photons engaged in whispered chatter as we walked in single file back through the void.

We approached the office. Moorefield stood at attention against the open door, his hands clasped below his belt, eyes focused along an invisible tightrope attached to the opposite wall. His body language offered an invitation to enter. I stopped at the threshold and caught the glare of Father Romano sitting on the opposite side of an eight-seat cherry conference table.

"Come in, Mr. Wheat." He pointed to the exact chair I was to occupy. Moorefield closed the door and stood in front, guarding any exterior light from exposing our rendezvous. I sat down on the edge of the chair, resisting the comfort of the soft leather back.

"Relax, Mr. Wheat. You're not in trouble."

"Yes, Father." A shadow spread across the table, covering us both. I turned and glanced at Moorefield, confirming the magnitude of his presence—a sentinel of monolithic proportion. My only thought at that precise moment was how long I could hold back my bladder.

"My boy, I have been watching you . . ." He shot a glance at Moorefield, hesitated, and put his head down with a chuckle. "I meant to say, we have been watching you all—watching to see where the trouble is. Which of you are student leaders and what adjustments must be made to keep our academy in peak harmonious shape. From what Mr. Moorefield tells me, you have been quite the model student, as was expected. Your father assured me." He ended the sentence as though a question, giving me time to confirm.

"It's early in the year, Father."

He laughed. "You mean there's still time for you to lose your way?"

"No, sir. That's not what I meant. I just mean, how much could you have noticed at that point?"

"In my experience, people have traits not easily recognized in the short term. Laziness, pride, academics, athleticism, fear, and determination. These, you need time to assess. However, leadership is usually an easy one to spot. A graceful confidence exudes from the man of wisdom and humility. Is that man you, Mr. Wheat?"

I stared, believing Father Romano was not expecting an answer, but I was uncomfortable with his assessment. Having been homeschooled through the lower grades, I lacked much experience in leadership. After all, who did I lead? I was fourteen. The extent of my wisdom included knowing how to stay out of my mother's way when she was cooking. However, I was also not socially impaired or made to feel insecure. I had not yet understood the concept of popularity or the disfavor of adolescent politics. That was all ahead of me.

Father Romano peeked over my shoulder and made the slightest nod to Mr. Moorefield. The door opened and he stepped out. The light rushed in. Father then leaned from his chair, clasping his hands on the table, and thoughtfully nodded in affirmation of his assessment.

"Tobias, I suppose we will find out if I am wrong, but I do believe you hold this trait. Perhaps latent and not fully developed into self-awareness."

"I don't feel like a leader, Father. I barely know my way around school. I haven't made any friends yet."

"No, and that is the grace of it. How many weeks has it been? It's obvious that you are not yet willing to sacrifice your intellect to the crowd. Feeling like you are a leader is often an illusion. True leadership is a gift given by the grace of the Lord, detected like a whiff of perfume; a missionary gift to be used to accomplish his will."

"Yes, Father," I mouthed. *If you say so*, I thought. *Where is all this headed*?

"Well, not necessary to convince you, Tobias. You will wear those shoes, or not. For now, I have a mission for you. The boy you met yesterday—"

"Mickey Sanders?"

"No. Mr. Lundergan."

"Oh. Are you expelling him for fighting?"

"Not at all. I've encouraged him to take some needed time out for a couple of days. I certainly do not condone fighting, Mr. Wheat, but he was fighting for honor—yours, to be exact, was he not?"

"Yes, Father."

"An excuse I will give him this one time."

"I'm glad to hear it. It wasn't his fault." My head was down as though I had misspoken.

"Do you care to tell me whose fault it was?"

"No, Father."

"Why not?" He pushed slightly away from the table.

"I'm okay. I'm not physically harmed. There's no need to punish anyone on my behalf, Father. I understand you have rules, and we must all obey them, but I don't want to rat out my classmates. That would be uncomfortable." I was hoping he would not have me turn anyone in. Even in an academy, a rat would always be shunned.

Father smiled. "There are many types of leadership, Tobias. You can lead men in the ways of war or business or on the field of play, but the greatest is moral leadership. Not simply knowing right from wrong, but knowing when to apply the right kind of pressure in a situation so righteousness prevails. Do you understand?"

"I think so," I said, but I wasn't sure. His words did not swell into obvious meaning.

Weeks later, perhaps years later, I felt the soft drizzle of understanding. I always thought imperative morals were fixed upon one compass. I found, as I aged, that many people have a wider understanding of morality as a variable calculated by need.

"In any case, the other boy is also taking time out," Father said.

"You knew?"

I guess I wasn't surprised. There were only forty of us, and Moorefield kept copious notes on our actions and conversations.

"Of course I knew. The question was a test of your willpower. You passed." Father smiled. "Tobias, I have something I need from you."

His words charged the skin on my arms to pucker into tiny bumps. I tried to smile back, but the slightest twitch of nerves became active in my cheeks. Internally, I drew a line and said, "*No. Choose someone else.*"

Then my lips moved: "Yes, Father?"

"I want you to befriend Chaff Lundergan." I felt like he had just slapped me across the face. He let the request hang in midair as though I were to pluck it, retrieve it, and bring it back to him. "Mr. Lundergan has an unsettled background. I'll let him share with you if he wishes. The important thing is, Mr. Lundergan needs a friend. He doesn't know it, but the necessity of friendship is a potent cure for what ails him. And not any friendship will do the trick."

"Why me?"

"The simple answer is: he likes you."

"Me?"

"Why does that surprise you?"

"He doesn't seem like the kind of guy that likes anyone, like he's bothered by being here. He keeps his distance."

"And you don't?"

It was true, I did keep a distance. Homeschooling was not a preparation for social contact. It was meant to keep the fertile mind unpolluted. Being immersed in a sea of testosterone makes you swim for the shallow end of the pool. But if the truth be told, I needed a friend as well; a goal I clung to like a favored blanket.

I didn't respond. His point was understood.

"For several days now, Mr. Lundergan has gone to the cafeteria to get his lunch, then off he goes to the East Hall stairwell, where he sits by himself on a step. Sad, but predictable. He doesn't think he fits in here at St. Joe's. That all changed a few days ago, when he found you. Talked with you. Ate with you. Fought for you. A very positive development."

Father gave me a few seconds to absorb the information. I recollect the events of the day, realizing Father Romano was right. Chaff did try to befriend me. "I guess so," I said tentatively. "Father, if he and I were friends, we would both be outcasts. No one—"

"Ah," Father interrupted. "That is the most important reason I want you to do this. Make no mistake. You can turn me down if you so choose, Tobias. To have the necessary impact on Mr. Lundergan's time here at the academy—to give him a boost into higher orbit—he needs more than a friend. He needs a mentor, a person—like you, Tobias—to emulate.

"I don't think you believe fitting into a particular group is of much importance. I think you are more fascinated with studying the groups than you are about joining them. Academics—sports—fellowship, these are the things that add weight to your backpack, Tobias. Am I right?"

I nodded. How could he have known these things about me? Moorefield must be a more potent spy than I thought. Only three weeks had passed since the beginning of the school year. "I suppose, Father. What if it doesn't go well?"

"It will go well," he said confidently. "Tobias, it will be a great act of charity for which you will be well rewarded." Father cast his eyes upward. I couldn't hold back my smile. "You may very well learn a few things from Mr. Lundergan. Differences can be attractions. And by now, you have learned that he is quite smart."

"How do you want me to do this?"

"Be yourself. Be an anchor, for now—a place of attachment. Everything else will take care of itself. Let it grow naturally."

CHAPTER 10

I would describe our relationship as anything but natural. The following day, after Father Romano's intervention, Chaff Lundergan returned to the academy. His participation in classes was the same apathetic and disinterested approach: short answers and lots of gazing out the windows. I wasn't the only one to notice.

Mr. Bonner took note of what he thought was an aloofness and an insult to his catechesis of ancient literature. He slapped a book down on his desk. Dust rose from the incursion. Twelve freshmen reflexively jumped in their seats. All eyes and ears were projected forward. Chaff only casually glanced away from the window, then resumed his inspection of the outdoors. Bonner moved to the front of his desk, holding his pointer out like a divining rod. It moved in a horizontal arc, taking its turn to point at each face in the room, stopping momentarily upon Chaff Lundergan. Squinting his disdain, he lowered the stick and spoke wildly as he paced.

"I understand that some of us are less stimulated by the classical research of great literature. Fetid minds wander upon the stuff of squalor and what belongs eventually to landfills rather than the spiritual philosophies of life." He pointed toward the windows. Confused faces squinted back. "Literature is not for the timid!"

Bonner struck the desk with his pointer. "It must be regarded with great honor to the many minds that have been brought to the fore—an offering to us men to distinguish ourselves, to enrich our lives. Could there be anything more dramatic, more classic, and more interesting than Homer's great poetic retelling of the Trojan War and

Odysseus's twenty-year journey home? What of Shakespeare's King Lear? Or Melville's great whale? Something must inspire you, no? Literature, men, exposes the great truths of the world. Is it a garden to care for or a desert to cross?"

Chaff interrupted the diatribe. "Everything we hear is an opinion, not a fact. Everything we see is a perspective, not the truth."

"Your words?" Bonner asked knowingly.

"They belong to Marcus Aurelius," Chaff replied.

Bonner was taken aback, brows rising to their highest point. He stared at Chaff, seeming to calculate a response. The rest of us didn't know what the hell Chaff just said, or why.

"You surprise me, Mr. Lundergan. Apparently, your ears have taken over the work of your eyes." Chaff smiled toward the window. "At such a young age, you have stunned me with your knowledge of the famous Emperor Aurelius. I have underestimated your mind."

"This 'being of mine, whatever it really is, consists of a little flesh, a little breath . . .' " Chaff added, as if to punctuate his grandstanding and take a bow in the limelight.

"Bravo again, Mr. Lundergan." Bonner nodded his head in appreciation. They were having their moment, bonded to an empirical understanding of the nature of man. "Class, this is what the classics may do for you. Let the words of Marcus Aurelius fill your mouth and taste their loveliness, then let them profit your minds, as was just demonstrated for you today." Mr. Bonner dismissed the class. Chaff headed out the door as fast as he could, as though he knew Bonner would want to talk to him.

"Mr. Lundergan, a word!" Bonner shouted after him. There was no response. Chaff headed down the hall like a missile in search of a target, ducking and veering through the throng of students.

The retelling of the episode would, no doubt, find its way through the same halls in the same fashion. Chaff was quickly becoming a legend. Under his skin, an uncouth toughness of attitude and poor manners rose like lava through an unlikely intelligence and suspicious education. It was as if he were a cursed beast waiting for someone or something to dispel his ugly nature for the real grandeur that lay beneath.

I was beginning to understand Father Romano's desire to find a safe place for Chaff to retreat to. Amazed by my own enthusiasm, I couldn't wait for lunch and my next encounter. My many questions were heaving up like field rocks in the frost of winter.

CHAPTER 11

I waited. Chaff never materialized. Then Father Romano's conversation came home about Chaff using the East Hall stairwell, out of bounds during lunch period. Moorefield was in the cafeteria on the upperclassmen side, breaking up an argument. I grabbed my soggy egg salad sandwich and headed to the stairwell and found Chaff sitting sideways on the top step, leaning against the wall. At first, he looked at me as though I had caught him in a crime, limbs stiffened, ready to bolt.

"You're not supposed to be here. You'll get in trouble," he said.

"Says the outlier."

He sat with his knees drawn up chest-high and his elbows resting on top, bouncing a makeshift aluminum ball against the far wall. He broke a half smile in reflex, then recovered. It was the first time I had seen a crack in the don't-bother-me facade.

"Can I join you?"

"It's a public stairwell."

"Let's hope not. I'm getting tired of being ushered into Father Romano's office."

Chaff gestured toward the lunchroom. "They give you trouble again?"

"Uh-uh. Just want to make sure you're okay."

"Weird, but thanks. How did you find me here?"

"Ah . . . Father Romano told me. Apparently, he knows everything that goes on in this asylum. Cameras possibly?" We paused and scanned the stairwell, but it was clear of any electronic surveillance. "More likely, Moorefield—I swear, he's a ghost—walks through walls."

"Father Romano thinks I need a friend."

The comment surprised me and I jerked my head in disbelief. I thought this friend thing was a covert mission.

"He told you that?"

"Yeah. Said you're a good guy and I should connect with you.

"That's why you sat at my table?"

"Yeah. You already saw how that went. Where I come from, Sanders would have been a piece of shit bleeding in some alley." He aimed at a place to spit but thought better and held back. "Anyway, you and I are nothing alike. I don't see the connection."

I ignored the comment and took it more as a challenge. He was right. We were nothing alike. The initial draw, besides Father Romano's request for my act of charity, was curiosity. Chaff appeared to be two people in one body. Both held mysteries pulling me in. Well . . . not in, but closer, where I searched for a glimpse of two heartbeats.

"How did you know that stuff in Bonner's class today?"

He openly laughed. "I thought Bonner's head was going to spin around on his shoulders. Either that, or he was about to adopt me like a lost puppy. Fun though."

Chaff hesitated, then asked, "What did Father Romano tell you about me?"

"Nothing. Said you'd tell me if you wanted to, like that didn't leave a whole world of questions."

"Well, I'm not sure I want to. Time to go." Chaff got up and slid the door open a few inches to scout the hallway. "Let's go," he said. We escaped from the stairwell and made our way to our next class.

***

Detective Harrigan sat unemotional listening to my story. Not every detail was shared and much of it summarized. "I'm amazed you haven't prompted me to rush to the end or fall asleep," I said.

"On the contrary. I'm fascinated." He took note of his watch. "Continue."

He yawned, leaving me a detestable curiosity about the man. Something was driving him, something more than an investigation. I'm no expert on how detectives work, but spending this much time with a witness-victim-suspect, or whatever I was to him, listening to an hour-long backstory didn't mesh with my layman's understanding of policework.

My story couldn't possibly give him the necessary lead needed to solve anything. For me, it was a catharsis, freeing my mind to remember the beginning of my friendship with Chaff Lundergan. I tried hard to ignore the end, at least temporarily. Harrigan wasn't digging for answers to anything significant. More of a prod, but not hammering me about the bank heist, as he called it. Or the murder, as I called it. There were facts I would not share. Not yet. But he didn't even bother to scrape at them.

"Are you waiting for something specific? A history of two fourteen-year-old boys managing to bond must seem innocuous."

"Like you said, I need to understand the relationship that brought you both to an unfortunate and illicit end. So, the stairwell . . ."

I continued waiting for some ulterior motive, some nugget he was waiting for. Nothing.

I continued.

"After that, the stairwell became a meeting place, a safe zone. The next couple of weeks, we got away with our rendezvous during lunch. No one asked where we were. But Moorefield knew all along we were there. Father Romano told him to leave things alone, allowing for the relationship to take."

"How'd you know?" Harrigan asked.

"There was a problem later. I told Father I didn't want to continue the friendship experiment. That's when I found out he and Moorefield were working behind the scenes to encourage the relationship. Explained everything."

"So, you became friends after all."

"Yes, but it was not easy. He was cagey. He was leery of my loyalty. I think he thought I was a spy for Father Romano. Things changed after the incident."

"Incident?"

"A couple of weeks later, we decided to stay in the cafeteria to eat. Chaff wanted to sit at the tables in the upperclassman area. I advised against the idea of it as an easy way to get our asses kicked. That's all I had to say. He put his head down and laughed. I asked what was so funny. He said, "Sounds like fun."

"Did he do it?" Harrigan asked, as though waiting for the punchline, almost enjoying the approaching danger.

"Yes, but I didn't go with him. I moved close, so I could see and hear what was about to happen. He picked a random table and sat down right in the middle. The seniors didn't have to stand in line for their food. They had attendants. After Chaff sat down, a server arrived and took his order. I think he named everything on the menu. I had to hold my sport coat up to my mouth to muffle my laughter."

Harrigan chuckled. "And?"

"The seniors who heard him ordering took note. The table became silent. They looked at him, cast eyes at each other, then at the freshman across from them, momentarily stunned. This had never happened before. Next thing, a guy named Blane Williams got up from across the table and yelled at him. His nostrils flared like a palomino driving hard on a Pony Express route. Both fists slammed the lunch table like hooves."

"What did he say?"

Harrigan was really enjoying my story, to my surprise, though my suspicions about his hidden agenda made my neck hair tingle. How could I be his only lead? He needed to be on the street, making calls, tracking down the whereabouts of the shooter, picking up debris for the forensics lab or whatever. Certainly not the detective I imagined from the dozen or so crime shows on TV. After all, aren't the characters modeled after real detectives? Amused by my own thoughts: *Is Harrigan a good cop or a bad cop?* swam in the hallways of my brain.

Harrigan snapped his fingers to bring me back to the conversation. "Hey, don't leave me hanging. What did he say?"

"Blane throttled Chaff with a hard stare, said, 'What the "bleep"? Get your puny freshman ass out of here, you muttonhead!' Then Williams yelled in our direction: 'Someone tell this muttonhead where he should be! You scrawny, bleating little goats better come retrieve your boy before we shear him and send him back crying for his mommy!' "

"What happened next was legendary. Chaff stood and told Williams to try. Told him it would be the sorriest day of his life. He sat back down. Blane was called out. He walked around the table and picked Chaff up by the shoulders of his jacket, pulling him off the bench and onto the floor. 'Now what, you little shit?' Blane said as he straddled Chaff's body."

Harrigan leaned forward. "Yeah?"

"I yelled at Williams—could hardly believe I did. Told him to leave Chaff alone. Williams bristled at me; an unfortunate distraction. Chaff punched Williams in the groin, causing him to fold like a cheap tent. Chaff grabbed his head and pulled him down and rolled over on top of him. The others were stunned. He got two or three hard whacks in before Moorefield came like a stroke of lightning and pulled Chaff off Williams with one arm. Moorefield set him down and held him back by the chest while reaching down to help Blane Williams to his feet. Chaff didn't fight or struggle. He looked at Blane and said, 'Now who's the little shit?'

"Moorefield marched them out of the lunchroom in complete silence. Nobody believed what happened. When Moorefield passed by, I told him it wasn't Chaff's fault, the other kid started it. Some dart of disdain shot out of Moorefield's eyes. I think he believed I started it—encouraged Chaff's incursion. Gave me the willies thinking I was in trouble and might be expelled. In the end, I think standing up for him was the beginning of my friendship with Chaff. But at that precise moment, I wanted nothing more to do with him. I believed he was unhinged."

"Sounds to me like the other kid needed an ass-kicking. I would have taken a piece of that myself," Harrigan said, like a true street thug.

"It isn't that. Chaff had conspired to put himself in the situation. He inspired the conflict and acted on it; the very definition of sin: Conspire, then act. Impulse is different—an involuntary reaction to unexpected acts. Chaff knew exactly what he was doing. The premeditation shook me."

Harrigan bobbed his head. "Yeah, that's what makes the difference between an accessory to a crime and a bystander. What are you guilty of, Mr. Wheat, criminal accessory or bystander?"

"You know, Detective, your compulsion for finding guilt is understandable considering your profession, but before you arrive there, don't you have to find evidence, or facts, or eyewitnesses? Maybe you should be somewhere other than here collecting that stuff."

"I'm a patient man, Mr. Wheat. I believe you have the facts I need. And when you are ready, I'll be here to receive them. My men will uncover the nature of the crime. Unfortunately, the FBI is in possession of the material forensics. But motive is the linchpin to solving any crime. If we know the *why*, we can usually reverse engineer the *who*."

"That makes a lot of sense. Thanks for clarifying."

"And for what it's worth, your story is entertaining. I might send out for popcorn and soda. And to be honest, so far, your friend's background hasn't convinced me of his fine virtues."

"Well, just so we are clear, I was there to support Chaff. He never got a chance to tell me why he was there." My voice turned slightly hostile.

Harrigan didn't answer. There was no mea culpa forming on his face. He put out his hand, open-palmed, to signal me to continue. So I did.

"I went to see Father Romano and told him it was all a mistake. I didn't want to continue trying to make a friend out of a crazy, unpredictable psycho. That was the moment when he leveled with me about helping the relationship along, and more importantly, why."

"So, what happened to Chaff and Williams?"

"Chaff was given his second warning and three-day cooling-off period. Coming back to school, he was nothing short of a legendary king to the freshmen. He thanked me for defending him. Said we would talk.

"Blane Williams was expelled. A week later, his parents got him back in, reminding Father how much they had contributed to the school over the years, and apparently, had a younger son who would be entering in the fall. To save face, Father Romano made a condition of admittance hinging on an apology. At the next assembly, Blane stood at the podium and apologized directly to Chaff and to the whole assembly for not showing better example as a senior. Humiliating, but good for everyone involved."

"Is that when Lundergan opened up to you?"

"Yes, an amazing part of the story, sets the stage for everything else."

The pain in my chest was climbing in intensity. I had to apologize and cut short our conversation.

"I'm going to have to take a hit on this medicine, so I don't know how much of this I'll get in before my next nap."

"One question," he said. "Did Lundergan ever tell you about his escapades on the Chicago streets when he was a kid?"

It was a weird regression. Instead of pushing the story forward, he wanted to go further back. "Yes. Eventually," I said.

The medicine took its effect.

CHAPTER 12

When I awakened, Harrigan was gone. My family had arrived and spread out around my hospital bed that had taken the place of my deathbed. Susan was holding my hand, smiling sympathetically.

"Hello again," I said, taking time to connect with each face. "Why so glum? Is there some news I should be worried about?"

A round of uncomfortable smiles.

"We're all worried about you," my mother said. "No news. Doctor Lantz is expected to come by in a little while. We should know more then. Your dad brought the paper." She turned toward him. "Marty, why don't you tell him what the paper says?"

"Stop!" Susan said. "This is not the time." A swordfight between eyes broke out. Susan would have none of it and was victorious. "My husband nearly died. He doesn't need this now." She pointed to the paper. Delores and Marty Wheat demurred.

"He's my son," my mother intoned.

"He's almost your dead son, Delores. The doctor told us yesterday that stress is the biggest danger to his heart."

"Dolores, leave it alone for now," Marty Wheat said as he placed his hand softly on his wife's arm. "Let's let them be for now." To Susan, he said, "We'll give you some time with your husband."

"Thanks, Martin." Susan gave him a quick hug. "Are you going to the hotel or down to the cafeteria?"

Dolores gave Martin one of her penetrating stares he was all too familiar with. "I think we will wait over a snack and coffee. Perhaps we could rejoin you afterwards?"

"Of course," Susan answered.

We exchanged goodbyes and they left after making Susan promise to call with Dr. Lantz's prognosis.

I studied my wife's face. A strong woman—imposing beauty needing no one's approval or compliment. Her short-cut, raven-black hair accentuated her polished, rounded cheek bones. She wore little makeup. It wasn't necessary.

"I did well," I said with an admiring smile.

"With what?"

"You. You're beautiful. I don't tell you enough."

She smiled at the compliment.

"It's nice that you still think of me that way."

"We've only been married for six months, not enough time for you to grow old and wrinkly."

"You better still think of me that way when I am old and wrinkly," Susan said.

"So what did the newspaper say?"

"The *Observer* reported on the incident. They had no facts so they went sensational. You can read it some other time." She lifted her gaze to the monitors above me.

"I don't understand what any of these monitors are saying but the nurse outside said you seem to be feeling a little better. Are you still experiencing a lot of pain?"

I nodded.

"I'm sorry," she whispered.

"Why should you be sorry?"

"I should never have let you go there. I know you were trying to help him, but it was nearly suicide to go in there. Now the police think you had something to do with it all."

"Have they bothered you?"

"A female detective, Samantha Ryan, came by the house yesterday after we left you. She asked if I knew you were going to the bank and what you were going to do."

"What did you tell her?"

"The truth. You were going to meet him, to talk him out of something. She asked what and I said I didn't know. That's true. I didn't. But, I don't think she believed me." Tears formed in ponds of regret. "She said I could be charged as an accessory. Is that what I am, an accessory to a crime, Tobias?"

"You and the detective want to know if I was involved; if I put on a charade, lied to you. Susan, you know better. The only thing I'm guilty of is bad judgment and trying to save him."

"Why didn't you call the police and let them handle it? You could have been killed. You *were* killed. The doctor said you were gone and that—" Susan's tears fell again. She collapsed into the side chair.

"I would like the answer to that question too," Harrigan said from the doorway. Susan was ready to react to the intrusion but he put his hands up to stop her. "I get it. I was checking in to see if your husband was ready to continue his story. Fascinating. Have you heard it?"

Susan reached for a tissue from the side table and wiped away her tears. "We are waiting for Dr. Lantz."

"I won't bother now. I wanted to let Tobias know we had a lead on the suspects. I'll stop back another time." Harrigan began to back out of the room, then hesitated. "If I may—these guys most likely skipped town, but they may also not want to leave witnesses behind. We'll continue to keep a man posted for now . . ." He nodded at us. "Tobias . . . Mrs. Wheat."

When Susan's tears ended, her angst took over. She paced around the room like she was looking for something. "I'm furious about him showing up at the worst times. Doesn't he have the answers he needs?"

"What are you looking for?"

"Something to throw at him if he comes back. First, he treats you like a suspect. Now he comes here about a threat to your life. The man is tactless."

"Don't kill the messenger, Susan. He's doing his job." I reached for Susan's hand, squeezed a little until she redirected her attention back to me. "It'll be okay. You'll see."

"Do you know them?" she asked.

"Yes, and so do you."

She paused and gave the comment a moment, then realized what I had said. "It was them?" Her face warped over the distasteful realization that those same men were responsible for my near death. They were also the men who entered her apartment at gunpoint months ago, threatened me and her, and kidnapped Chaff.

"My God," she said.

Doctor Lantz arrived. The interruption distracted Susan from any further reaction to what I told her. The less Susan knew, the better. Her safety kept me guarded about anything I told her.

Lantz distracted us, discussing my improving condition and what to expect in the near future.

CHAPTER 13

Detective Harrigan returned after lunch a week and a half into my recovery. A small plastic plate with red Jell-O was the only remnant remaining on the roll-away. He sat down. “Looks delicious.”

“Help yourself. The estimate around here is about four hundred a day. Three semi-decent meals, bathroom breaks, a shave, and someone to rub your legs. Not bad. Checking in is a bitch though. Watch out for the cover charge.”

“About the same price as a day in the slammer. All the same amenities, except everyone rubs you the wrong way.”

“Funny.”

“You’re a lucky man, Tobias. I spoke to Dr. Comstock.”

“Why him?”

“Well, if you had died, the medical examiner would answer our questions, but as it is, we consulted the only other person who got a look at your insides. Dr. Comstock shared an X-ray of the damage, pre-op and post-op. Lundergan was shot with an AR-15 rifle. Shoots a .223 caliber round. Small, but leaves the muzzle at three times the speed of a handgun. Someone meant business. Comstock surmises the round struck his upper torso, cutting a path through his aorta before exiting. Even if missed, the cavitation would do enough damage to surrounding tissue to lay him down. He most likely bled out.”

I cocked my head to the side. "Thanks for the physics lesson. I don't play with guns, so none of that sank in. He was shot. He's dead. That's all that matters."

"Maybe," Harrigan said. "But physics, as you say, explains what happened to you."

I ignored his comment, recollecting something he said in his explanation. "What do you mean *most likely* bled out? Wouldn't you be aware of the cause of death by now?"

"His body was removed from the crime scene by an FBI forensics team. Not examined locally. According to the medical examiner, Constance what's-her-name, the FBI told her he lost too much blood. He was suspected of a previous crime. They needed to match DNA, so they took the body in a hurry."

"FBI?"

"Don't be surprised. They have jurisdiction in a bank robbery. Although, I'm not sure why they don't care to visit you," Harrigan pondered, turning to look out the window for a moment as if he were having a revelation of his own. He let out a huff, like something dawned on him. He turned back around but was no longer fully engaged in our conversation, still mulling over a thought.

"Not a bank robbery," I reinforced. "Besides, Detective, I thought you were the lead in the investigation. That doesn't add up."

I pondered. Maybe they backed off when they realized it wasn't what they thought. On the other hand, why take the body?

Harrigan shrugged. "Got me. That's for the boys in the tower to figure out. For now, it's being treated as a bank job and a homicide. I still want the reason why you and Mr. Lundergan were there, who killed him, where they are, and what they wanted."

Diamonds. They wanted the damn diamonds. It was my turn to phase out. The information was a lot to take in. Chaff doesn't have a family. Someone to be there—at his funeral. I wondered if there would be a funeral. Where would they bury him?

"Is it possible to contact them?"

"Who?"

"The FBI. I want to arrange his burial. I'm his only family." My head tilted into a helpless gaze. The reality was setting in. It wasn't only about me getting shot. "My friend is dead. I will never see him again. I have to contact them."

"I'll see what I can do," Harrigan said. "I might have a contact. I worked on a task force with the FBI years ago."

I took note of his comment. Something Chaff told me a year ago made me wonder. An informant on the task force, he said. They never identified him but had suspicions. I shoved the thought away; too provocative.

"Can I ask you another question about the shooting?" Harrigan nodded. "If the bullet exited, how did you know the round was an AR-15? Did you find it?"

"That's the funny thing I wanted to tell you earlier. The doctor showed us the round he removed from you.

Same bullet. Seems you might be right, your friend saved your life, although Dr. Comstock swears you both should be dead." Harrigan held the X-ray up toward the ceiling light. "See that?" He pointed. "The object of your discomfort. The bullet entered your chest sideways, shattering your rib cage. He removed bone fragments from your heart. Tiny arrows. He said they acted like a plug, keeping your heart pumping long enough for him to operate and repair the damage."

"So, you believe that Chaff was innocent?"

"I didn't say that. I said he saved your life. However, you can continue to convince me. The last time you were about to tell me an important part of the story before you pressed the deadman switch on the morphine injector."

"Not morphine."

"Effective, nevertheless. You were out in seconds." Harrigan sat down and pulled his writing pad out of his upper pocket, then prompted me to begin again with the wave of his hand.

Memories resurfaced.

"Things settled down after the Blane Williams incident. In fact, Chaff seemed almost normal. Academy life became routine. I joined the soccer team. Chaff tried cross-country. He was successful—responsible for a new school record. We were inseparable in those days. No one dared to give us trouble. He ate a lot of dinners at my house—stayed over, went to church with us. Mom and Dad wanted to adopt him.

"Then, one day late in our senior year, I opened my locker and found a note someone slipped through the metal grill."

"From Lundergan?" Harrigan asked.

"No name. The note read, 'Tell your friend to bring it to me or else—he'll know.' "

Harrigan sat up in his seat like it had just happened and he needed to spring into action. "What the hell? *It*? What was *it*?"

"I don't know."

I did, but I still wasn't sure I wanted to say anything. If what Chaff told me was in the case actually was, that much money could make a person do bizarre things.

"What did you do?"

"Nothing at first. I thought he got himself into trouble with Mickey or Blane or someone who thought I held sway over Chaff. I figured anyone could easily go to the source."

"And?"

"The next day, I got another note. This time from Chaff, saying 'practice field at five pm.' The soccer team practices at three thirty, so I was there. He was sitting up high in the bleachers alone. I climbed up and sat next to him. He was smoking a cigarette.

" 'Not smart,' I told him.

" 'The least of my troubles,' he said. Then he threw it down and stomped it out as if he was trying to blend it into the cement step.

" 'I'm ready,' he said.

" 'Ready for what?'

" 'To tell you my story.' "

"Okay, good. What did he tell you?" Harrigan asked with great interest.

CHAPTER 14

"Chaff grew up on the street. His father was jailed for a bank robbery in West Virginia when he was two or three."

"Runs in the family," Harrigan said.

"Just listen. His mother became an alcoholic. A lot of visitors—men visitors—put some food on the table for a while. By the time he was twelve, he was in and out of school, on the street learning how to pickpocket along with other petty crimes that got him into juvey a few times. He got hooked up with a gang on the south side—the kiddy gang. That was the name they gave themselves. A couple of older kids being run by a very unpleasant crew of miscreants exploiting them. He tried to get out."

"Seems like a theme."

"Possibly." I disliked Harrigan's sarcasm, but I regretfully understood his point of view.

"Let me guess," Harrigan said. "They wouldn't let him."

"Right. Once in, in for life. Anyway, there was this guy the kiddy gang was told to follow."

"The syndicate?"

"No, the guys working for them. Somewhere along the way, they decided they wanted a bigger cut. They took matters into their own hands. The boys—Chaff's kiddy gang—were told all they had to do was steal some item a courier was carrying and bring it back to them. When the item went missing, the plan was to blame it on the kids if anything went sideways. It was supposed to be easy."

"Huh. Not easy enough?"

"Exactly."

"How did the kids find out they were being set up?"

"The older boy overheard one of them talking in an ally."

Harrigan looked away, like he had finally figured something out.

"What was the item?" he asked.

"I didn't know at the time. I asked, but Chaff wouldn't tell me. Said it would be better if I didn't know. It didn't take much to put two and two together—courier, syndicate, diamonds, cash, but I left it there. Figured he would tell me in time.

"It turns out the police and the FBI were also following, tracking a money laundering and diamond smuggling operation—the syndicate you mentioned earlier. By the way, how did you find out about the syndicate?"

"You underestimate my detective skills, Tobias. Occasionally, I leave the donuts behind and squeeze in a little work." Harrigan laughed at his own joke.

"You are here twenty-four seven. How do you have the time?"

Harrigan gave me one of those polite smiles like when you want to avoid violence in mixed company. Sarcasm is a ploy meant to keep others at arm's length until its effects are reversed, an inexcusable assault. His knowledge of the syndicate pushed all my alert buttons. I remember him saying he was on a task force with the FBI. I suppose it's possible to have innocent knowledge.

"The grunts on the street keep me informed. Let's return to the story."

I took a drink of water to stall a little longer and flush away my immediate concerns about the integrity of the man I was talking to. His deflection twitched a nerve. The pause produced no facts I could hang on; no circumstantial evidence either. Just a feeling—a weird intuition I usually credited to Susan.

I pushed my concerns to the side, deciding for the moment that my near-death experience and the criminals that caused it were responsible for my paranoia. Distrusting Harrigan wasn't helping. He was the detective, I was the victim. I needed to let him do his job. I adjusted my mental position, then continued with my story.

"When the FBI were about to step in, Chaff and his buddies struck and stole the guy's case right out from under the nose of the police—everyone. Now the kiddy gang were the ones being followed. The plan fell apart and the case got moved around. The police never recovered it. The bad guys never put their hands on it. Chaff got caught. After grilling him for hours, not getting what they wanted, he was carted off to a detention center and was held there for a week."

"If true, he was too young. That would not have happened," Harrigan insisted.

"You would think. Apparently, Chaff and his friends interrupted a major investigation by undercover agents and all. They wanted to make sure he was kept quiet until it was all over. They claimed it was for his safety."

"Yeah, sure," Harrigan snorted. "Maybe they were saving him to rat out the other guys. What happened next?"

"What happened next is no one ever knew what happened to the stolen Halliburton case and Chaff was thrown a lifeline."

"The case is gone?"

"That's what I believe."

I held back the truth.

"The investigation ended and became a cold case. The police couldn't find his mother. She vacated without a trace. No other relatives."

"Abandoned," Harrigan guessed.

"Correct."

Chaff told me he didn't feel abandoned. He felt relieved. But I never believed he felt that deep down. I don't think he ever wanted to see her again, but possibly he wanted to know if she missed him—belonged to him.

"Because of his age, social services got involved. They tried to find a foster home but no one wanted him because of his record, and twelve-year-olds are not high on the adoption list. A priest named Father Toomey convinced the authorities to let him take Chaff into a home for boys run by Catholic Charities."

"He escaped?"

"You want to tell the story?" My turn for a little sarcasm. Harrigan nodded and I continued.

"It turned out he liked the place. He and Father Toomey became friends—sort of a father figure, no pun intended. It also turned out Chaff is smart—untrained, uneducated—but very smart. He spent the next two years changing that status, studying the classics and learning his ABCs.

"A couple of years later, Father Toomey contacted his friend Father Romano in New Jersey, whom he is friends with from as far back as seminary, and begged the favor of enrolling Chaff at St. Joe's Academy for Boys, a charitable experiment. Father Romano agreed and set him up with an older couple from church. Not as foster parents. They were alone and had an extra room. Father paid them a stipend for food and board to watch over him."

"An interesting turn of events," Harrigan said.

"Agreed. The transfer was hush-hush, meant to keep Chaff safe. I never knew any of this early on; in fact, not until a few weeks before graduation, although I guessed he had some kind of extracurricular education. The guy was frighteningly smart."

"You found this out when?"

"After the note showed up in my locker and we had the chat in the stands that day. I was amazed. I asked Chaff why he decided to tell me. He said someone was looking for him, and he had to go away. Whoever wrote that note scared him. It came out later that Chaff was afraid they would come after me to get to him. It was a total sacrifice."

"Which begs the question, as you said. Why not go to the source?"

"They were watching. Aware he and I were friends. They didn't care about Chaff, only what he could tell them about the missing aluminum case. He was afraid they would use me as leverage."

"Did he have it?"

"Have what, the case? No. I mean, I don't think so. He never said anything to me one way or the other."

But he had. I wasn't sure if the lie came across my face. It was the second time I refused the information.

Harrigan's eyebrows raised. He made a note. "So, he leaves the academy . . ."

"No. I talked him into staying. I told him he needed to go to Father Romano and tell him what had happened. Father was aware of his background and invested in keeping Chaff out of harm's way."

"What about the bad guys?" Harrigan asked.

I laughed out loud. "I couldn't believe it. Moorefield?"

"Yeah?"

"In real life, a bodyguard procured to look after Chaff. Turns out Moorefield is ex-Secret Service, ex-FBI, retired. I wouldn't be surprised if the guy was also a SEAL. He's amazing. Father Romano was his pastor, confessor, and friend. Hired him under the guise of vice principal but with the express special duty of watching Chaff's back.

Father Romano was aware someone might show up at some point.

"In fact, Father Toomey had contacted Father later on and said a couple of roughnecks pressed him about Chaff's whereabouts. He didn't give up any info, but there was a break-in after. His office was torn up, and they might have found some note or something that led them to St. Joe's. Father Toomey couldn't be sure. Chaff and I were kept in the loop and told to bring any information or observations of danger directly to him or Moorefield."

"This Romano was his guardian angel," Harrigan said. "Along with the FBI guy."

"*Father* Romano," I corrected, "and yes, he was. Once he explained it, Chaff felt a little better. Leary, but willing. From that point on, the bond between the four of us thickened. A crazy time, to be sure."

"How long did it last?"

"There were a couple small episodes, but nothing Moorefield couldn't handle. He had a few retired friends—the R66 squad, as he called them." I had to laugh at the memory. "Chaff's safety became a fun retirement project. Moorefield was intense, but without him, this story would have ended sooner."

Worn out at this point, I needed a nap along with a shot of pain meds. The family was expected. Harrigan was unusually gracious this time. He said the story was helping him, although I couldn't figure how. He stood and asked if he could return in the morning. Then he asked two last questions.

"Does the name Johnny Willow mean anything to you?"

"No, who is he?" I winced like someone had stuck my temple with an ice pick. I knew exactly who Johnny Willow was—a violent maniac. I held back to see what Harrigan could tell me.

"You might know him as 'The Woodshed,' " he said, dead-faced. I got a shot of adrenaline, but I managed to return the same expression. Harrigan didn't wait for my answer before asking his second question. "So, Chaff Lundergan never had the case?"

Again, he didn't wait. He said, "I'll visit again tomorrow," and left the room.

CHAPTER 15

The next morning, I opened my eyes to find Harrigan standing outside the open door to my room talking to the officer he posted, the man's back toward me. I overheard Harrigan's instructions:

"Here's a couple of photos. Watch out for these guys; they may take matters in their own hands—extensive training. Don't underestimate them. Anything suspicious, you call me," he said.

"You think these guys could show?" the officer asked.

"Doubtful, but better to be wise about the possibilities. The worst case, make sure you're faster than they are."

"Yes, sir," the officer said. The man looked over his shoulder and saw me looking at him. For an instant, we caught eyes. He reflexively touched his gun holstered under his arm. Harrigan then aggressively pushed him out of my line of sight, landing him against the outside wall. "What's wrong with you?" I heard Harrigan mutter to him, then he poked his head around the corner of the door frame. "Hey, you awake?"

"Yes. What was that all about? Are you seriously thinking they're still around?"

He let go of the man's jacket and sauntered inside the room. "Assuming I stole a bunch of green? No. I'd be on my way to a private beach somewhere—way south. Like you said, no green were taken. I would still be far away from here, but then, you can never underestimate the stupid. Assuming your bad guys came up short of any money, or the exotic lost case, they might just be pissed off."

"The man out in the hall . . . he looks familiar."

My comment had an effect. Harrigan hung his head, pressed his lips tight, and gulped down a deep breath. He glanced to the side where the man was standing. He seemed annoyed. Looking at the man, he said, "Yeah, he gets that a lot. One of those faces, I guess." Harrigan changed the subject, looking back at me. "By the way, after I left you yesterday, I paid a visit to Father Romano. Your wife put me in touch with him. He's staying at the rectory at St. Peter's, not far from here."

He waited for my reaction. Smiled. Then he put his hands in his pockets and took a wide stance. His broad body was imposing. "He told me an interesting story," Harrigan said. "About an encounter you may or may not have had with Johnny Willow, aka Woodshed. You want to confirm or deny?"

"What did he tell you?"

Harrigan leaned against the wall. "I would rather hear it from you."

"You should leave Father Romano out of all this. He's a holy man; here to give me comfort."

"He appeared more than willing to help. Said he owed you. You said you didn't know Willow. I'm interested in which one of you is telling the truth. He's got the edge."

Father was in his sixties when I entered St. Joe's. His short, white hair put on like a laurel wreath around his balding intellect. The last I heard, he was retiring from his active role at the academy, but the man I knew was never meant to retire—a leader of extraordinary means, an educational pillar of the community.

The day we met, his imposing stare captured my attention and held me. I was having an audience with the king of a small country. Stout. Strong like a hundred-year-old oak, but limbs of kindness sheltering you from all dangers, physical and spiritual. A decade of rosary beads adorned his side pocket. Taking confession with him during those years was a warm embrace direct from the Lord. Chaff felt the same. Father allowed a rare friendship, unusual, between the sheep and the shepherd. We may have been a project in the beginning but in the end, we were his adopted children.

"Of course, he thought he was helping." I squeezed my eyes shut, remembering a not-so-fun incident. "Yeah, I may have met the man. It was senior year, graduation a week away. College was set. Chaff and I were both accepted at Duke with plans—major in public relations and journalism. After that, we would open our own PR firm. *The Chaff and the Wheat Public Relations.* It was a good plan."

"What happened?"

"The guy you mentioned yesterday—he showed up."

"Let me guess. He went after Lundergan," Harrigan suggested.

"No. He came after me. We were driving by then. He caught me in the senior parking lot. Put a hood over my head and shoved me into a car trunk. They took me—"

"They?" Harrigan interrupted.

"I counted three voices. Not sure, but that's what I figured."

"You get a look?"

"They never took the hood off. I never knew where they took me until the whole thing was over. They tied me to a chair. I heard the cock of a gun, felt the metal against my head. They said if I wanted to survive and if I wanted my family to survive, Chaff needed to cough up the whereabouts of some case. Said they had waited long enough. They didn't believe me when I insisted it was the first I heard of a case. I didn't know what was in it; I didn't know where it was, and I didn't care. That got me a bloody lip."

"How did you know Johnny Willow kidnapped you?"

"I didn't, but they said if I didn't yield, I would be taken to the Woodshed. They made it clear that it wasn't a place."

"How did you figure?"

"They said *he* would make me talk. Afterwards, I would be dead, lame, or catatonic. The threat was laced with a bit more vitriol than what I'm saying. I didn't know he was your guy until you mentioned the name."

"You get hurt?"

"Knocked me around a bit. Bruised me, scared me, nothing more. The big one burned the palm of my hand with a lighter and said, 'The fire is getting hotter. You feel it?' "

"You remember anything else?"

"Yeah, I remember peeing myself before things got quiet. They all left. I sat for hours in my own stench. A homeless guy found me the next morning. Removed the hood and untied me. I gave him twenty dollars to keep his mouth shut and found my way home."

"That's it? You didn't call it in?"

"Until I could speak to Chaff, I didn't want to make trouble. I went to Father Romano and Moorefield the next day; told them what happened. Moorefield said he would take care of it. The same day, Chaff was gone. No goodbye. No explanation."

"Gone . . . hmm. Moorefield?"

"I'm not sure. I didn't see Chaff again for a few years. You're going to ask me where he was all that time and I can't tell you. It's not pertinent to the story anyway."

I wasn't going to tell Harrigan. At least not now. It wouldn't help build sympathy for Chaff. He didn't question me any further, like he knew the answer. I suspected as much. He was connecting some dots, but from what little I shared, I couldn't figure out what that could be.

A nurse stopped in and said it was time for my CT scans to check how my heart was doing. The timing was helpful. Harrigan left me alone, giving me time to catch my breath. Before he left, I asked if I could have a copy of the mug shots he left with the officer outside my door. At first, he was confused. "Mug shots? Oh, oh, yeah." He handed me a copy and said, "The big guy is Trevor Masters, 'The Baker.' A long rap sheet. Very unpleasant fellow. See you tomorrow. The other guy is much nicer but just as lethal."

I remembered them. The chill returned, seeped in under my skin. The nurse brought me an additional blanket.

CHAPTER 16

A Year Earlier

The next day, Harrigan walked in and took his seat. "Can we get to the meat and potatoes today?"

I gave Harrigan a long stare, not sure what to do. He wanted more. He wanted details of what Chaff's role was before he was killed. My brain equivocated.

"I know you aren't sure what to share with me, Tobias. I'm the law and you don't know where you fit in this whole affair, but your friend is dead. It can't be any worse for him. I can treat you as a witness or a suspect—your choice. But I think it's in your best interest to cough up what you know."

He was right. Chaff wasn't in more danger. What was I protecting? Who was I protecting? I fast-forwarded to the crux of the story.

***

A year ago, I was sitting at my desk in front of my dorm window at college, heavy into *The World According to Rhetoric*. Final exams a week away, and like the other eighteen hundred seniors, I was immersed in cramming, black coffee, and unhealthy snacks.

A soft persistent knocking interrupted my mind, annoying as all hell. I turned to rush into the hall and scream at the guilty idiot. There in the frame of my door was a face. I couldn't believe who it belonged to.

"Chaff, what the hell?"

I was startled to see him and jerked my head back as if he were a ghost. He stood in the doorway leaning against the doorframe, staring at me with a shit-eating grin, wearing a blue Duke hoodie, jeans, and a pair of Nikes. His ruddy cheeks were puffed up by an exaggerated smile and his red locks leaked out the sides of his hood.

"Should I take a bow? You look like you're ready to applaud."

I didn't know what to say.

He held up a hand and waved. "Surprise."

"To say the least. Damn! Is that really you?"

"Hold on, let me check. Yep, it's me."

"How did you find me?"

"I stopped a pretty girl in the mall. Described you: Blond hair, blue eyes, dimple on the right cheek, wire rims, one awkward whisker, but otherwise kind of handsome."

"Some random girl knew me?"

"She had no idea. I had to stop at the student center and inquire at the desk."

I couldn't laugh. He was standing there like a mirage. All I could do was close my eyes and hope he was still there when I opened them. *Three years.* It had been three years since we had seen or spoken to each other.

"At least one of us made it to Duke. You doing the PR gig like we imagined?"

I ignored the question. "What are you doing here?" I rushed him. Chaff put out a hand. I slapped it away and hugged him, grabbed his shoulders and ran my eyes from head to toes. "Shit! You look like you belong here. Did you—?"

"Nah, I took a quick tour of campus. Checked out the Blue Devils store—cool stuff. I bought this hoodie. Hey, great to see you, man. You haven't changed." He glanced at my desk full of open books. "Still a dweeb with a big brain," he teased.

Chaff's grin evaporated. Turned serious. "This is a great school. I'm happy you made it and wish we were here together. Anyway, I'm sure you have questions. I'm all yours for a few hours. Is there anywhere we can grab a beer?"

"Damn right I have questions. It's been too long. I thought you were dead. I can't believe you're here!"

"Dead man walking, actually. Has it been that long? Come to think of it, you're a bit different." He bent down and took a close look at my chin. "Is that a second whisker?"

I pushed him away and threw a rolled-up piece of paper at him. "Bastard. What do you mean dead man walking?"

"I'll explain, but not here. C'mon."

I was hesitant. I wanted to machine-gun fifty questions right on the spot, but he had stepped out and was walking down the resident hallway toward the stairs. I grabbed a jacket and followed.

It was midday. We went to Louie's Grub Hub on Plum Street just off campus. Took a booth and ordered a pitcher of beer. The place was tired and worn. Tabletops gouged, water stains on the ceilings, a chipped linoleum floor, probably fifty years old and the cheapest spot on campus. Most of the effort was placed in the food—big burgers, sloppy tacos, and great chili. Perfect college food. Freshman girls waiting tables to help pay the bills, an added bonus. Louie was past fifty, but he had an excellent eye for hiring.

I took a longer gaze at Chaff's face and his red hair—*man on fire.* I remember calling him that after I saw him scare the crap out of Jonathan Palitan back at the academy in ninth grade. He'd put on a little weight, his cheeks were fuller, and his belt hung low beneath his stomach. He was still youthful and solid though. Confidence still beamed through his eyes. He'd developed a tic I hadn't noticed before. His cheek fluttered every now and then. He rubbed at it when it happened, said it was an old injury from an alley fight.

"Are you finished staring? I'm not back from the dead or anything." Chaff coughed a chuckle.

"Don't make me pinch you. So, where have you been?" I asked the obvious.

"Mostly? Chicago."

"You went back? You back in the—?"

"The business? No. Why would you think that?" His head lowered reflexively and his eyes wandered left and right, betraying a hidden truth. "Hardly. How many times do I need to remind you I was twelve when I was a part of that stuff? I'm not even sure a twelve-year-old can qualify as a genuine bad guy. Maybe a punk, but come on."

"I seem to remember a seventeen-year-old when your friends came after me. They were looking for you . . . for the case, the one you told me about. They beat the shit out of me, then left me for the rats and cockroaches till some homeless guy found me. After it was over, you were gone. Now, here you are. What should I think?"

"Not that."

"Okay, so what upstanding line of work have you been engaged in since the thug reunion?" I was pushing him and felt bad about it, but I needed to know what was up.

Chaff laughed, an uncomfortable laugh, more of an understanding grunt. "I guess I deserved that," he said. "But, no. I didn't go back. You, Romano, and Moorefield drilled that life out of me. So much so, I went in the opposite direction."

I wasn't sure what Chaff meant, but he appeared to be sincere. "You became a priest?"

"Something like that . . . You're a jerk, Tobias." Our faces dropped into the fun of our repartee. Something we both missed in our friendship. "By the way, I never told you about the case. You knew we stole an item, but I never told you what it was. How did you hear about it?"

"Initially? My mom. She came to school one day a couple of weeks after we connected and had a sit-down with Father Romano. She asked about you because we were hanging out a lot. Said you looked sinister."

We clinked beer glasses.

"She never told me directly, but I overheard her telling my dad one night after dinner. There was a theft—some briefcase a businessman was attached to. You and a couple of friends snatched it and you got caught, but were too young for the authorities to hold. Placed in a juvenile program. They never found the missing item. Nothing more after that. I waited for you to tell me more. You never shared the details and I didn't pry."

"You're okay, Tobias, my best friend, but I didn't think you could handle knowing about my background at the time. The academy was like being sent to Mars. Off-world for me. Everyone was alien. I didn't know how to function or who I could trust. You were the most unlikely kid to connect with, squeaky-clean; I thought I was going to slip and fall down just being near you. You turned out to be okay. Very okay. But then." He glanced out the window, lifted the blind an inch, focused on the street, then turned back.

"I should have charged you for all the protection I gave you for those four years," Chaff chided.

"That's okay. It would have been a wash to help you navigate the life. Teaching you how to blend in was harder than teaching a two-year-old how to use a fork and knife."

"Touché"

"Getting back to your unannounced departure, Moorefield went silent about where you went."

"We were protecting you."

"Me?"

"Yeah, those guys weren't fooling around. They would hurt you even worse if I didn't leave when I did. My exit had to be clean and you had to be in the clear—unaware."

"Clear—clean—unaware? Jeez! You sound like you are part of a spy ring. I thought the stolen case deal was old stuff, back when you were twelve or something, eight years ago. Isn't that over?"

He ran his hand through his hair. A subtle exasperation released in a heavy sigh. "I wish. I thought so. Spy ring? No, but you're close."

I pushed back from the table. "Like that doesn't have to be explained. How close?"

"I'm working up to that. You deserve an explanation," Chaff said, behaving like a person who was not ready to tell you the truth. His face swelled with a now-or-never decision-making palsy, breaking through the mind's defenses and getting closer to the *now*.

I interrupted the verdict, or whatever was pending in his thoughts. "Why did you come back? I mean, I'm glad you did, but why now?"

"I need your help." Chaff's smile was gone. "I want to tell you all about it now. You good with that?"

"Why wouldn't I be?"

"Because once I tell you, you won't be able to un-hear it. I could be putting you at risk."

"Spit it out."

***

Trevor Masters held the phone to his ear and kept his eyes peeled on the Grub Hub. His black hair hung wildly over pockmarked cheeks and a ruthless gaze before dipping into his coat's leather collar to hide his face.

"He's here. I'm staring at him."

A voice at the other end of the phone crept into his psyche and restrained his savage desires. "Do not approach. Not now. You understand?"

"Yeah, for now. I'm tired of chasing this little weasel. Time to heat things up. Don't make me wait too long."

"Is Wheat with him?" the voice asked.

"Yeah. You think he handed it off?" Masters snarled his lip as he spoke into the phone.

"Just follow for now and don't get made. We don't want them to run."

"Got it." Masters put his phone in his left jacket pocket, then landed his hand on the nine millimeter lying next to him on the car seat. He would put him down if he had his way. Years had gone by and they were no closer to finding the case. It was hard for him to maintain his impatient surveillance.

Masters didn't like taking orders. Never did. He was part of Johnny Willow's crew, which is a form of possession—*Willow's crew.* The thought tortured his mind for years, envious Willow had the connection and not him. The syndicate people were getting impatient. Willow was on a tight leash and a constant threat of not finding their lost merchandise. Merchandise he originally meant to keep lost until his plan to deep-six the kiddy gang got screwed up by the feds. Chaff Lundergan was the only one left who knew the whereabouts of the damn case. However, Willow was unsure. Masters was confident.

Masters thought to himself he never would have lost the score in the first place, and the kid would never have survived this long if he made the decisions. The syndicate pulled the plug on their involvement in any new handoffs and threatened a certain retaliation if they didn't recover the assets. Patience was running short all around. Trevor's thoughts swirled into a kind of chaos between taking orders and giving orders, imagining his own outcome and his own payday. He had taken care of the other punks years ago. Lundergan was way past his life expectancy. Who did he think he was?

CHAPTER 17

Chaff glanced out the window again, appraising the street, the cars, and the people. His demeanor prompted me to gawk too. What was I supposed to see? At three in the afternoon, the sun washed through the window and fell on him like someone turned on a switch illuminating his face. He had to hood his eyes with his hand, but then turned away.

"Excuse me." Chaff waved at our waitress, a young, pretty brunette with a ponytail; couldn't have been older than seventeen. She pranced as she approached the table like she was about to be asked out by an upperclassman. "Can you put these blinds down for us? The light is so bright, I feel like I should be dancing on stage."

Her infatuated smile evaporated. She stretched her thin, delicate body over the table to release the blind. The youthful curvature drew our eyes before Chaff and I glanced at each other with competing admiration. "Is that okay now?" she stepped back and asked.

Chaff smiled and made it obvious as he searched for her name tag. "Yes, very okay . . . ah—Caitlin," he said, venerating her figure with his eyes. Caitlin stared like she was standing on the shore looking out to sea. "That will be all then?" Her final hope for more attention.

"Yes, thanks," Chaff said before dispelling all hope and returning to our conversation. Caitlin backed away—expectations dashed—and melted back into the cacophony of the morning Grub Hub patrons.

"Cruel," I said.

"On a different day . . ." He glanced back in her direction. "This is more important."

My interest was piqued, but more like I was reading a crime novel and not inside the story myself, pages flipping without my help.

"Okay," he began. "Most of what I'm going to tell you, I learned later—much later. It was a surprise that they had found me at the academy after all that time."

"Who are *they*?"

"Not important. Not yet." Chaff paused like he was having doubts about telling me. "Tobias, I know you are going to have questions—a lot of questions, but you need to trust me. Time is not my friend. It would help if you would just listen. Most of this story you have already heard."

"What you told me about our senior year in the stands?"

"Yeah, but I'm going to tell you again—more details. It explains where I've been for the last few years. You good with that?"

I nodded. Chaff took a deep breath and looked at me like it was the beginning of an interview for a secret security clearance. His earlier comment, *you can't un-hear it*, resonated in my mind. Maybe I didn't want to hear. Maybe I wanted to remain a naïve best friend. This wasn't like reminiscing. What Chaff was about to tell me was a whole other part of his life, a hidden epilogue to the guy I knew. I followed his eyes out the window as if I recognized what he was afraid of. Finally, he began.

"I was twelve. I lived mostly on the street. The reason is a whole other story—another time though." Chaff flipped his hand in the air as if to wave away that part of his life, but Father Romano filled me in back in the day when he was trying to convince me to befriend a troubled student from Chicago.

Chaff's father was in jail for a bank robbery; died there. His mother abandoned him, left him on the street.

"I was running with two other guys, one of them older, Jimmy Scariff, the other more my age, Blake Elliston. Jimmy had a connection with a big outfit. At the time, I didn't know who, but it was where he got his orders from."

"With whom?" I asked. Chaff cocked his head with a disapproving grin. "Sorry, continue."

"He had us running these small jobs. Snatch and grab stuff. I was paid in cash. At the age of twelve, I thought I was rich." He made a self-deprecating face and laughed. "I was the lookout. When we found our mark, we jumped on our skateboards and created enough confusion to dislodge wallets, purses, shopping bags—anything they were carrying that might look expensive. We would skate in different directions, hook up later at a secret spot. No one knew where except us, not even Jimmy's connections. Secret to this day.

"We honed our skills as successful little thieves; had a couple scrapes with the law, but usually ended up with a warning or a threat to send me to jail. Like I said, I was twelve; the exact reason for using the kiddy gang. That was never going to happen. If they caught me, I would hang my face in a mea culpa, add a few tears, and they would send me home."

Chaff blew out some bad air at the sound of the word *home*.

"About three months into our crime wave, Scariff told us about a much bigger job and a much bigger payoff, but he said it was dangerous. He told me to sit this one out. I said, no way." Chaff lowered his head, taking in the memory. "I was so full of smart-ass smack back then. Anyway, Scariff agreed, but only as lookout and jump man."

"Jump man?"

"Yeah, I was to be the distraction. Skate by the mark, jump and flip my board a few times in front of him, then roll up and put my hand out for a tip, like musicians on the street. Performance pay. That would freeze-frame the event. The others would strike and I would skate away. They never told me what they were supposed to steal."

"The case . . ."

"Yes. A guy named John Harwood was the mark."

"You knew him?"

"Not at the time. Now, I do. So, listen. It turns out that he is a hired courier by an African syndicate smuggling something into the country. Harwood never saw the contents of the metal case handcuffed to his right arm. Neither did we, but Harwood was well aware that he carried something of immense value—probably illicit. It didn't matter. The service he offered was reputed to be efficient and safe, with no questions asked. He and his security man were experienced and carried out his missions with zero failures. His compensation was paid half at the start and half at the end."

"Hold on. Security guard? Handcuffed? That doesn't sound like a wallet and purse job. Holy shit! You weren't terrified?"

"Not at all, just fearless, and happy to be a part of something. Although Jimmy, who was only sixteen, became my giant older brother—protector, enforcer. I worshiped the ground he walked on. *Nothing bad will happen*. That's what he always said to me and Blake."

"Except this time," I interjected. Chaff ignored my comment and continued.

"For a week, we watched Harwood and noted everywhere he went. His destination was always the same. He walked a half mile through the city in random directions, but he always ended up on the west side of the Chicago River and down the ramp of the Union Station parking garage. A black van waited with tinted windows. Like a robot, he and the guard turned with their backs to the van. The door slid open and Harwood and his guard were hooded before being escorted into the vehicle. A half hour later, Harwood and his man were driven back to the contact point and told to wait five minutes before taking off their hoods."

"How could you know they would drive him back?"

"Luck. After they took him, we hung out and skated in the garage. Practiced jumping stairs, shooting down ramps, and gliding the rails. The van returned. We hid behind some cars. When Harwood got out, the case was still attached to his wrist. Most likely, an exchange. They took off their hoods and started walking back.

"The return trip was more direct, a ten-minute walk to the Sears Tower. We all followed. A well-dressed Black man greeted him just outside the main doors in the swarm of people that came and went. "Thank you, John," he said politely in what sounded like a slight British accent, handing him a white envelope. "I'll take it from here."

Harwood would hand over the case to his contact, smile, and return to his office, wherever that was, where he would wait for another assignment, which happened often. We monitored him repeating the process three times in one week. The same guy would hand him a silver Halliburton briefcase. He would handcuff it to Harwood's wrist and send him on his way."

I took a giant swig of my beer without taking my eyes off Chaff. I felt immersed in a thriller, disturbing images of my best friend on every page.

"Let me jump ahead. This past year, I found out what Harwood was doing." Chaff stuck his fingers in between the blinds and spread them open. His glance out the window was longer this time.

I snapped my fingers. "Hey, Chaff. What are you looking for? What's out there?"

"Never mind," he said without turning his head back to me. "All good."

"So, you monitored him?"

"Right." Chaff's eyes refocused on me.

"This is where it gets interesting. It turns out that the West Africans in Sierra Leone were laundering uncut diamonds offshore for years in exchange for weapons. The country was steeped in a civil war."

"You're kidding, diamonds?"

"Blood diamonds, named for the wars they financed."

"I can't believe—" Chaff gave me a patient stare that said, *when you're done?* "Right. Continue."

"Even after their war ended, it continued. It did not go unnoticed. A lot of diamonds made their way to the States. The FBI, in concert with a Chicago PD special task force, were watching a local syndicate suspected of involvement in the scheme. Chicago wasn't the only city this was happening in, but it was the nexus."

"So, you're saying you got caught up in a diamond smuggling ring? Jeez!"

"Diamonds would come in and be transferred by courier to a middleman before the cache was sold on the black market to retailers. Cash would come back. Everyone took a chunk out of the diamonds' value, but in the end, some unsuspecting groom would pay six thousand dollars for his fiancée's half carat ring of mediocre quality. Meanwhile, the diamond digger stood in an underground mud pit unearthing the stones for a buck and a half a day. At twelve, none of that mattered."

"Now?"

"Now, I care a lot. You'll understand when I finish."

I relaxed my posture and sank back into my seat.

"The courier was the lowest man on the totem pole. They—the FBI—wanted the outfits tugging on both ends of the string. So they surveilled, tracked, and waited for the right moment." Chaff snickered at me. "You keep staring at me that way, your eyes are going to fall out."

"Sorry . . . an unbelievable story. You have my attention and my imagination wrapped like a sausage. These are not details a twelve-year-old would be privy to. How did you find all this out?"

"I found out a lot of things over the last year and a half. Not as a twelve-year-old."

Chaff continued. "The FBI tracked the exchanges to a syndicate on the South Side.

"Mafia?"

"Not unless the Mafia were Africans. Tejan Cole of Sierra Leone runs it. Bad guy. Diamonds are small, if you haven't noticed. They can get lost, in pockets and greedy hands. Cole keeps a tight grip on the shipments and who has their hands on them down the line."

"Is he still around?"

"I'll get to that. I'm telling the back history right now. The syndicate operated through an intermediary to keep out of the lens of the authorities. And, at this point, they were watching too. They had information about the task force from an inside informant."

"So, there was a spy. Did they ever find him?"

“We have our suspicions. A dirty detective—maybe.”

“We?”

Chaff held his hand up. “Later. Level two was to engage Johnny Willow’s crew, a lean, three-man outfit trusted to carry out any lucrative gig where danger and violence were optional. Tejan Cole hired them. Level three, Johnny’s idea: He engaged several young lost boys as informants, lookouts, and petty thieves who worked for the equivalent fee of free candy and a rush of adrenalin. His boys knew the streets and shadows, rode bicycles or skateboards through the city scouring for victims.”

“That was you. I mean, your gang?”

“Yeah.” Chaff’s gaze lowered into an imagined hole of guilt and shame. “Tobias, you know that’s not me anymore. At twelve, for God’s sake—stupid and angry . . .”

“Of course. No apology necessary.” I reached over and tapped his hand. “Keep going.”

“For this job, Willow hired Jimmy Scariff—us, in effect. Jimmy was sixteen, like I said, a young thug, in and out of the juvenile system multiple times. That’s what we all were—thugs. Assuming no one intervened, we were all on a one-way ticket into the criminal world where the odds of surviving much beyond adulthood are minimal.

“The day came. We had our plan to intercept Harwood. At the precise moment that he was about to cuff the new item, me and Blake flew over the edge of the steps, splitting the crowd and causing enough shock to freeze Harwood from receiving the case for a split second. When heads turned, Scariff flew in on his bike, splitting Harwood and the guy handing off the case. Snatch and grab. That's how we did it."

"Where's the case?" I asked, still pulsing like I was the one working the heist.

"Jimmy took it to our secret spot. Funny thing . . . I never saw Jimmy again. Not long after, the police caught Blake and me. Kept me in jail for two weeks."

"They can do that?"

"They said it was for my safety. That's when I found out about the task force. It's also when I recognized a guy on the task force. I saw him talking with Jimmy one time a couple of days before the job. Never thought more about it until much later.

"They turned me over to Social Services, who dropped me in St. John Bosco's home for lost boys with Father Toomey. Catholic Charities ran it. A year later, I was baptized—a side note, not an important part of the story," he said, smiling. "A year after that, a deal was made to ship me off to New Jersey—St Joe's Academy."

"Good news. Mazel Tov. So, Blake ended up with the case. Then what?"

"No. Blake was killed in a hit-and-run a couple of days later. I didn't find out until the police released me. They made it obvious that it wasn't an accident. Gave me the news along with a lecture about where my life was headed. No one ever found Jimmy, so I figured he ended up with the case. Probably handed it off like he was supposed to, but that's not what happened."

I was riveted, wishing—praying—that none of it was true and I was just being entertained by a terrific story.

"I'm listening."

He split the blinds again. "Shit! You see that black BMW over there near True Value?" Chaff asked, nodding his head in that direction.

I stuck my fingers in the blinds and made an opening. "I think so. Some guy just got out. You know him?"

"We have to go. Now!"

I left ten dollars on the table and started for the door.

"Uh-uh. This way," he said, grabbing my shirt. I followed him into the Grub Hub kitchen, dodging a couple of surprised cooks and a busboy holding a giant tray of dirty dishes. We made our way out the back door and into the alley.

"What's going on?"

"Shut up for a minute. I have to think. How the hell did they find me?"

"Who?"

CHAPTER 18

We didn't talk for several blocks as we weaved between apartment buildings and dorms. Adrenalin flowed through every muscle. Not from fear. Not yet. Confusion was more like it, since I didn't understand what we were running from.

Chaff's story about the last few years was disorienting enough, but to be drawn into its reality was nightmarish, at best. My eyes widened to their peripheral max, fingers tingling, as I scanned for some hidden danger. *What am I supposed to be looking for*?

We stopped. Chaff put his head down and pinched his nose. He gave the illusion of concentrating on our next move. A drip of sweat rested on his upper lip and across the center of his forehead. I realized I, too, was sweating from the adrenalin rush, with pitted underarms and clammy hands.

"What are you thinking?"

"If we keep running, he will find us. We need a plan. Give me a moment."

"Chaff, I have a car. Let's go back to my dorm."

"No. I don't want them to identify you or recognize your car. I should never have come. Putting you in danger like this was a bad idea. Damn it! I never wanted it to be like this. I just wanted . . ."

We were standing beneath the stone archway of the Duke University Library. The shadowed tunnel gave us momentary cover. Chaff paced. When he spoke, his words were directed down and ahead of his feet as if talking to himself. “Think. Think.” He tapped the side of his head with an open palm.

“I have a friend,” I said timidly.

“What?”

I was hesitant to involve her. “I said I have a friend, with an apartment off campus. We’ll be safe there. Let me call.”

“She? Never mind. How far? How will we get there?” Chaff’s eyes continued to rove in all directions looking for his—our—nemesis. He didn’t appear to be afraid. A frightened man is incapacitated mentally, not sure of what to do, where to run. But not Chaff; he was alert, watchful, and ready to react. It was the same look I remembered from our early years at the academy when he was the new kid. He was always ready to strike or defend, unable to trust his new environment. Feral reflex.

“She can pick us up near the stadium,” I said. “Chaff? Did you hear me?”

“Does *she* have a name?” he asked, without being deterred from his vigilant assessment of the immediate area.

“Susan.”

Chaff slapped me on the shoulder, relieved. He nodded. “Good plan.”

“The stadium is a ten-minute walk from here.”

I called Susan for a location for pickup. I would explain later.

We walked with our heads turning, scanning for the black BMW. Duke is a sprawling campus not easy to navigate if you are unfamiliar with the layout. I took us through a couple of buildings where there would be a second exit that merged us into the student crowd on the other side.

"You know your way around this place."

"It takes four years to figure it all out."

"Susan?" He left the name hanging.

"What about her?"

"Are you and she a thing?" Chaff stopped, holding me back with his arm across my chest. "Look! Is that the black Beemer?"

A car was moving perpendicular a block ahead of us. "Not even close; a Hyundai, and the driver looks to be about seventy or so. Man, you're really spooked. What kind of danger are you . . . I mean we, in?" Chaff's paranoia became contagious, causing me to be skittish every time I saw a black car on our way to the meeting spot.

"Like you said to Susan, I'll explain later. Right now, let's just go to your girlfriend's apartment." He redirected his attention to our surroundings. Chaff's fingers latched onto the corner of a stone wall running along the front of the science school. He poked his head ever-so-slightly around the edge. "I think we're clear. Let's go."

I pulled on his shirt sleeve. "This way."

***

When Susan saw us racing toward her car, she put her window down and asked what was going on. I couldn't answer right away since I didn't know myself. The story was unfinished, and Chaff never told me who was following him.

Without answering, we hopped into the back seat of her bright-red Jeep Wrangler. Chaff's uneasiness about our flashy getaway vehicle was written all over his face. He slouched down and I parroted the action. Susan glanced in her rearview mirror, our reflection missing. She turned around with a puzzled face.

"Something wrong, gentlemen?"

"We'll fill you in at your apartment." I gave her a pleading look. Susan rolled her eyes and turned back around, putting the Jeep in gear and letting her annoyance find its way to her gas pedal. Our heads bounced off the back seat from the sudden torque.

Susan's apartment was large for one person. The furniture was simple, even sparse. I had seen Susan's apartment a couple of times, but as Chaff scanned the interior for the first time, I became aware of how skeletal it all was. No television. No throw cushions on the single couch sitting awkwardly near the center of the room. No other furniture, not even a lamp or a coffee table. Homemade curtains, or something gauze-like hung over the windows, and a toaster was the only visible utility on the Formica countertops.

"Nice," Chaff said, bobbing his head. "Roommates?"

"Oh please. It's awful. No need to be graciously insincere." Susan tossed her books on the round kitchen table to show her displeasure. She skimmed the surroundings as though a design was taking shape. "It was meant to have roommates, but I like living by myself. It's been a work in progress. I just haven't progressed." Her voice echoed a bit in the open space. I hadn't noticed the effect until now.

Chaff and I sat at the kitchen table and waited while Susan brought us a couple of beers. "Do I need to ask again?" She moved a chair and sat down, one arm across her chest and the other holding a can of beer in front of her face. Legs crossed. An irritated look—awkward silence. She asked again, "What's going on?"

Chaff took the lead. "I'm Chaff Lundergan, an old friend of Tobias."

"So . . . you're Chaff Lundergan." Susan locked on Chaff's green eyes. It seemed like she was dredging up shallow memories from listening to me reminisce about our early years together at the academy. Her expression was cold and intimidating. "Tobias told me about you. You guys met at the academy. He said you were a hothead, *man on fire,* always getting into fights—a fish out of water. Are you a fish out of water?"

Chaff glanced over at me. "He said that?"

"Hey, I was just referencing your red hair. Honest," I said.

"Among other things," she said, continuing to hold the can as a protective shield.

"Hmm. Well, those things are probably all true. I was quite a handful back then before I took the leap across the tracks, or out of the water, as you say. That is, with the help of Tobias. He was—is—a best friend. Always there."

"You mean he was forced to be a friend by Father . . . what's his name?" She expected my correction.

"Father Romano," I said. "Susan, we were not forced."

The introduction was going in the wrong direction, not as imagined.

"Yeah, you were," Chaff shot back, letting out another snide laugh. "Cellmates at first, friendship came later. But, yeah, I was rough then. Since, I have learned a few things thanks to Tobias and his inspiration. I'm a better man today."

"Then why were you being chased?"

She placed the beer on the table and sat motionless and expressionless, prepared to resist anything Chaff had to say. I had seen that face before at a campus political rally we attended. She didn't want to go to the event, saying, "Liberals have nothing to say that I want to hear. They're crass, self-centered, and parrots of other people's thoughts." Curiosity being a human condition, we went anyway.

I watched as she stood with the same gaping scrutiny for ten minutes listening to "the idiot with the bullhorn," as she put it. She grabbed me. "Do you believe this?" Then insisted we find something better to do.

Her question and accompanying attitude were not lost on Chaff. "An excellent question." Chaff glanced at me and smiled—stalling, deflecting. "I take it you and Tobias are not casual friends. He's shared a lot with you."

I gave Susan a pleading look, hoping to neutralize the conversation.

"I'm at a disadvantage," Chaff went on. "You're more familiar with my history than I am of yours. Tell me, how long have you known Tobias?"

"What's that got to do with anything?" Susan huffed.

She was well aware Chaff had skillfully turned the conversation around. She stood, a clear irritation on her face. Susan didn't know what to do with her annoyance or why she was having such a reaction to Chaff's sudden arrival. I had described him as my best friend, but best friends don't disappear for years, then magically reappear, and they don't need to be rescued from the shadows. I understood her reaction. I wanted the answer to Chaff's question as well.

"We've known each other for half a year."

"Ah . . . I see." Chaff puckered his lips. "I've known him for—what would you say, Tobias—seven years? Eight?"

Susan bit her lip, realizing Chaff was positioning the importance of his relationship with me. Damn if he wasn't competing.

"By now, you may be aware he snores like a lion," Chaff teased, hoping to break the ice between them.

"Some friendships are a matter of convenience, like when you need something, say a rescue car, or when you need somewhere to hide," she said. "Say an out-of-the-way apartment."

I walked out of the kitchen, grabbing a bag of chips off the table. "Where are you going?" she asked.

I put my hand up in surrender. "The two people I love most in the world are like a couple of dogs sniffing at each other." I crunched a chip. "Come get me when you are done, and I'll properly introduce you. In the meantime, I'll be on the patio."

"Wait," Chaff interrupted. "I should be the one to go. I didn't mean to cause any stress. Susan has every right to wonder about me. I crashed her world, and she's right, I do have a suspicious past, which is unfortunate and still connected to the present." He cast back to Susan. "You're right, I need Tobias's help. I've known Tobias for a long time and I thought I could . . ."

"Chaff, stay, please. This is nonsense. No one needs to go."

I was afraid if he left, he would be gone for good. I turned to Susan, entreating, "Give him a chance, Susan. Needing help is not a crime, and it's what friends are for; it goes both ways."

I met Susan at the beginning of my senior year at Duke, six months ago. Our initial bond was so strong that time sped up, producing roots, plants, and buds so quickly we embraced each other like a married couple of twenty years. We shared everything. Although she had not seen a picture of Chaff, she had a sudden recognition, but only of the embellished past and not the present.

It was my fault.

The present is new to me as well, having not seen or heard from Chaff for years. Memory has a way of producing a scaffold that rises around a person—around a relationship—continuing to build a structure that is incomplete. My relationship with Susan was titillating, full of exciting new adventures, but my love for Chaff—my history with Chaff—was intertwined in a brotherhood that could not survive without both parts, both stories.

I couldn't let him leave.

"I have a class to get to." Susan was miffed. I could tell she felt shoved to the periphery, her eyes downcast. I knew she was only reacting to the past and Chaff's sudden and portentous appearance. She grabbed her bag, her keys, and headed to the door, turning back to Chaff for a second. "If you are still here when I return, I'll fix something to eat. Tobias will introduce us." She gave a forced smile.

"I would like that," Chaff said.

I walked her to the door and tried to kiss her. She turned and gave me her cheek. I lowered my voice. "Susan, I have questions too. Let me find out what's going on and we will talk. I promise. He's a good guy."

After she left, Chaff gave me a funny look, begging for an explanation. "What was that all about? What'd you tell her about me?"

"What?"

I was embarrassed about how things went.

"It wasn't an ideal first meeting. She means no harm. Susan is protective, if nothing else, and it seemed natural to tell her about my history—family, friends, and interests. I might have over-embellished, but come on . . . You do have a bit of a sordid past."

"Yeah, aware." Chaff gave an understanding nod. "She's beautiful."

"Thanks. I would have told you about her, but I was distracted by running for our lives. Were we running for our lives?"

"No. Maybe. I'm not sure. The guy is a psycho. His name is Trevor Masters. We call him The Baker because he's such a hothead. He's looking for me because he thinks I have something that belongs to him."

"Do you?"

"Yes."

Chaff stood and paced around the kitchen, then leaned against the counter between the sink and the stove with folded arms. He lifted himself to the counter, letting his legs dangle, drew his lips in and blew out a rush of air. "So, you remember the case we've talked about?"

"Yeah, you said Scariff never handed it off."

"I have it."

"What? For a moment, there, I thought you said you had it."

"Yes, that's what I said."

We stared at each other in a weird, three-second contest of eyebrow raises. I didn't know where to go next. I waited for an explanation, but it was not immediately forthcoming. I couldn't wait any longer.

"First, how did you acquire it, and from your reaction and our little frightening escape from the Grub Hub, I take it someone else wants it? What the hell? Eight years later, they're still chasing it?"

"Well, friend, that's why I need your help."

***

"The little bastards got away."

Masters spoke into his phone like he was pumping toxic gas through the mic. "We need to do this my way."

"Don't be stupid. We need Lundergan alive," the voice insisted. "Stick with leveraging Wheat."

"That didn't work before."

"That was over three years ago. I don't think he knew anything at the time. I'll bet he still doesn't. Lundergan's smart. He won't give up the whereabouts to anyone. It makes him vulnerable. Wheat is special to him. Go back to the college and wait. You get Wheat, and we'll get Chaff to open up. But, Trevor—"

"I know, Johnny. I can't kill anyone," he said with disdain. His upper lip rose at the corner. "Not yet."

"Exactly. I'm sending Wallace to help."

Masters knew Johnny always trusted him to get the job done—the nasty part of the job, but he didn't trust his judgment nor his restraint. Masters was bothered by it and felt second-guessed and second-ranked. He did take pleasure in administering pain and could lose sight of the real objective of obtaining the information pain produces.

"I don't need Wallace. Tell that homo to stay put. This is my job. I'll do it alone."

"You know, Masters, one day, Wallace is going to get tired of you calling him that. I would watch my ass. Don't mess up!" The connection ended. Wallace was standing next to Willow listening to the conversation.

"He'll never see me," Wallace said, then headed out the door.

Masters smiled. The thought of how he would torment Tobias Wheat and lure Chaff into a trap was like an anticipated holiday. He had to prepare his mind, refine his technique.

CHAPTER 19

For the next half hour, Chaff explained that he was working with the FBI. I nearly choked on the revelation. After the ordeal with Johnny Willow's reappearance at the academy, Moorefield took over and set things up. It took a year of planning and training before being placed undercover. Protecting me was the key motivator. Not the only reason, as I found out later, in Chaff's winding explanations for his absence. Learning about his FBI connection was startling. The revelation took a moment to sink in.

"Yes. After those bastards took you, senior year, to get at me, Moorefield went into action. He made some calls and the next thing I knew, I was sitting in a safe house with two babysitting FBI agents."

"Moorefield—our Moorefield?" I said in disbelief.

"Moorefield is connected. I couldn't believe it either. After I got over the shock and surprise, he gave me a big-daddy speech about where I was headed, how smart I was. Told me I needed to decide what I wanted to do with my life. Turns out he was an FBI officer before he did the Secret Service stint. All connected though. He said he was part of a task force in Chicago at the time tracking the smuggling operation."

"Moorefield was a plant . . ." A revelation I mumbled to myself. "He followed you to the academy?"

I rubbed my forehead trying to rearrange the bits of information Chaff laid out and the knowledge I thought I understood from back then. I felt naïve. Disoriented. I paced in the small space of Susan's kitchen, running

Chaff's story through my skull like sludge through clogged pipes.

"Yes and no. Moorefield was the vice principal, a job he took after retiring, but my arrival at the academy and the alert he received from his old team got his attention. Moorefield became complicit when they suggested reopening the investigation. At first, he—I mean they—were using me as bait. Down the road, someone would come for me, and they would be waiting. Moorefield was in the perfect position to facilitate."

"Father Romano was okay with that?"

"Father Romano believed Moorefield was retired from service. At first, the only thing he knew was what Father Toomey had told him. A complete act of charity to take me; but Father Romano suspected the possibility of trouble. He didn't know what kind or how dangerous, but he didn't take chances. Considering my background and Moorefield's experience, he made Moorefield my protector. The whole thing fit right into their game plan. Moorefield laughed about it when he took me into his confidence."

"Three years? Wow, a long time to be protecting someone."

"Yep. I had no idea until your kidnapping and release. Moorefield told me, at the time, they all but gave up. The task force disbanded. Surveillance of the syndicate fell off the top ten lists. Until Willow's men took you. That's when I was whisked away and—"

"And found your way to the FBI," I said, finishing his thought.

"Yep."

"Moorefield. Where is he now?"

"Fishing, I suppose, or whatever retired FBI-Secret Service-Vice Principal guys do when they hang up the badge. Second time around for him. He handed me off after the agency got me settled and explained my role. Told me he was proud of me. Haven't seen him since."

"You're an agent?"

"An agent? No." Chaff laughed. "A mole . . . undercover. Wired at times." He pointed to his chest. "They talked me into getting back in with Willow's crew to find out who his benefactor is. At first, I said no. I didn't think Willow would go for it."

"What changed?"

"You. My FBI handler convinced me, if Willow couldn't turn me, they would come back for you. Our friendship became a liability. Figured I would give up information about the stolen case if they had leverage on you. You asked if I was back in business. You're half right. I have been undercover with the bad guys for the last two years. And there is no easy way to get the stink off."

"Chaff, is all this about protecting me? You gave up college for the FBI and an undercover get-yourself-killed stint. Damn! I'm sorry."

"That, and paying back some debt to society . . . to Moorefield, Father Romano, Father Toomey . . . you. Life would have been so much different had it not been for you guys, for the academy. I felt grateful, but there had to be some penance to free me from the life—that life—to truly be severed from their crimes. My childhood is what it is, but a little ball of anger is still wrapped up in my stomach. I guess I wanted to rid myself of that world once and for all. And don't be too sad. They promised a full ride to any university I want if this all works out."

I was dripping with emotion.

"Hey, don't go all crybaby on me. Besides, working with the agency people is actually exciting, like I almost have a real job. Something meaningful. They even pay me. I'll be okay."

"Yeah, but don't get yourself killed doing it. I won't be okay with that."

"Never," he said.

I swallowed whatever emotion was left and we slapped a high five in solidarity.

"So, they let you just walk right back into their crew, no questions asked?"

"I didn't say that. Besides, you have to realize, I was never technically a part of his crew. I was the youngest member of the kiddy gang. Scariff reported to Willow, not me. And I only saw him from a distance."

"Still, they had to be wondering where you had been all that time and why you were coming to them now."

"You're right. First, I was taken to the Woodshed. He beat me like my drunken father, said I caused him a lot of grief and messed up his relationship with the source, which, of course, was the Africans. So to answer your question, Tejan Cole's men are very much around."

"The Woodshed?"

"Willow's handle."

"I remember the name," I said. "Those goons who kidnapped me said they were going to take me there—to him. Scared the piss out of me."

"It should have. The guy has no conscience, no code."

"I think he was there that day at the warehouse. I counted three voices."

Chaff rubbed the bridge of his nose with his thumb and forefinger, not massaging a headache. More likely, holding back the pain of his memories. I'm not sure which memory haunted him the most: his street family or the family that put him on the street. Either way, living a lie for three years couldn't have been easy, acting out a criminal life that, given different events and outcomes, could have easily been his reality.

I moved to the sliding glass door in the kitchen, put my hands in my jeans pockets and stared outside, looking at nothing. I poked around inside my mind, rewriting everything I thought I knew about Chaff and the events back at the academy. I bounced my forehead lightly on the glass door, surrendering to this new reality.

Chaff shifted on the countertop. I heard a crack. "Shit! Don't tell your girlfriend."

"Oh, she'll be coming for you now," I laughed. "Don't worry, I'll take the blame. How did things work out in the end?"

"Johnny was suspicious of me. They all were. After eight years, since the ordeal with Harwood, the gullible factor was zero. I acted all innocent. Told him I was aware of his watching me and wanted to know why. He glared at me funny, like I was being stupid. Couldn't believe I walked right in. It took several days to convince him I didn't have the case, had no idea where it might be. Took a few more to make him believe I wanted to be in with him. I don't think he ever trusted me, but I was in."

"You *did* have the case though?"

"Not at first. Between what the FBI told me and what I gleaned from working on the crew, I got an education about the goings-on and with whom. Johnny had me doing pickups and drop-offs. The FBI wanted to know how the operation connected to the syndicate and the source of the smuggling. They were working closely with Interpol. For two years, I fed information through my handler, but for the last year, I have been trying to make my way out."

"You became the courier?"

"No. He didn't trust me for something that big. Besides, the syndicate changed tactics. No laundering anymore, at least not through a third-party operator. They opened a wholesale outlet and did their own cutting and selling, direct to retail, under the name Capital Imports."

"Doesn't sound illegal," I said.

"Sure, if the diamonds aren't first smuggled out of African mines. Legit on this side of the Atlantic once they're off the boat. Not so on the other shore. So, to answer your original question about the object, do you remember me telling you about the secret spot?"

"Yeah, the one no one knew about."

I pulled two more beers from the fridge and noticed the time on my watch. "She'll be back, I'm guessing, in about an hour. Her class had ended by now, but if true to form, Susan will swing by my dorm room and leave me a funny note. It's a thing."

Chaff laughed. My cheeks reddened a little. "What can I tell you? They call it love, man. You should try it."

"I don't know what to say, dude." He continued to chuckle. "Tonight's note may not be so friendly after our recent intro."

"Yeah, yeah, yeah. Just forget I ever said anything. You were saying? The spot?"

Chaff continued. "We found an abandoned paper mill the *Tribune* used back some fifteen years ago, three miles south of the city. We got inside through the loading dock. A cool hangout."

Chaff shifted his head off to the side, his eyes glaring into the past for a moment. He was smiling through the memory.

"None of that matters now. The place is huge. You could get lost inside, especially with the dim natural lighting from some high windows. We practiced our skills on the smooth cement floor, built ramps and rails. It was our own personal training facility and secret hideout. I even slept there when I couldn't go home." I noticed his fingers grip the edge of the counter slightly, remembering the reasons he couldn't go back.

"No one ever came around?"

"Nah, I think they marked it for demolition, but never got around to scheduling. Still there. As I said, I went back and found the case stuck behind an old vault on the second floor of what used to be the office overlooking the work floor. It was our secret hand-off spot for payments. The vault was impossible to open, so Jimmy would hide things behind it. He called it the back shelf. We called the vault room the boy's suite."

"Why didn't you turn it over to the FBI when you had your chance? Do they even know you have it?"

"The one thing the street taught me is never to trust the guy who has more to lose than you. If I give it up, I'm a dead man. If I don't, I'm a dead man walking. If the FBI has it, I'm the target of revenge. So, for now, let's just say I'm hatching a plan to stay alive."

"Did you look?"

"Yeah, I looked."

"Well?"

"How does two or three million in uncut diamonds sound? Maybe more. I'm no expert on diamonds."

"You—have—got—to—be—kidding me!" I feigned falling with weak legs. Not my fortune, but knowing Chaff had it, standing there with him somehow made me feel complicit in the crime. The temperature in my cheeks rose and a slight vertigo set in.

"You okay?" he asked, laughing at me.

I wobbled and grabbed the back of one of the chairs. "I don't think so. Not what I expected."

Chaff became serious.

"Tobias, I told you I needed your help . . ." He let the statement hang as he reached into his back pocket and pulled out a small manila bank envelope. Handing it to me, he said, "This envelope contains a key and an explanation. Don't lose it."

"What is it?" I held the envelope in my hand like something contagious was hiding inside.

"It's the key I hope will save my life. Will you do this for me? It's the only thing I'm asking of you for now and you're the only person I trust."

CHAPTER 20

The door opened. Susan stood there in the doorframe. A strange, ghostly foreboding look. Body stiff. Her movement was hesitant.

"Susan? What's wrong?"

I put the envelope in my back pocket.

A voice from behind her growled, "Move."

Trevor Masters appeared like a daemon shadow. He pushed at the small of her back, shoving Susan further into the room. He slammed the door closed with his foot.

"Hello, gentlemen," Masters said. "Am I late for the party?" His left hand gripped Susan's shoulder, stopping her a few feet in to assess the room. "Anyone else here?" His eyes panned left and right.

Chaff and I were frozen in place. I shook my head. "No," I said. I observed Susan, near catatonic. Her pupils were dilated, sucking in all the light in the room.

My chest beat in wild rhythms, arguing with my body to run or fight. My brain was a different story, unable to comprehend the moment, questioning the reality before us. I noticed a bruise on Susan's cheek. It drew me out of my frightened daze.

"Your cheek . . . He hit you?" I asked, starting toward her.

"Not so fast, college boy. Step back." I realized then that he had a gun. "I was waiting for you back at your dorm when your girly friend showed up. We had a disagreement." Masters smiled with animosity. "Then she thought better of our relationship and brought me here."

Chaff said, "Let her be, Trevor. I'll go with you. There's no need for any violence."

"Go with me so you can talk your way out of it again? I don't think so. I think we can solve our little mystery right here, right now. Where is our property, you little shit? You made fools of us for too long. I know you have it!"

He pushed Susan again, this time with more force. "Sit!" He pointed the barrel at the small couch in the living room. "You too!" he said, pointing the revolver at my chest. "Make no mistake. I'm not here to play nice, so don't get stupid."

Masters turned back towards Chaff. "On your knees!" Trevor walked cautiously into the kitchen, still looking for who else might be in the apartment.

Chaff complied and knelt on the tile floor next to the kitchen table with his hands up. "Trevor, you've been chasing this idea about the case I'm supposed to have for years. It's not true. I don't have one and have no idea where it is. I've told you that. Johnny believes me. He's moved on. Why can't you?"

"Shut up! You're lying. You may have convinced Johnny, but I never believed you. Never! You're going to tell me where it is right now."

"Or what? You're going to kill me? How stupid is that? If I did know where, killing me would be unwise . . . and stupid."

I slid my hand over the top of Susan's thigh and turned it palm up. She allowed it, letting her fingers find their place in mine. She squeezed so tight that my knuckles ached. Chaff was lying. Why didn't he give him the case? *We will all be dead. No witnesses.*

Chaff seemed calm, like he was pulling a splinter from the lion's foot. It's how I knew him: methodical, unemotional, and able to find the weak spot in his enemies, real or perceived, then take advantage when they least expected. It reminded me of the pummeling he gave Blane Williams back at the academy freshman year. When Blane looked away for a second, Chaff took advantage and ruined his day.

From my vantage point, Masters had no weaknesses. He had the gun, which appeared small inside his massive grip. He had the leverage, and he was in control.

Chaff continued. "Killing any of us will bring the police, the feds, Johnny, and worst of all, the syndicate, down on you. Killing is not how they like to operate. They smuggle and cheat, but always in the shadows, Trevor. You know that. If there is any necessary killing, they'll go all pro."

Masters appeared frustrated by Chaff's commentary. He cocked the gun and held it against Chaff's head enough to make him tilt to the right. Masters gritted his teeth, stretching his neck muscles like he was arguing with himself, wanting badly to pull the trigger. He swept back a few greasy strands of hair and snapped his neck with a sharp thrust, cracking a vertebra. I heard the pop!

"WHERE IS THE CASE?" Masters demanded.

"Somewhere back in Chicago, you idiot, hidden by Jimmy Scariff or Blake Elliston, both coincidentally dead. Any idea who killed them?" Chaff said in an accusing tone. "Unless you have a psychic that can communicate with the dead, I don't think you're ever going to find what you're looking for."

"Scariff told you." Masters hated the game Chaff was playing, written large on his face.

"You might remember that I was sitting in a jail cell at the time. First to be caught, last to know. So how could I know where he hid the damn thing? Everyone was gone when I got out—all accidentally killed. I say accidentally, because who would be dumb enough to kill the only guys who could tell you where the case was hidden?"

"Yeah, who would be that dumb?"

Another voice drew everyone's attention. They all focused on the door. A short, stocky man with white, crewed hair stood motionless, his attention on Trevor Masters. His hands hung at his side, the right one canted towards the back of his leg holding something. His countenance was upscale, confident, tanned. He could have walked out of an LL Bean catalog wearing a white, cotton, button-down tucked neatly in pleated, black, linen slacks. A brown, pebbled belt and brown leather slip-ons over white socks added the remaining flare. The contrast between him and Trevor Masters couldn't be starker.

"Wallace! What are you doing here? I told Willow I didn't need any help. Get out! I'm handling this." Trevor uncocked his weapon and stood back like he was caught stealing.

Susan looked at me with renewed fear floating over her water-soaked eyes.

"Who are these men?" she whispered.

I wasn't supposed to know the answer to that question, but after spending the day with Chaff, they were well planted in my memory. Chaff was undercover, but I couldn't say anything. Susan had no choice but to suspect the worst: Chaff was a criminal. Men with guns were in her apartment. Our lives hung in the balance.

Wallace eyed Susan. "We won't bother you anymore. You can relax."

"No!" Trevor yelled at Wallace. "We can't leave witnesses."

"Pack that gun of yours in your pants and there will be nothing to witness. Lundergan said he would come with us. Isn't that true?" He aimed a finger at Chaff.

"Exactly," Chaff said, putting his hands down and slowly rising off his knees. "That's what I told Trevor when he arrived. I'm visiting with my friends, but I'm ready when you are."

"Good," Wallace said.

Masters and Wallace stared at each other for a few uncomfortable seconds, sizing up each other's intent and abilities. It felt like a gunfight was pending before Masters decided to stick his gun behind his belt. Wallace raised his right hand, barely exposing his weapon, and placed it in the small of his back. The duel was over, for now.

Wallace and Masters escorted Chaff. He turned in a quick flash to say, "See ya, buddy. Glad we caught up. A *key* moment, man." Chaff winked at me, then walked out between them.

The door closed. Susan and I sat on the couch for several seconds, expecting them to return. The whole episode was surreal. We embraced. Susan's tears streamed out of a full, trembling cry in my arms. I peeked up at the ceiling and prayed my thanks to God and a request to save Chaff Lundergan from unholy men.

CHAPTER 21

Present Time

"An interesting tale, Mr. Wheat. Charming, wistful, violent, and quite revealing." Harrigan's attitude shifted from solicitous to pathetic intolerance. He couldn't even look me in the eye. A strange and sudden change came over him. While searching for something in his coat pocket, he asked, "You never saw him again until last Thursday?" He pulled a cigarette from a black-and-gold case and hung it above his right ear, replacing the small case in his vest. Harrigan regarded his watch, slapped both thighs and stood, stretching. "I'm a bit stiff from sitting, but I thank you for the pleasure of that story," he said, speaking with zero sincerity.

"I never said I hadn't seen him before. You're leaving?"

"No, you didn't say, but then . . . some things are understood through observation."

"You knew?"

"Yes, of course."

Harrigan stared at me, uncomfortable, like he was debating some decision. His last remark about *things understood* stunned me. "Have Chaff and I been under observation?"

He flinched, probably realizing he had given too much away. He attempted to deflect my question by ignoring it, stating his conclusion. "The forever infamous case of diamonds is not yet found, but believed, at least by your story, that Mr. Lundergan did in fact have it. He's been lying for the better part of a decade. That kind of information could piss somebody off—maybe get someone killed."

Did he just threaten me?

"Implied, maybe, but I never knew. No one knows what I have told you, Detective. That's between us, right?"

I did, but at this point, I was not at all comfortable yielding or confirming any more information. The man had taken off some outer shell and revealed a different personality, more threatening, accusing, less detecting and more probing.

"Yes, of course." Again, no sincerity. His answer was an afterthought, like he had to agree verbally, but the real intent rested on a thin layer beneath his words. "The envelope he gave you . . . It had no answers? No revelations about the whereabouts of the case?"

"I thought this was a murder investigation, Detective."

"I don't exactly know what it is at this point." He pulled his wrinkled sport coat back and rested his fat hands on his hips, revealing both his badge and his holstered weapon. "We no longer have a body. The money did not belong to the bank. You told me it belonged to the deceased. The perpetrators got away. Of course, the only person close enough to tell us what the hell happened is lying here on a bed instead of a slab, having told me events from nine years ago created the deadly circumstances that occurred here in Charlotte a couple of weeks ago. Not a lot to go on except that you might have some key information you're withholding."

I winced at the word *key*. "So now what? You invalidated everything I told you."

"Now? I leave. Thank you for the good times, Mr. Wheat. I'll be heading back."

"Back where?"

Harrigan flashed a penetrating stare that moved in slow motion into the distance, like I had been removed from in front of his eyes without his noticing. *Another mistake*?

"Harrigan?"

He moved to the door. He opened it only far enough for him to squeeze through. Like a shadow leaving its body harbor, Detective Harrigan was gone. Seemingly put off about the lack of information he wanted. Something beyond what I could give him, or chose not to. Or maybe he had what he needed. He left with no further next steps.

I considered his comment about *heading back*. I had no reason to believe it meant anything, but it didn't stop me from an intuitive cautionary shiver.

Nurse Spriggs opened the door. "Time for a check, Tobias. How are you feeling?" she asked with a genuine, pleasant smile that made it easy to understand why she had become a nurse.

"Exhausted."

What she did not know was the cause of my exhaustion. It was a psychological fatigue from my hour-long journey back through my early days and unwitting entanglements. Harrigan's interrogation was not so much a manhandling but an orchestrated prompting. I felt like I had been given an enema, spilling the intimate details of my life, then flushed, made to believe they were meaningless. His demeanor. That stare. I believed he wasn't coming back. Having given up so much information, rcgrct crcpt into my stomach. I needed time to consider the implications and put all the small, incomplete pieces in order.

"To be expected. But if it's any consolation, I can see your condition is improving. I overheard the doctor recording his notes. He may release you tomorrow or Saturday into the care of your wife. Happy news, right?"

"Yes, happy news," I repeated. As she bent closer, placing the inflatable blood pressure cuff around my arm, her perfume drew my senses. Her black hair fell forward. She swept one side back behind her ear and cocked her head to protect against the effects of gravity. "I'm sorry. I'm supposed to wear my hair pulled back, but I was in a rush this morning. My sitter called in sick, an impromptu bring-your-child-to-work day."

"I won't tell. Bring him by later. We can chat. How old is he?"

"He's a she—Bethany, and I would like that. Thanks," she said, relieved, smiling.

"I like your perfume," I said, hoping she didn't take it the wrong way.

She didn't look up from the meter as she pumped air into the neoprene cuff. "It's body wash. We're not allowed to wear perfume. Is it too much?"

"Not at all, a nice distraction from the linebacker smell that permeated the room for the last hour or so."

Her smile had not faded. "He walked down the hall with the other guy a moment ago. That's why I have come in now. I didn't want to interrupt before."

"Wait. The other guy? You mean the officer posted outside my door is gone too?"

"I guess so. There's no one there now."

That brought back my earlier questions about the efficacy of Detective Harrigan. Apprehension followed my speculation. I remembered his comment about having been on a joint task force with the FBI. I shuddered at the coincidence, but then, I don't believe in coincidence.

CHAPTER 22

Doctor Lantz decided against my departure on Friday and held me over the weekend. I was disappointed. I had been given several opportunities to stand and walk. Nurse Spriggs held my arm tight as if to save me from falling over the edge of a cliff.

"Thanks for the support," I said.

"In no time, this will be your wife giving you care," she said. "You're doing well. Recovering this fast from the kind of wound you suffered is amazing. The doctor said it's because of your youth and conditioning. That's excellent."

"Yeah, I can leap tall buildings, but I'm not faster than a speeding bullet."

"Keep trying, Superman."

"Hey, don't make me laugh." I stopped halfway down the hall and glanced back over my shoulder at the doorway of my room. "Can I ask you something?"

"Sure."

"Do you find it odd the police, or whoever he was, is no longer outside my door? Like, what changed?"

She looked at me pensive; knowing. "I do. In fact, a few of us talked at the nurses' station this morning. Is it possible they caught the men that did this to you and there is no more danger?"

"Nurse Spriggs, are you questioning my gullibility?"

"Of course not. Why? Is there more danger?"

"I don't know." I glanced away from her eyes, lost in my own thoughts. She didn't press me for an answer, then walked me back to my room, her left hand grasping my arm and her right arm around my waist for support. We walked like an old couple strolling along the beach. My thoughts went there with Susan at my side, hoping for the freedom to live our lives without the constant fear of grown-up bogeymen under the bed.

By Monday morning, I could feel more freedom of movement, able to roll, sit up, and reach out without the previous excruciating pain. What remained was more of an ache from extensive bruising. I had also cut back on the need for extra jolts of medicine, clearing the fog in my head. The body is an amazing instrument providing for its own healing, intervening when attacked by violence or disease.

A blond, faux wooden nightstand sat next to my hospital bed. One of the drawers was slightly open. I reached over and pulled, letting it hang at the end of its leverage point. I couldn't help but smile. Susan must have come when I was sleeping. Inside were a few pairs of underwear, socks, tees, a toothbrush, and a travel tube of toothpaste. My cell phone sat on top of the tees. "What, no razor and shave cream?" I muttered to myself.

The door opened only a few inches and Nurse Spriggs stuck her head in. "She left that in the bathroom for you."

She hung on the door with her hands, never fully entering. "The doctor said we can remove your catheter today and see how you do without it. I hope that cheers you up."

"I have detachment issues, but I think I can handle being unchained."

She smiled at the comment, waving her index finger at me like she was correcting a child.

"That's why your wife put the razor in the bathroom; but no showers yet. We will continue to wash you at your bedside for now."

"My wife . . . is she still here?" I asked.

"I believe so. You were still asleep when she arrived. She may have gone to the cafeteria."

"Thank you."

I reached for my phone, stopping halfway, grunting. A spasm of pain shot through my chest. I held my breath, waiting for it to subside. Nurse Spriggs rushed to my bed but there was little she could do except offer me her sympathy.

"Let me get that for you, Mr. Wheat."

"Please—Tobias," I said, straining. "We've known each other forever." The pain was subsiding. I wasn't expecting the reminder.

"Okay, Tobias, your injury is not something that heals quickly. I think you will be sore for a while longer. Here." She handed the phone to me.

My chest muscles deflated, releasing their grip. I laid back and Nurse Spriggs engaged the motor that raised my bed. I touched the screen and the LCD lit up to reveal six icons indicating different apps and a Google search bar. The message app showed I had fifteen messages. I went through them one by one, well-wishes from friends and fellow associates from my PR firm, Pike and Associates. Some serious outpourings, prayers being offered, and such, but mostly, humorous one-liners meant to raise my spirits:

>;*I knew you were a heartless bastard.*

>;*If things go south, can I have your car?*

>;*Your wife made eyes at me. What does she know?*

All in good fun, but I had to resist working into any sustained laughter for fear of the pain. Nurse Spriggs saw the wide grin on my face.

"I'm glad you're feeling better, Tobias. I'll leave you to your comics and check in on you in a little while."

I nodded without looking up, so engrossed in the messages and emails. I got to the last message with the most current timestamp and realized it was from Susan.

>;*Tobias, please don't ever leave me. I won't be able to endure it. Our marriage is so young, I hardly had time to know you, to love you with all I have, and to hold your hand a thousand times—ten thousand times. Is that selfish of me? I don't care. Please get better and come home to me.*

The message was beautiful and swung me from the ecstatic happiness of friendly humor to the ecstasy of raw love touching the ends of every nerve, producing goose bumps and glassy eyes.

We got married only six months after school. After our encounter months earlier with Chaff and those men, we were thrown into each other's arms with a new intensity that made us realize how precious life is. We didn't want to wait any longer than we had to. Parents on both sides were advocates of our plans. Since both of us are only-children, the thought of grandchildren made the willingness and planning by gleeful mothers effortless. Only one thing got in the way of a perfect outcome.

Chaff had given me a phone number to call him in an emergency. A wedding wasn't the emergency he was anticipating. I asked him to be my best man, and he agreed. Susan found out what I did, putting a pall over the event. She recoiled emotionally. Chaff was on his best behavior and his presence was uneventful, but Susan kept looking for shadows and monsters to come crashing in.

While our vows were spoken in the sanctuary of Saint Thomas Aquinas Catholic Church in Charlotte, her eyes moved over top of my shoulder. Chaff sat off to the right, opposite the bridesmaid in witness to the sacredness of our sacrament, a sacredness she felt was defiled by his being there, as she confessed to me that evening. Reluctant, she said she would try to accept him as a friend. Call it intuition or a woman's sixth sense, but she harbored an uneasiness about the future of our relationship. Her eyes twitched anytime Chaff's name was mentioned.

The last thing Chaff said to me at the airport before leaving was that he was getting out. He didn't need to explain. We hugged. I felt joy at the news and told him I would be anticipating a different future in our friendship. He slapped me on the shoulders and said, "Me too, dude. I'll be in touch."

That was six months ago. No contact until last Thursday. I had received a letter from him a month earlier with news and instructions. He phoned me in the morning to tell me he had changed his mind. I didn't share that information with Harrigan, or anyone else.

I cleared the message screen and stared at the Google search field. Detective Harrigan's surprising departure and the removal of the officer he had posted outside my door left me in a vulnerable state. It also moved me from curiosity to a feeling of impending doom.

Seconds later, the information popped up on screen; the phone number for the Charlotte police department a click away.

Susan stepped through the door.

"Excuse me, sir. Has anyone seen my husband of late?"

CHAPTER 23

Susan bent and kissed me on my forehead and brushed my hair with her fingers. "I'll bet you're looking forward to a proper shower."

"Do I have an odor?" I replied. "The nurses do the best they can at bedside, but shampooing hasn't been on the schedule yet."

"I'll bet they do, and no, you don't smell, so tell the nurses to stay away." We both laughed and held pleasant chatter without the dark depressions left by the criminal world. Bridges formed, letting us step over the crevices of greed and hatred. We held each other's hand and greeted each other's eyes, love traveling freely between us.

"I guess this isn't the most attractive you've ever seen me."

Susan sat down on the chair next to my bed but remained on the edge of the seat. "I'm not thinking about that, Tobias. I'm just happy that you're alive. Did the detective get everything he needed to find those men?"

"Harrigan? Yeah, I think Detective Harrigan got everything he needed." I had a sudden flash of angst.

I didn't want to clue her in on what I was thinking. Not until I checked things out. Even then, it would only scare her. If I was right, she would be in danger of being anywhere near me. I had to think of a way to get her out of town for a while.

Susan got up and moved to the edge of my bed. She reached for my hand but didn't make eye contact, then found my wedding ring, twirling it with her thumbs. Her demeanor shifted from enthusiasm to concern. Something was on her mind, and my guess was something other than my health. Something bothered her, but she was hesitating, deciding whether to open up. Our innocent moment had passed and the sun hid behind clouds.

"Susan." I reached up and touched her chin. "What's wrong?"

"I found something in your office," she said, pouty, as if personally injured. "It surprised me."

"A mouse . . . no wait, a rat." She didn't smile. "What then?"

She let go of my hand, reached for her purse, pulled the handles apart, and unzipped it. An envelope rose inside her hand. My name and address, no return. Across the face near the address on both sides was marked with a stamp: Confidential. "Why didn't you tell me?"

The envelope held an article from the Chicago Tribune dated a month earlier. The story was only two paragraphs with the headline: *FBI Stings Smugglers*. The byline from someone named Ryan Smith. I remember thinking when I read it that it was a ten-year investigation by the FBI and a huge takedown. I thought it would be more prominent—front-page material like SUPERMEN SAVE THE CITY.

They took down the syndicate and all its tendrils across the country—New York, Miami, San Francisco, Vegas. Capital Imports shuttered and a hundred and fourteen men were taken into custody in one day. A big get for the FBI, and all they got in notoriety were two paragraphs and a nondescript headline by a junior reporter.

Also inside the envelope was a note from Chaff. The investigation was over, but Willow's crew didn't go down with the ship. The FBI failed to extract him before the big bust, which left him vulnerable, and the only way out was to run.

To Susan's chagrin, having read the letter, he was running this way and would contact me when he was in town. That meant the crew wouldn't be far behind. His last sentence brought me the most fear: "I will need your key," which could only mean he was going to give them the case and hope to save his ass—and mine.

"I tried to tell you, but I didn't want you to be scared. I know how things affected you from before. You couldn't sleep—looked around every corner. And those pills you took just so you could sleep; it was an addiction. Also why I wanted you out of town, why I sent you to stay with your parents in Atlanta."

"I'm your wife. You should have told me. I would have talked you out of getting involved. And now look at you. I nearly lost you, Tobias." Tears streamed down her soft, white cheeks in prisms of love and anger and regret. She reached for a tissue from her purse.

"No, don't wipe them."

Susan's face contorted. "Why?"

"They're beautiful tears shed for me, each one a diadem—a little wet pearl of love."

She smiled, holding back a sniffle, her glassy eyes advancing toward me with equal amounts of relief for my recovery and trepidation for the future. "You should have been a poet," she said, wiping the wetness from her face.

"It's over now. No more tears. No more fears."

"Okay." She gurgled a short laugh and her face brightened.

I tried to move the conversation as far from recent events as possible.

"Have you been to the house since you got back from Atlanta?" I asked.

"Yes. Your mom and dad are there with me. No one knows what to do, Tobias. We all act so helpless." Susan waited with a blank expression, expecting an answer.

"The doctor said that I may go home soon, possibly tomorrow." I breathed heavily, knowing my next comment would not make Susan happy. "I want you to go with my mom and dad."

"Where?" she asked. Her eyes hooded over, taken aback by my statement.

"Home to New Jersey. It will be a comfort to them to have you there. You said it: no one knows what to do, and if you are all there when I come home, you'll all be hovering—ineffectively. We'll all feel helpless."

"What about you? Who will take care of you?" she asked. Susan was ready to argue this one out.

"They are setting me up with a day nurse. I'll be okay, and I will heal much faster without the"—I tried to lighten things by laughing—"moping and tears and what-can-I-get-you questions. You'll see."

Susan pulled her hands away, visibly angry. She got up. "Not funny," she said, staring down at me, repelled by my reasoning.

I wasn't convincing. She knew it was something else, something hidden. She held my eyes like my mother did when I was caught in a lie. At the age of ten, a terrifying gaze. Today, it was equally chilling.

"It's not over, is it?" More of an accusation than a question. "You're trying to protect me," she accused. "You think they could be back and you want me out of town—again. Is that it?"

"I'm not sure. It's possible. Susan, if that were to happen, I don't want to give them any leverage with my family. I—"

She interrupted. "What happened to no more fears?" I couldn't blame her for the question or the anger. "You were patronizing me before—manipulating me." She turned and peered out the window, but the light had changed. The darkness arrived and mirrored her dark emotions. Her reflection stared back at both of us, her arms wrapped tight around her and a face full of resentment.

My head dropped like a dead weight, chin to chest. I kept my eyes closed for an extra second and tried again, slowly stating the obvious in a low, controlled tone. "It's the right thing to do until this is over. You know that."

I forced conviction into my words, matching her resentment with a huge reality check.

"You saw those men. They're unhinged—unpredictable. I didn't want you to worry, but it is what it is and I want you to be safe. Be mad if you want, but I wouldn't be able to live—wouldn't want to live—if anything happened to you."

"What would you do if they did come back? Who protects you?" She turned and paced at the foot of my bed. She began to complain, but her words were not aimed at me. "This is not how I wanted my marriage to begin. You nearly died. Very bad men are stalking you. What are we going to do? What—"

"Susan. Susan." I called her name a couple of times before she stopped her tirade, giving me her attention, burdened and hurt. "I want you out of town. Will you do that for me?"

The tears flooded out again.

"I have a plan."

Susan agreed with the caveat that my plan was sufficient; that I would be safe. I told her what I had in mind. I would call Moorefield. He would know what to do. He would protect me. She never met Special Agent Moorefield—retired. She heard the stories. Susan knew him as a protector, seasoned and capable, and most of all, devoted to my safety. She acquiesced.

CHAPTER 24

After Susan left for home one last time to pack and collect my parents, I finished what I intended to do and called the Charlotte police—city and county. No one by the name of Harrigan was on either force. They explained that the FBI took over the case right from the beginning. No one from their side was investigating. But nothing explained where the FBI was and why they had not been to see me.

I was duped. I realized why Harrigan was so patient when listening to the whole story of my relationship with Chaff Lundergan. I told him everything. He now knew, or surmised, that Chaff had the case and now he believed that I knew where the damn thing was. I didn't. Now that Chaff was dead, I became the only thing standing in his way—their way. He was working with them. He had to be. Detective Harrigan was the informant from the task force. That much was apparent, and I was now the object of their disdain.

I made another call to the Chicago PD and asked to speak with Detective Harrigan. They said he was not in. Out on personal business. They asked for my name so they could leave him a message. I declined and said I would call back. That confirmed it. *Son of a bitch!* I could feel the rush of blood running through my damaged heart and up the sides of my neck, pulsing like a flooded stream, pulling my thoughts along random walls of depression and anger.

I yelled into the air, "Damn! How could I be so stupid! Why didn't I ask for his badge when he first arrived?"

I'd painted a giant target on my back. They wouldn't kill me until they got what they wanted—not much consolation there. I had one more phone call to make, but first, I needed to make sure I still had the key.

I pushed the call button. A moment later, an unfamiliar face entered the room. "Where is Nurse Spriggs?" I asked.

"Home with her sick daughter. I'll be taking care of you today, Mr. Wheat."

"Tobias."

"Well, Tobias, my name is Sam, short for Samantha. You should be getting out of here soon enough. Do you have plans on where you will convalesce?"

She was nothing like Spriggs, tall and all woman through every curve, but not over-feminine—solid as a rock, not an ounce of fat. I would stand at attention if she demanded. Her black strands pulled back in a tight bun, black-rimmed glasses framing her intense, sky-blue eyes. Nurse Sam Ryan, RN on her name tag. If General Ryan, I would believe it. No pleasant smile, faux or otherwise. I'm simply the patient in room 213, the object of her morning task.

"Home for now. I live here in town. A loft."

"Ah . . . someone to take care of you after you're released?"

"Home care for now. I think they call it Angel Care. A friend might stay with me."

"I would guess your wife?" She seemed surprised.

I didn't answer. Lack of trust kept me quiet about Susan's whereabouts.

"So, how can I help you?" Nurse Ryan asked. I forgot why I summoned her. She glanced at my hand, still grasping the call device. "Call button?"

"Oh, yes, ah, can you help me find my clothes? I need to retrieve something from my jeans."

She walked over and opened a narrow closet door. A blanket and an extra pillow were shoved into the upper shelf. At the bottom were my folded jeans, T-shirt, and Duke Jersey resting on a pair of black Nikes. Susan must have taken them home to wash out the blood. That couldn't have been easy for her.

Nurse Ryan retrieved my jeans and handed them to me. The pockets were empty, as I guessed. Susan had left town by now and until I could get home to find it, I was helpless, even a bit panicked. If they went to my loft and found the key, I would no longer be of any use to them.

"Lose something?"

"Yeah, I did. My house key is missing. My wife removed it. Probably at home. Inconvenient," I said.

"Did you check your drawer? Your wife may have left it there."

"True, but I highly doubt she would have."

I only doubted it because she wasn't aware of the key. If Susan found the envelope in my jeans, she would drop it on my dresser at home.

"I'm sure it'll turn up," Nurse Ryan replied.

I couldn't help but notice that Nurse Ryan hesitated, putting her hand up to her ear. She paused, her eyes narrowed, then she turned to leave. "I'll check on you later." She ran from my room.

Her abrupt departure was weird. She didn't bother to check any of the monitors, take my blood pressure, my pulse, or any of the repetitious routines of Nurse Spriggs. I couldn't put my finger on it, but something about the name Ryan. *Where did I hear that name before*? I could swear she was wearing an earpiece and communicating with someone.

I swung my legs over the side of my hospital bed. This time, not so painful. I was glad about that. They removed my catheter and medicine drip on Saturday morning, preparing me for discharge and home care. I rubbed the Band-Aid covering a worn vein in the crease of my elbow. For the first time in over a week, I stretched and felt some freedom of movement. In fact, the only thing I was connected to at this point was the oxygen feed forked into the bottom of my nose and a blood pressure cuff on my right arm. I disengaged both devices and stood.

Standing made me dizzy, so I remained in place for a moment, holding myself on the food tray stand until I regained my balance and a clear head. I opened the nightstand drawer and searched among the few items of clothing.

"Sweet Jesus!" There it was, under my white T-shirt. "I love you, Susan," I said aloud and kissed the envelope, drawing my appreciation into a satisfied smile.

Suddenly, the door swung open, slamming into the backstop. Nurse Ryan rushed in. "Good, you're up. Put your jeans on! Hurry, and don't argue with me."

The folds in her brow said it all. She pulled the door closed and kept a vigil, watching through a narrow opening. "Not a nurse," I said as I moved to the closet and slipped on my jeans, putting the envelope in my back pocket. The quick movement made my chest throb. I threw off the hospital gown and barely got the T-shirt over my head when she grabbed me by the arm. I pulled in the opposite direction to grab my phone and felt the power of her grip. She noticed what I was reaching for and relented. Then she reasserted her hold, dragging me out of the room.

"We are moving, now!" She reached underneath her nurse's dress and lifted a .38-caliber pistol from a holster on her thigh.

"I hardly know you," I said. "That was awesome."

She rolled her eyes at my lame, out-of-place attempt at humor, then reached up to her ear. "Coming to you. Back stairwell."

Back to me:

"FBI, Special Agent Ryan. Here to protect you from a very unpleasant guest headed this way. Can you walk?"

I nodded. "I wondered where you guys were."

"Not now. Let's go."

The revelation that Nurse Ryan was Special Agent Ryan was not surprising; made perfect sense. She being an untouchable, cold beauty. But I felt safe in her commanding ways like a child to a mother.

We moved down the hall, her gaze moving in all directions. She continued holding my wrist like I were a two-year-old toddler. Her touch, oddly enough, made my pulse quicken from the grip of exhilaration in the sudden circumstances, and in being saved by a real-life wonder woman.

Only days ago, I was just a PR man writing copy for businessmen and women, lawyers, and local politicians. A day later, I almost died of a criminal's bullet and now I was running at half-speed down a hospital hallway dragged by a beautiful special agent of the FBI hollering at innocent bystanders to clear the way.

A shot rang out. Agent Ryan flinched, letting out a guttural expletive as the round grazed her right arm then continued in flight, piercing the doorframe we were headed toward. People screamed, ducking down into the crevices of the hallway. I was stunned, cowering with arms flailing uselessly in front of my face. I briefly recognized the man that was posted outside my door, obviously with different orders this time. "Holy shit!"

"He's not aiming for you. They want you alive."

Ryan shoved me to the left side of the hallway, twirling off to the right, crouching low, holding her arm, firing back. Two shots. One missed, hitting the fire alarm, setting off the loud, pulsing bell. Two more shots rang out from the man. Not aimed at me. They wanted me alive. That much was clear. Special Agent Ryan's return fire this time hit her target—shoulder shot, just above and to the right of the heart. The shooter dropped, letting out a loud curse, rolling on the floor—still viable, but enough time for us to push through the steel door.

Agent Ryan was bleeding; a few drops hit the floor. She looked through the small door window. "He's up! Damn!" The fire alarm pulsed in loud spats, adding to the drama and making it hard to concentrate.

Then, like something dawned on her, she said, "I have an idea." She squeezed her arm on the top step, the second and third, letting her blood sprinkle in random spots on the stairs going down before retreating to me. "Quick! We're going up."

She was clever. When he entered through the door, he would believe we had gone down the stairs, giving us needed time to escape. But where? Wouldn't we just be cornered when we ran out of stairs?

Going up was difficult, straining my chest and my breathing. The fake Nurse Ryan spoke again into her comm, telling everyone listening that the new extraction point was rooftop. "Chopper! I repeat, chopper!"

CHAPTER 25

We had no sooner lifted off when the roof door swung open. The man was holding his arm, in obvious pain. Despite that, he stopped and pointed his gun at us. He took one futile shot that pinged off the front fuselage, then lowered his weapon and watched as we peeled off over the rooftops of Charlotte. Agent Ryan spoke into her headset. The whooping rotors made it difficult for me to hear.

"You have him?" she said to someone at the other end of the connection.

A second later: "Okay, fix him up for now. We'll interrogate later." Another pause. "No. They can take care of me in New York. It's just a flesh wound."

She patted the pilot on the shoulder and said thanks, shifting her gaze to me. "You okay?" She glanced over my shoulder, pointed to her headphones and nodded. Another headset hung near my head. I put it on and adjusted the slider and mic. The whooping faded into a background noise. I held both sides of the headphones and listened to the pilot's voice communicating with someone on the ground—air speed, fuel check, nautical miles, altitude and expected fly time. "Roger. See you on the ground."

The channel changed and I heard Special Agent Ryan's voice. "Can you hear me?"

I turned toward her and nodded. She pointed at the microphone. "You can speak."

"Oh, right." I adjusted the mic closer to my mouth. "Where are we going?" I asked with a raised voice.

"New York. Two hours. Will you make it?" she said with fake sincerity.

"Yeah, I think so. I grew up pretty fast back there—a big boy now."

She hinted at a smile, then said, "I love saving men."

I think she was being funny. A dry humor, taking advantage of my nervousness and disorientation. Her voice was clear, and sounded as if it was emanating from inside my head. She lifted the small, flat cubby door between us, pulled out a bottle of water and handed it to me. "Let me know if I need to hold your hand or anything."

"Funny." I laid my hand out, palm up. She held an amused, sarcastic grin, enjoying the exchange. "Some kind of exit down there. I didn't think my emancipation would be so exciting. Thank you for saving my life. That seems to be a repeated theme these days. Everyone is getting their chance to save Tobias."

I pointed at her bleeding arm. "You're leaking nails."

She beamed because of the reference to how tough she was. "That was my first gunfight. You train for years for that one moment and it comes out of the blue. I'm not sure it's toughness or just programmed to win."

"Ah, I knew you weren't real; amazing what they can do with robots these days."

"Hmm, a sense of humor. I don't like that in a man."

"Sorry. You get what you see. I'm glad you're programmed to win. So, we're going to New York?"

"Yes, we're going to the city, someone we want you to meet. Not planning on it this soon, but under the circumstances, we don't have a choice."

"Who's we?" I asked.

"The thirty-five thousand people who work for the FBI," she said in a deliberate and dry tone. Ryan wasn't used to being at the other end of the question. "Did you recognize the guy?"

"He's been hovering outside my door for over a week. Working with a guy named Joh—"

Agent Ryan cut me off. "Johnny Willow. We know."

"You mind if I take a look at your credentials?" I put my hand out like I was looking for a tip.

"Trust issues, Mr. Wheat?"

"The last guy sat in my room for several days drilling me as the local detective on the case. Turned out to be from Chicago. Probably working with Willow's outfit. So, yeah, I may have some trust issues."

"Detective Harrigan," she said flatly, handing me her shield and ID. The picture didn't do her justice but she was legit. "He's a detective. A good one in his day until greed snuck up his pant leg and doubled the size of his balls. Harrigan hoped to cash in on the diamond trade. He played both sides."

"The task force?"

"Yes. That's when they turned him. Frankly, we didn't put it all together until he showed up in your hospital room."

"Anyone you guys don't know about?"

"Ten years on the case? No, I don't think a loose cluc can be found. We know who they are and what we're dealing with. We hauled in the whole operation. These guys are outliers. Just a matter of time."

"Can I ask you, where were you guys? If Harrigan is not the real detective on the case, where was the first string? Charlotte PD told me the FBI took over the case but you guys were nowhere to be seen. Considering what had transpired, I was a sitting duck, along with my family. You put us at risk."

"We were there. No one was at risk. And it was a good move to get your wife out of town."

"Where? And how did you . . .?"

"In the hospital—nurse on duty." She pointed with her finger to be emphatic. "Dr. Lantz is Special Agent Lantz. Spriggs?" Ryan put her head down and laughed. "She liked you."

"Shit. Nurse Spriggs is FBI? You're kidding. She still likes me, right?"

"She's a talented agent. Fresh from the academy. It was her first undercover work. She'll do well in time."

"So, the three of you?"

"All told, we had five in the hospital and another eight in the immediate surroundings. You were never alone,

Tobias. Harrigan showed up, and we figured it was our chance to see if he would lead us to Willow. After we shut down the smuggling ring, Willow left town. Harrigan got information that we were closing in on the operation and must have given him a heads-up. Willow and his crew vanished. With the operation gone and Lundergan dead, you became their only lead—and ours."

"Lead? What do you mean? I have nothing they want." I didn't want her to detect the lie in my face. My eyes diverted below to the stream of traffic on Interstate 95. I'm sure my mother and Susan would have nothing over Ryan's frightening charm.

"Tobias, your room was bugged. We heard it all. That's how I found out where your wife was. No need to go all secretive on us now. Besides, another witness that saw what happened told us everything."

"Who? I don't remember anyone else there."

"You're going to meet him. Patience. We want to corroborate on your stories."

Nobody knows what happened that day. I stared into the clouds that rose above us, reenacting the event in my mind. A few pedestrians when we came out of the bank, a car or two, but the shot came from a hidden spot—a corner of the building. The only person who saw what happened was Chaff, no longer a witness.

"Why are we flying so low?"

"Two reasons: Doctor Lantz's orders. He felt the air pressure at altitude could have a negative effect on your heart, and Bell 429s are fast, but they only have a range of plus four hundred. We'll be landing in a little while at

Quantico to refuel. You look like you could use something to drink, maybe some food."

Special Agent Ryan was still dressed in her nurse outfit with a noticeable red sleeve. In these last weeks, I thought I'd seen enough blood to last a lifetime; so close to the surface, so easily released from the body. Some only lose blood, others lose their lives. How much blood does it take?

Chaff died. I lived.

We landed. Several agents on the ground came forward with a wheelchair. Doctor Lantz stood on the tarmac, waiting. He was the first to speak when I got out of the helicopter and the turbine shut down with a diminishing whir.

"How are you doing, Tobias?" he asked. Sincere, but the relationship had turned to an awkward understanding about his alias. We shook hands. "I guess you were told."

"Ah, yes, recently informed. A bombshell, only a couple hours in recovery."

"Sorry for the deception. I am a doctor, if any consolation; in fact, I remain your doctor."

"Not a problem now, Doc. I'll live. But Nurse Ratchet could use some of your expertise." I nodded behind to Special Agent Ryan, unlatching herself from the seat buckle. He raised his eyebrows when he noticed the trail of blood.

“An interesting reference. It fits,” he said with a broad smile. He reached for Ryan. “C’mon, we’ll fix you up.”

Agent Ryan was not as amused. “Don’t touch me or I’ll shoot you. I’m fine.”

“I thought nurses were pleasant creatures eternally caring with good will towards all.”

She slapped his hand away and jumped from the cabin. “Take care of Tobias. Get him something to eat.”

Lantz laughed, shaking his head. “Always tough as nails, Agent Ryan.”

“That’s what I said!” I looked back at her for a reaction.

She gave us a disapproving *I’ll-kill-you* face before moving away, speaking to someone on her cell phone.

CHAPTER 26

We were prepping to be in the air 40 minutes later. I only had time for a sandwich and a soda. Dr. Lantz did not approve. He checked my vitals and gave me a shot of B12 before walking me to the chopper. I was surprised when he jumped in with us.

"Worried about me, Doc? Should I be worried too?"

"Your recovery is going quite well. Your injuries were severe, and we will monitor you closely, but worry is not one of my medical treatments. There are other patients to take care of where we're going. I'll be monitoring you all. Your nurse will be joining us too."

"My nurse?"

The blades started their initial rev. Doctor Lantz nodded towards the tarmac. A woman dressed in black cargos, a tight T-shirt and a pistol strapped to her right thigh trotted toward us. Her hair pulled back in a ponytail, swinging wildly as she ran, she carried a small duffle bag and approached the chopper with a broad, white smile.

"Hello, Tobias. How are you doing?"

"Nurse Spriggs? Holy hell. This just keeps getting better and better." I turned to Agent Ryan. "Any more surprises today?"

"Maybe one more," she said, then gave the signal to our pilot to lift off. She pulled Spriggs on board. "Julie, glad to have you along." The rotors spun up and lifted us into flight. The torque was strong and I had to catch my breath.

She grabbed a set of phones. “Has Tobias been brought in?”

“Hey. I’m right here and, yes, she told me. I can’t believe it. You were such a great nurse.”

“I still am,” Special Agent Spriggs said. “I’m an agency field paramedic.”

“The gun?

She followed my eyes to her holster. Smiling. “For the most difficult cases, when there’s no hope and I just have to put them out of their misery.”

“You and Agent Ryan should team up and put on a show. What happened to sweet Nurse Spriggs?”

She put her hand to her heart and said, “Still inside.”

Doctor Lantz opened a medical journal and studied its contents. He put on his wire-rim glasses. He ignored our repartee. I read the title: *Heart Valve Surgery for Patients and Caregivers*.

Special Agent Spriggs touched my knee and said, “It’s not for you. No need to worry.”

“Who?” I asked.

“Someone who might need”—she peeked over at the book’s title—“heart valve surgery.”

I was temporarily relieved, feeling bad for the poor guy who might need the surgery. “Something happened to him? Is he going to make it?”

"We hope so. They're doing everything they can. He was stabbed in the chest, among other physical assaults. Barely hanging on." She glanced at Special Agent Ryan, a sympathetic look, but I didn't know why.

"Tobias," Ryan said.

I gave her my non-verbal attentive smile.

"We have a little over an hour left. Would you be willing to recount the events from the day of the shooting? It might help our investigation."

"What specifics do you want to know?"

"Why were you there? And just so we are clear, we know about the diamonds."

I was surprised by her comment. "Chaff told you?"

"No, but he should have. I told you, we had your room bugged at the hospital. We didn't know about the collateral from the Chicago involvement. It made sense when Harrigan kept asking about it. That's what he is after, what they're all after. The motive is clear now. Their little smuggling ring is no more, since we shut it all down, and the misplaced diamonds will give them a nice stake to start over. What we don't know is what is supposed to happen. Who fired the shot? Where are the diamonds?"

"That's a lot of questions."

"That's what we do."

"So, let me get this straight. The FBI has no idea about the original theft and murders?"

"Skimming from the syndicate is not smart. They're ruthless. To answer your question, we didn't know. Willow is a dot on the *i* of the smuggling operation. We wanted to put him out of business along with everyone else."

"They're ruthless? I thought you shut the syndicate down."

"We removed a sizable tumor but there are still some nasty remnants out there. The Africans are resilient if nothing else. Our first priority is to shut down all the operations on this side of the Atlantic."

"But you said the Tejan guy is here. Did you capture him?"

"No. I said he runs it. Tejan Cole was on the no-fly list. His loyalists ran the operation. We put them out of business. But Cole may have found his way into the country. We may see him reengage in the future."

***

I gave a five-minute summary of the events leading up to the day and told her about the letter and key Chaff gave me a year earlier back at Duke before the crew came for him.

"What did the letter say?"

I removed the folded letter from my back pocket and handed it to Agent Ryan. She grabbed it from a corner, holding it like a dead rodent. "Your friend take an origami class? How many times can you fold a piece of paper?"

I didn't answer. She finished unfolding it, read it, and handed it back to me, never breaking a facial expression. "So, the money was meant to be a wedding gift for you? He knew they were close behind and wanted to make sure he handed it off to you before anything happened. But something did happen."

"Yes." I tilted my head, trying to fight the memory.

"And the key—he didn't say in the letter, but probably the box key where the stolen merchandise is. That's what he came back for."

"I knew Chaff's virtuous side, Special Agent. His motivations were honest, intended to protect me and Susan, give us a gift, and get away from the bad guys."

Ryan was unmoved. "There were two deposit boxes and two keys. You were going to meet and exchange keys. Very interesting. You get the money. He gets the diamonds."

"It wasn't like that. He was going to turn over the diamonds to the crew to get them to leave us alone."

"The letter doesn't say."

"It's the truth. I spoke with him that morning. That was the plan, but he changed his mind. He wasn't going to give them the diamonds. Chaff heard them talking before he went into hiding. He told me they wanted to kill everyone, diamonds or not. He decided to turn them over to you guys if he could get to them first."

"A convenient story."

"Well, Chaff's dead, so it's the only story you have."

She and Special Agent Spriggs exchanged glances. Ryan stared out the window with an aloofness, considering my comment, then turned back to me. "You're right. It's the only story we have. Please, continue."

"We arrived at First Citizens. Chaff asked for my key. He gave me his, and said I was to hold it for safekeeping; that he would let me know when he needed it. He opened the deposit box, one of those large ones. Pulled out a duffle bag, and we walked out of the bank. That's when he tried to give it to me, said it was a belated wedding gift. I refused to take it."

"So the key you had all this time was for the box holding the money?"

"Correct. He always knew how precarious his situation was. The key was a gift for the worst-case scenario."

"Where was he going?" Ryan asked.

"I never got that far. When we were outside, Chaff's eyes shifted over my shoulder. I saw the panic in his face. He grabbed me and turned me around a hundred eighty degrees. A shot blasted out and he and I both collapsed. I woke up in the recovery room of the ER and never saw him again. They said he died. It was Harrigan who told me the FBI stepped in and recovered his body. Is it true?"

"Yes, mostly true," she said.

"Mostly?"

She waved the back of her hand at me. "Go on."

"Harrigan also said the same bullet that hit Chaff hit me."

"Also true."

"Where did you take him?"

Another glance towards Spriggs. "To our forensics lab."

Her answer gave me a shiver, imagining the cold body of my best friend lying on a metal table in a refrigerated room with his chest exposed, vacant of life. I didn't want to see him that way, hoping he would be released and given a proper Catholic funeral and buried in sacred ground.

Ryan regained my attention. She aimed her stare at my hands, still holding the envelope and letter. "I assume that envelope contains a key. What do you intend on doing with it?"

"As I said, it was Chaff's intention to turn it over to you guys. It's yours now." I handed it over.

"Smart move, Tobias."

Nothing more was said until we landed and made our way by ground to 26 Federal Plaza. The wheelchair once again unfolded for me and we rolled to the front of the building. The etching on the glass front read: Federal Bureau of Investigation, New York. The least of all the locations in the world where I would ever dream of entering.

She knocked on the glass door and said, "Bulletproof," like it was a favorite toy. Then Ryan presented her security card to the guards in the lobby and a thumbprint to open the elevator door. I didn't pay attention to what floor we were dragged up to but when the door opened, stenciled in red at the top of the opposing wall were two arrows. To the right, New York field office. To the left, Hospital, Forensics, and Cafeteria.

"The FBI has a hospital?"

"Not technically," Spriggs answered. "It's a forensics lab. Usually nothing alive. There are exceptions though."

CHAPTER 27

We moved down a hallway, block wall to the left, clear, heavy glass to the right supported by thin metal pillars. Several people at workstations, not noticing us.

In the center of the lab was a male body on a metal gurney, a thin, white cover waist-high, feet and toes extending, a pale blue. A tag hung from the right toe. A technician wearing protective yellow-tinted glasses, blue gloves, and a white coat over gray scrubs bent low, pulling an overhead light close to the body. I came to a stop, watching him cut through the unfortunate person's sternum with a scalpel. I shielded my eyes with my hand and turned away.

"Spriggs, is this one of your exceptions?" I asked.

"No. I assure you; that one is absolutely dead."

"Is it—?"

"No, it's not him."

I was relieved, but if she had said it was Chaff, I would have blown lunch right there. Even with the glass partition, the remnants of formaldehyde and sterile alcohol laced the air as we moved further down the hall. "They need some serious room scents around here."

"You get used to it," Spriggs said.

Ryan added a comment. "We would rather capture them than kill them. The smell is a reminder of our failures. We're good, but not perfect."

We continued through a maze of hallways and two checkpoints. Doctor Lantz trailed behind, reading notes from a blue file folder. "This is good, very good," he said, drawing a look from all of us. He lifted his head, smiling. "Sorry, talking to myself."

"Well, we heard you," Ryan said. "What gives?"

"If this latest assessment is true, our patient might improve well enough; we can operate. First the heart and then plastic surgery."

"We can interrogate?" Ryan asked.

"If that is what you must do. It would be better if his convalescence was less stressful. He needs rest."

"Yeah, I can attest to that," I said. "Interrogation is not restful. Who are we talking about?"

Agent Ryan stared at me and Doc Lantz, her steely eyes burning into our frontal lobes. "We're the FBI. We interrogate—investigate. We are not a convalescent home. There are no nurses or candy stripers here. Do you see anyone here looking like that?"

Lantz and I shook our heads in the negative.

"Right. That's what I thought," Ryan said. "Now, your job is to wake him up. I'll take it from there."

"Tobias . . ." She softened just a bit. "In a moment, things might come as a shock to you. My apologies in advance for the secrecy. For now, close your eyes or hang onto Spriggs in case you faint at what you are about to see."

Agent Spriggs shot me a sad face and rubbed my arm. "You'll be okay—after the shock that is."

"Crap. If your comments are meant to scare me, they're working."

Doctor Lantz noticed my clammy skin and touched my neck with two fingers. "Your heart is racing." He looked at Special Agent Ryan. "There's no reason for him to witness this."

She shrugged.

We approached an open door. An agent suited in black, wearing a white shirt and black tie, stood just outside the frame, hands crossed in front of him, a white coiled wire attached to his ear. He stood motionless, not blinking.

Doctor Lantz moved in front of me. "Stay here, no need for you to come in." He shot a defying glance at Ryan. One more time Doctor Lantz told me to stay, then he and the others walked into the room.

I couldn't hear anything. Feeling antsy, I spun the wheelchair around a couple of times, back and forth. *What's going on in there*? Another couple of minutes went by and I decided to roll my chair into the open door, stand up to look at the others. Big mistake.

"My God!"

I staggered back, grabbed the sides of the doorframe, and froze. Agent Spriggs moved quickly towards me. The man lying in the bed was broken and wrapped from head to foot. So badly beaten and lacerated, I couldn't make out a face. The bile in my stomach churned and I immediately had to back out of the room, falling into my wheelchair.

"What happened?"

Before anyone could answer, I heard Special Agent Ryan attempting to talk with what remained in that bed. I couldn't believe how brazen she was.

Spriggs whispered to me, "Special Agent Tommy Spears, undercover as a mid-level enforcer for a drug cartel operating on the East Side. His cover was blown, and they did that to him a week ago. Left him for dead."

I whispered back, "That's who Special Agent Ryan wants to interrogate?"

"Not exactly. She and Tommy were partners before he took the undercover job. I think she just wants justice for him. She's been hoping he'd come around, at least long enough to learn who did this. It's sad to see him like this. Ryan's pretty broken up, trying to keep it together. She's amazing, able to handle stress, but I think I can see the timber cracking with what they did to Tommy. She wears a stiff attitude like an exoskeleton; not who she is underneath."

"Shouldn't he be in a hospital?"

"He was," Spriggs said. "They did what they could. Said they didn't think he would make it past the next twenty-four hours. We brought him here. It's been three days. Dr Lantz is calling in specialists, heart and plastic surgery. That's what he has been reading up on."

It was sad—horrible, in fact, the image engraved on my mind, although I was happy to learn Ryan had a heart. The personality she wore is a necessity for the job, but I had thought it a permanent persona; a hard-ass feminist with man issues. I realized it was a façade keeping her from crumbling at the worst moments. I felt sorry for Tommy Spears; no one should have to go through that. But I felt sad for Special Agent Ryan too.

I noticed her glassy eyes when she came out of the room. She leaned against the wall just outside, arms grasping at her chest. A few moments later, she slipped on her mental flak-jacket, wiped her face, and waved us on to our next stop a couple doors down. Just outside the door, Special Agent Ryan approached me. "Can you stand?"

"Yes."

"Come with me." She held her hand out and helped me up. "I want you to meet our witness."

She kept her arm around my waist. Her grasp felt somewhat maternal, reassuring, a person I had not met until now. Agency was removed for the moment, walking with Samantha Ryan and not the Special Agent.

"Hold onto me if you need to."

"What do you mean? Why would I—" I reached the door and looked into the eyes of a ghost. My knees went slack. Ryan grabbed my shirt and my belt simultaneously and held me in place until steady. Spriggs moved to my other side. "You okay, Tobias?"

"No! I'm not okay." I pointed at the face staring back at me. "He's alive? That's him?" I wiped my face, trying to improve the image, removing any doubt about who I was seeing. My throat swelled, making it hard to swallow, fighting back tears.

He spoke first. "Tobias, they told me you would be coming," he said so casually. "How are you?"

"They told me shit!" The weakness in my knees returned.

"Dude, that's the same open-mouth gawk on your face that day at your dorm. Precious," Chaff chortled, putting his hands out like he did the day he appeared in my dorm doorway. "Surprise."

Chaff Lundergan was alive, sitting up and making fun of me like nothing had happened while I stood there like a rubber doll ready to collapse in disbelief with two FBI special agents holding me up.

"Bloody hell!" I shouted.

"Bloody hell? Where'd that come from?" Chaff started laughing, holding his chest through the pain. It was contagious. I laughed with him, not for the banter but as an outlet for my feelings of awe and wonder. Tears sloshed around my eyes. The laughter spread to the others and the room filled with buoyant amusement and a smattering of relief. A very different engagement than the room we left a moment ago.

For me, laughter is a substitute for angst held back. I had to fight through undulating waves of emotion—shock, happiness, gratefulness, disbelief, and the gut-twisting involuntary spasms defying definition.

Finally, I regained my balance and tugged at Ryan and Spriggs to release their holds. "I always wanted to say that," I said. "I watched a Bond movie in the hospital."

We laughed again as I rushed to his bedside and knelt beside him, clasped hands like arm wrestlers. It's a grip I would never forget and didn't want to let go of.

"You were dead, you know? Everyone said you were dead."

"You were there, man. Did I pee myself?"

"No . . . I don't know! What?"

"Because if I didn't pee myself, I wouldn't be dead."

"How would I know, being all shot and everything, lying in my own pool of blood?"

I couldn't help myself. The tears made their way down my cheeks. The emotions kept flowing. I was happy, angry, and overwhelmed. Chaff Lundergan was lying in a hospital bed, attached to every tube and vessel that held me in place as early as this morning, twin victims of one bullet. Chaff's resurrection defied the known facts and my own observations, but who am I to argue with second chances—mine, his, and Jesus Christ's himself?

Everyone appeared to be amused by our reunion, but Special Agent Ryan had a more visceral reaction, failing to hold back her own joy watching us reconnect. It couldn't have been easy after seeing Tommy Spears earlier. I think she was happy one of us had a happy ending. Her tears were comforting on two fronts: for the joy she shared with me and for the glimpse of humanity under the exoskeleton.

Chaff and I felt a mutual relief at the strength of our hold. "They said you were touch-and-go too," he said. "Good to see you're okay, sidekick."

"Ha. Good to be seen. That was one hell of a shot, had both our names on it. But see us now, a near-death experience to talk about." I turned to Doctor Lantz. "So, he's going to be okay, right?"

"Yes, I believe so. The two of you are young and healthy—strong hearts." He shook his head, a disbelieving look. "Though you both defied death. Miraculously," he added. "The bullet shattered your rib cage, but before it did, it blasted through Mr. Lundergan's lung and nicked his right atrium. Neither one of you should be here."

Chaff and I fist bumped and fake exploded fists, smiling like we had defied the devil. I had the urge to bend down and hug him, but the monitoring connections, intravenous feed, and oxygen made it awkward to attempt. Susan felt the same way after I awoke.

"So, who are your girlfriends?" Chaff asked, nodding to Spriggs and Ryan. Their faces straightened. He noticed Ryan, still in her nurse's uniform. "You're bleeding. Did you miss someone's vein or did some doctor get upset with you?"

"Uh-oh," Spriggs mumbled.

"What?"

Agent Ryan bent down and grabbed Chaff's hair and pulled his head back in mock anger, morphing into a fake smile. She was not pleased with the chauvinistic comment. In a soft but deliberate voice she said, "Look, you little prick. The doctor says you should be dead. I can fix that."

"Agent Ryan," Doctor Lantz cautioned her.

She let go of his hair. "We understand each other?"

"Roger that," Chaff said, smiling back.

She stepped back, regretting her reaction. Spriggs moved to comfort Ryan, putting her hand on her shoulder. "Sam, I know what you are going through. He didn't mean anything by it."

Ryan nodded her understanding, then introduced herself. "My name is Special Agent Ryan." She dried her tears with her hand and sniffed back the wetness in her nose and throat. She nodded at the dried blood on her nurse's uniform. "I saved your friend's life today with a little bloodletting . . . and excellent shooting, if I do say so myself."

Ah, the old Ryan was resurfacing. Super-agent once again.

"I'm assigned to what remains of the cleanup operation. For the two of you, it amounts to saving your lives again. Doctor Lantz and Special Agent Spriggs are here to make sure you don't die inconveniently before we find your team of creepy jackals. The two of you are expected to cooperate."

"It's true, Chaff. They came after me at the hospital. Special Agent Ryan saved my life—shot one of them—and flew me here to see you. I didn't know it would be you though."

Chaff seemed to ignore my comment, still focusing on the words *your team.* "They're not my team, Agent Ryan," Chaff said, his tone serious. "You guys came to me over a year ago. You asked me to go camping with the creepy jackals, as you put it. I did what you asked and the FBI got a big score. I got a bullet. So, take your attitude and shove it." A malicious smile took shape. "If you want any more of my help, you'll bring me something."

"Bring you what?" Ryan asked, glancing over at Spriggs.

Chaff raised his head, giving some thought to the question, like he didn't have an answer, then refocused on Ryan, "A burger and fries." He turned his head toward me but kept his gaze on Ryan. I smirked into his peripheral vision.

"Make it two."

Chaff turned to Doctor Lantz, not giving Special Agent Ryan a chance to respond. "I've been here for days. Do I need all this shit attached to me anymore? I feel fine. I'm fine."

CHAPTER 28

Chaff and I were left alone to catch up. Spriggs went for food. Lantz was consulting somewhere, and Special Agent Ryan was called to a meeting with the Executive Director of the Criminal Investigative Division, Mike Garrity. Chaff drifted off to sleep from a final draw of pain medicine, leaving me to sit, staring in awe of my friend and the miraculous outcome of events.

I was still having difficulty coming to grips with Chaff's resurrection. My thoughts leaped into the unknown: death is not something you prepare for. There is no practiced reaction, only natural, spontaneous emotions that rise in its effect. The soul doesn't wave goodbye or dip a wing as it takes off. The awareness of death is in what the body doesn't do. It no longer animates. It no longer responds to camaraderie or memory or laughter—or love. The body fails. And then you begin to accuse yourself for all the squandered milliseconds of a relationship taken for granted that you thought would expand into the future. I had traveled the dark byways of denial, anger, regret, and complacency—no other dark shaft to explore.

Now, as life had returned to Chaff's body like a morning tide rolling back to shore, I needed to clear the emotional wreckage left by the false testimony of my senses. Death had been mocked and I never felt happier. My eyes closed around a pleasant dream and all the wasted emotional discharge.

"All right, boys, time to wake up!" Ryan's voice bellowed. I reentered consciousness. I could hear hands slapping together and my eyes sprang open. Special Agent Ryan's white, bloodied uniform was gone. Her pantsuit, dark black. It reminded me of *Men in Black.* She was clicking manically at the end of a ballpoint pen. I was waiting for the memory wipe. An unfamiliar man stood behind her.

"I'm awake."

"What about the undercover boy?"

The small, aluminum-rimmed clock on the wall said 5:00 p.m. I figured we slept for a little over an hour. "He should be coming around soon. That is, if he had the same medicine they gave me. It usually wears off by now."

My timing couldn't have been better. Chaff woke, groggy, licking his lips and otherwise trying to regain his faculties. I knew the feeling and poured some water. He chugged it fast. "More," he said. I poured a second glass and nodded at our visitors.

"You boys catch up on old times? By the way, your cold burgers are on the table there. Spriggs was offended you didn't leave a tip."

"You mean old times when we sleep in our own beds and there are no FBI agents in our rooms and no one tries to kill us? Oh, yeah, we're all caught up," Chaff said, sarcastic as ever.

"So, you were just dreaming," Ryan countered. She looked over at her associate. A slight bob of her head projected pleasure with her retort. The man held a blank expression and she regained an unsmiling pose. "Boys, I want you to meet Mike Garrity, Executive Director of the Crime Division. We have a plan. The director wanted to meet you and see what you thought about the strategy."

Garrity held out his hand. “Hello to both of you.” A firm squeeze let us both know he was not here to kibitz. Chaff reached for one of the bags and unwrapped his sandwich, devouring it in four bites. He licked his fingers and grabbed a napkin.

“Dude, you going to eat yours?”

“Nah, you can have it.” I pointed to his cheek. A drip of ketchup was dangling precariously. “You want me to smack the back of your head to get it to fall?”

He laughed. “Dude, that was funny.”

Garrity and Ryan saw no humor in the exchange. They stood with hands clasped in front of their suits like they were waiting for us to finish our last meal before execution.

I said, “You wouldn’t be bothered to share your plan with a couple of wounded twenty-somethings if your strategy didn’t involve us.”

Garrity spoke. “You’re perceptive, Mr. Wheat. You are at the center of it. Mr. Lundergan, on the other hand, until further notice, will remain dead.”

“On your mother’s grave,” Chaff retaliated. “If Tobias is in, I’m in.”

“The choice is not yours, Mr. Lundergan. This is a directive you will obey, in restraint if necessary.”

“Obedience is an act of love. Slavery is obedience under the dictate of force,” Chaff retorted.

I was amazed once again at his ability to sift effortlessly through his mind's library of tomes pulled from ancient volumes.

"Saint Ephraim," Garrity responded with a satisfied smile.

Chaff was taken aback. An amused Garrity heard the quote. He clapped his hands twice in soft appreciation; his confidence oozed.

"Don't be surprised, Mr. Lundergan. I've read all the Church Fathers through to Augustine's *Confessions*—fourth century. One of my passions. Obedience was one of his," he said, hoping the point was made.

"I'm impressed."

"He's not here to impress you," Ryan snapped.

I found it easy to misread her tone as harsh or resentful, but on duty she is devoid of emotional language. Hers is efficient, verbal minimalism.

"Mr. Lundergan, if impressing you is necessary to make you fall into line, I accept," Garrity said. "I'm not trying to cut you out. I am protecting you. Your condition is serious, and things are likely to get rough from this point on. The suspects we are after also know you and they think you are dead. That plays in our favor—in your favor too. We have the key. We know the bank. Tobias here will draw them out of hiding by agreeing to give up the key. We snatch them when they go for the thing they have been after all this time. It should be an easy grab. Then you will be free to rejoin the living."

"I can tell that you haven't given much thought to this plan, Agent Deputy Commander," Chaff said.

Ryan let out a loud hiss, about to blow a gasket. "Executive Dir—"

Garrity held up his hand and stopped her in mid-sentence. He regarded her with a nod. He turned back to Chaff. "Can you elaborate?"

I was equally interested in his reply, since I'm not fond of being at the center of anything that involves guns.

"I know these guys, and I'm the only one that can finger Johnny Willow. No one has seen him. He stays in the shadows and lets his henchmen do the dirty work. He's smart. You will never see him."

"Doesn't Mr. Wheat have knowledge of him?"

I answered, "No. I only heard his voice—I think—over a year ago. The henchmen I know, at least two of them. Violent. Unpredictable. Scary as hell."

Chaff followed up. "There you go. I'm the only one that knows who he is. Believe me, he'll stay back. You'll never see him. It won't be as easy as you think. Cashing in on these diamonds has been on their minds for ten years. They're not going to fold up without a fight. Masters will shoot first and think about it later."

"Okay, do you have a better plan?" Garrity asked.

"You're not serious," Ryan said. I thought she was going to punch a wall. "You're asking a man who spent the better part of his life with the very criminals we're after?"

Garrity never said a word. He squinted at Ryan with a kind of telepathy, because she immediately stepped back and swallowed her indignant attitude. It became clear Garrity was a listener. He's the kind of guy who is not satisfied until the light shines through every facet.

"That was the FBI's plan. Not mine," Chaff answered. "I would have been happy with normal."

"Mr. Lundergan," Garrity said. "Please continue."

"First, I will go with you. I agree my inconvenient death is an asset in this situation, so I'll hang back inside the bank, unseen." Chaff put up his hand, anticipating my objection and giving me a hard stare that said, shut up for now. He reengaged Garrity. "Tobias goes in to the bank. They'll be watching. Here's the switch: Tobias never comes out. That will draw them out, but not Willow. He'll stay back. Your guys on the inside protect Tobias and take down the villains." He turned and winked at me.

"Does Tobias get to say anything here?" I inserted.

"No," both Chaff and Ryan snapped in tandem.

"That's what I thought." I sat back and listened to the strategy taking shape, wondering how two severely injured, heart-lame patients were going to hobble through a dangerous intervention by the FBI. I was about to be set on the hook as bait, and Chaff was the one casting me out into the deep.

"How exactly do we take down Mr. Willow?" Garrity asked.

"My resurrection comes into play at that point. I leave the bank through the front door casually—maybe in a wheelchair for maximum visibility and vulnerability—carrying a knockoff Halliburton case on my lap down the sidewalk and into a car; one with a bug. You can provide that, right?"

Garrity nodded.

"There's no doubt Johnny will be watching. When he realizes it's me, he'll follow. I head out of town, transmit what car he's in, pull over and wait like I'm going to hand over the case and you guys intercede and take him down. Simple. Easy. No one gets hurt. Game over."

A slight hint of a smile leaked from one side of Garrity's cheek. He turned and questioned Agent Ryan without saying a word.

"It could work," Ryan said, nodding in agreement, surprised that Chaff's plan swayed her. "With a little more detail and planning, of course."

"Of course," Chaff acquiesced to keep the peace.

"Put it in play," Garrity said, then turned and left the room.

CHAPTER 29

After everyone was gone, we sat and talked, waiting for Doctor Lantz to arrive and officially release Chaff. Agent Ryan was assembling her team. Garrity returned to his tower or wherever deputy chiefs go to mull over their assessments and decisions. I was still reticent about Chaff's plan, but I understood. He rationalized well. However, the world of master plans is littered with schemes and blueprints that never succeed.

"Are you sure about this?" I asked.

"Why? You're not?"

"I'm sure about what we are supposed to do and what the FBI is supposed to do, but you can't predict what Willow will do. Should we send him a note with instructions?"

Chaff fixed a stare that shot straight through me for a few seconds, then contemplated some thought swirling around in his head. One of his notorious self-assured smiles flashed across his face.

"I know that look," I said.

"You know, it's not a bad idea."

"What?"

"Sending a note. Instructions, like you said. After all, how is he going to know you will be there?" He swung his legs over the side of the bed and pulled off the oxygen tube. He was still attached to the line in his arm, a process familiar to me. Chaff glimpsed at the line, then at me.

"Okay," I said. "But if you bleed out, it's not my fault."

I withdrew the needle and placed a white napkin from his food tray over the puncture wound. "Hold this."

"I'm impressed with your nursing skills."

"Careful, wise guy."

Chaff laughed, reengaging his plan to send Willow a message.

"I still have a phone number. Assuming it hasn't been ditched, we tell him when and what we intend to do. We give him specific instructions. If he wants the diamonds, he'll follow the directions. That's brilliant—you're brilliant. Help me find my clothes."

"I was being sarcastic. I think it's a horrible idea."

"Reason?"

"He's not supposed to know you're alive."

"Exactly. That's why you're going to call him."

"Me?"

"Yeah. You call. Tell him you found his number on my phone and you reconsidered. You're ready to give up the diamonds. Give him the date and time." Chaff chuckled, then added, "Tell him to come alone."

"He's not going to believe me. He'll know about the gun battle and the FBI."

"If he asks, you say they held you for a little while, questioned you, and let you go. You're scared and just want to be left alone and you're willing to cooperate. Trust me. He wants that case more than anything on the planet. The FBI still thinks he wants to cash in. The truth is, he's afraid of Tejan Cole."

"He's here?"

"Yes, and he's a real threat to Johnny. Believe me, Johnny will buy any story you give him. Tobias, I'm serious, this will work."

"Shouldn't you tell Ryan what we're planning?"

"Sure, right after we actually put the plan in play. Screw Ryan. She sees us as the B-team. She'll run in the opposite direction of whatever we say."

"How do you still have your phone? They took mine as soon as I entered the building."

"The doc brought it back to me two days ago. He said they cloned the SIM card and sanitized all FBI-related data. They also turned off the GPS location service so it couldn't be traced. I asked him if it was bugged. He said no, but the little nervous twitch in his cheek said yes."

Chaff scrolled through his phone's contact list, stopped, and handed it to me. "This is the one."

"Fanny? The contact name is Fanny?" I laughed.

"A long story. Now call."

"Now?"

I felt flushed. I wanted to run from the room. I would rather take a job cleaning dirty toilets than speak to this scum on the phone.

Chaff's arm remained extended, holding the instrument of my disdain in front of my face. I don't know why, but I had a flashback to the days when we were in Father Romano's academy. Chaff had saved me on more than one occasion from intemperate pubescent boys. I owed him.

I took the phone and made the call. It went to voicemail. I tapped the speaker icon so Chaff could listen:

"Leave a message, asshole—two second pause—*well, what is it, asshole?"* Then a beep.

So, I left a message. "It's Tobias Wheat. Is this the asshole looking for a certain silver case you lost in 1998? Back to the future is calling. If you still want the item, meet me alone at First Citizens Bank in Charlotte tomorrow at four p.m. It will be turned over to the FBI if I don't see you, Mr. Willow. I don't care about ownership. I just want to be left alone. Don't be late. The bank lobby closes at five. This is your one and only chance. Asshole out."

I clicked off and eyed Chaff for approval.

"Tobias, that was perfect. I don't know where you pulled that from, but very convincing. And funny. It was hard not to laugh. Now, will you please help me find my clothes? Time to tell Agent Ryan what the B-team did. They're not going to be thrilled with your next-day setup—not much time to prepare."

"I was nervous. It was the first thing that came to me. Should I call him back?"

"Yeah, go ahead. Tell him you're going away for the weekend and you will see him on Monday."

"Ha, ha. Maybe I should invite him to lunch. How are we going to find our special FBI friends? We don't know our way around here," I said.

"There's a guard outside the door, isn't there?"

***

"You did what?" Ryan was shaking mad. "Frick'n idiots!" The words bellowed, ricocheting off her office walls.

Several agents outside of her office stopped what they were doing, distracted by her outburst. Ryan got up from her chair and leaned both hands on the edge of her desk. I thought she was going to climb over instead of around. "Who the hell do you think you are?"

If I had a red cape, she would have charged at us.

She lifted the front of her desk a couple of inches in the air and let it slam back to the floor. Chaff turned around and waved to the underlings outside with a smile, then closed the door.

"You're embarrassing yourself, Agent Ryan," Chaff taunted.

I never saw anyone's eyes widen quite as far. I put my head down so she couldn't see my smirk. Nails, darts, or bullets were flying out of her mouth through sounds that were unrecognizable forms of speech. She held her hands up in a mock throat hold, sneered, and fell into her chair, arms limp and dangling on either side. "That's the dumbest thing I ever heard. I should arrest you both for interfering in an investigation."

"We're trying to help," I said. "Besides, how are you going to get them there on the day and time of your choosing? It was the smart thing to do."

Ryan raised her voice. "There is nothing smart about putting my agents' lives in danger!" She paused, squeezing her eyes closed, and calmed herself, then leaned forward. "Tomorrow is tomorrow, damn it! How the hell are we going to set up in"—she looked at her watch and counted—"less than twenty-four hours? We're over four hundred miles away. There isn't enough time to put all the parts in motion. You've compromised the operation. You don't even know if he received your message, let alone agreed to it."

I moved forward and handed Special Agent Ryan the phone. The screen displayed a text message: "I'll be there."

"Damn." Ryan continued to stare at the screen. "We still don't have time. Assembling a team, flying them to Charlotte, setting up to execute—it can't be done that fast." Second-guessing herself, she picked up her landline. "Teddi, get me Conrad Smith." She slammed the phone down.

"If anyone can get this done fast, it will be Conrad. I will circle back to you after we talk. For now, the two of you can rest. Teddi will get you settled." Agent Ryan motioned through her office window to a young woman just outside her office. Chaff and I started for the door. She wasn't finished.

"Gentlemen, stay out of trouble. No more surprises or I'll personally see to it you're both incarcerated. You get me?"

No reply was necessary. We made our exit.

CHAPTER 30

Teddi took us to a medical suite, separating us into different rooms. Mine held a standard medical exam table with two monitors coupled to one side, a stool with rollers at the foot of the table, and a sink and closet on the wall nearest the door. The overhead lighting and white reflective paint forced me to squint. She handed me a folded hospital gown and told me to get comfortable on the table.

"What's this?" I asked.

"You never saw a hospital gown?" she said sarcastically. "Warm in the front, cool in the back. Doctor Lantz will be here to give you a checkup. Nothing to worry about."

I made a quick inspection. "No obvious torture devices or probes, so that's comforting."

"Don't get too comfortable, Mr. Wheat. We're the FBI, and we are always probing something." She smiled maliciously and left the room.

I knocked on the wall separating our rooms. "You there?"

A muffled voice sprang from the wall. "Don't look. I'm naked."

I laughed at the joke. It made me reflect on our early chemistry back at the academy. Chaff's repartee was anything but friendly then. He was hostile, not just to me but to everyone. The construct of trust had not been born in him at that point in his life. There was a wildness about him, starved for affection. His early years conditioned him to pounce on the weak and take what he could. We were opposite in every way. Our relationship was imperfect—humorless. His DNA was still sending out instructions.

Father Romano's tutelage, the spiritual forces of Saint Joe's Academy, and our unlikely friendship made their way into Chaff's psyche. Those few years together changed us both for the better. I became less naïve, less sterile. Chaff's personality grew branches, obscuring his feral childhood. Obscured, not buried. A contentious knot hides inside that can be untied by the right set of circumstances; the animal within aroused and fearsome. I liked to believe we had a symbiotic nature holding us in proper balance and control, a counterbalance to unnatural aggression.

There was a knock on the door. Doctor Lantz announced himself and entered the room. I was still holding the gown. "Sorry. I was distracted by the stark accommodations, the lack of artwork, and the anticipation of a pat down by Nurse Spriggs. Is she still around?"

"Tobias, I appreciate your penchant for cynicism, but assuming you are still planning on engaging in this foolish plan, I need to examine you. Granted, you and Mr. Lundergan made a remarkable recovery. However, your injuries were severe. I don't recommend your participation."

"Except for the pain from surgery, what is the worst that could happen?"

"Blood clot. Infection. Pneumonia, lightheaded dizziness, or a tear in your wound from too much stress, to name a few. Additional bed rest is what you both need. I've made my concerns and recommendations known to Special Agent Ryan."

"And?"

"Minimally, she has only agreed to wheelchairs during tomorrow's operation."

"That ought to make the bad guys feel confident, don't ya think? Maybe the entire team of special agents should be in wheelchairs. It will confuse the shit out of them. Wait. You said tomorrow's operation. Does that mean we're on?"

"That's my understanding. Act funny if you like, but this is serious, Tobias. Consider what I said."

The exam lasted no more than fifteen minutes. Doctor Lantz was pleased with the results. Nurse Spriggs arrived a few minutes later to change the dressings on my sutures. She also wrapped my chest front to back to give me extra support should there be any need for quick or stressful movements, considering what we were about to engage in.

"How does that feel?"

"Feels secure—comforting. Did you . . .?"

"Yes, Chaff received the same treatment." Then she added, "You are both putting yourselves in danger. You had heart surgery just over a week ago and now you are going on an FBI operation? Not smart. Why the hurry?"

"How long do you think the FBI is going to babysit us? At some point, you're going to send me home. Believe me, I want to go home, but until these guys are caught or satisfied, my wife and I will be in constant danger. What are you going to do about Chaff? Witness protection? No, this all must come to a head soon. Now would be good."

Spriggs didn't bother to counter. She finished the final touches. "Doctor Lantz and I will be onsite, just in case. Don't get this wet." She touched my cheek. "Be safe. Your wife needs you back."

She left, and I put my clothes back on. I opened the door leading to the hallway and Teddi was waiting with two wheelchairs. Chaff was already seated. "C'mon, I'll race ya."

"Where are we racing to?"

"Apparently, the Hilton in Midtown. Teddi here lined up some sweet accommodations for us. Unfortunately, the list of rules promises a very boring night for two single guys with a perfectly good sympathy-getting story sure to arouse the pub patrons. No leaving the room, no alcohol from the cooler, no Jacuzzi. What are we supposed to do, sleep?" He turned toward Teddi. "Did I get that all right?"

"A novel idea," Teddi said. "I could set you up in a motel room in the Bronx though, if the Hilton doesn't make the grade for you."

"No, no, no. The Hilton sounds fine," I said. I motioned to Chaff, making a slice at my throat. I couldn't wait for the day to end. Sleep sounded great.

***

It was around six in the evening. I was no sooner through the door of our hotel room than I found one of the double beds to crash on. My incisions kept me from leaping. I crawled up on the bed on my knees and eased myself lower, then rolled over onto my back, wincing through the process.

I didn't notice where Chaff landed. The last sound I heard was him calling room service. An hour later, I felt a hand shaking my ankle.

"Hey. Tobias. Wake up. The food arrived. Waste not, want not."

I grunted. My mind was telling me I was hungry. My body was telling me it didn't give a damn. After the battle was over, I rolled to the side of the bed and lifted myself off.

"The food had better be good. What'd you order?"

"Everything we are not supposed to have: burgers, fries, beer. Lots of beer. C'mon, drag yourself over here."

We sat at a round table in front of a large window four stories up. When we had finished feasting, Chaff got up and pulled the drapes back, exposing The Avenue of The Americas busy with the human race. "The city that never sleeps, and we can't stomp around in it. What a shame."

His gaze appeared to be more than the simple framing of city life. It was a contemplation. His head drooped down to the street where people moved in opposite directions.

"Wealth and virtue severed from poverty and ugliness by choices benign, until you see clearly what you are not," Chaff said, thinking aloud.

"Was that original?"

He gave me a crooked smile.

"What are you?" I asked.

"A late bloomer, I suppose. The ugliness creeps and virtue is like a new organ that hasn't found its place yet. I'll get there."

He stood deep in contemplation, looking out at a world in motion. Chaff was no longer among the ugliness of the criminal underworld, no longer under its influence. For the first time in a long while, I think he saw the world differently, more promising, more available, but with remnants of selfish inclinations. A failed father and broken mother gave him nothing to take with him into the world, naked in a blizzard of moral dilemmas. No lessons to ponder. All he had—would ever have—he had to take from the world. I prayed that a bullet in the heart changed his desires.

"Be glad you're here and not out there."

"Why?" He turned his head.

"Because that's where the criminals roam and the sky is always gray. New York has its moments, but in an ugly and weird way more often. Too many cabs. People will climb over you to climb up the ladder. They never sleep because the city turns them all into zombies." I put my arms out and made a dead face.

"Cynicism does not suit you, Tobias. You have always seen the good in everything. What happened to you?"

"You're right. Doctor Lantz noticed too. It's all this stuff: Willow, the FBI, you, and Susan. Who can forget that? It's depressing."

"Eat your burger. It's all going to be okay. I promise."

My phone started to vibrate on the bed where I left it. Chaff was closest. He got up and retrieved it. “It’s Susan,” he said. “That should cheer you up.” He tossed the phone to me.

“Susan? Hey, I was just thinking about you. How—”

“Very touching.”

A man’s voice. What?

“Who is this?” I stood, knocking my chair backwards. “Where’s Susan?”

“She’s right here with your parents, Dolores and Marty. We’re having a little get-to-know-you party. You want to come over?”

“Shit! Harrigan!”

CHAPTER 31

I threw the phone down on the table and jumped back from it. "He's got her! Harrigan's got her . . . shit! Shit! Shit!" I pressed my temples with the palms of my hands. Impotent to do anything. An irrational fear held me in place, staring at the phone's lit screen as dread washed over me.

Chaff picked up the phone and touched mute. He handed the terrifying call back to me. "Tobias, you must talk to him. Find out what he wants."

"I know what he wants. Isn't it what everyone wants? This is your fault."

Chaff didn't react. He shook the phone at me. "Talk."

I took it, holding the frame like it was infected. Stared at the screen, waiting for Harrigan's face to pop up in a threatening hologram. Then I turned off the mute and held it to my ear. "What do you want?" I said, grit in my voice but toothless in my bite.

Harrigan said, "I want peace and love and happiness for all God's creatures. Isn't that what we all want?"

His sarcasm drilled into my skull.

"The important thing is how we interpret those things that make us happy. Wouldn't you agree, Tobias? I imagine returning your family in good health would make you happy."

"Let me talk to my wife," I demanded.

Muffled voices argued in the background. "Like I told you, scream and I shoot Dolores. You understand?"

Susan agreed. "Tobias, is that you?

"Susan! Yes, it's me. Are you okay? Is everyone okay?" I was shaking with anger or fear or nerves—so helpless.

"Yes, please give him what he wants so this can end. We're okay but scared."

More noise on the line. "Hello? Susan?"

Harrigan snatched the phone away.

"There you go," Harrigan said in mock friendliness. "Your wife would be happy if this all could end. Everyone wants what I want; peace and happiness. Now, my turn. Let me tell you what is going to make me happy. Your wife has wisely spelled it out for you. Give me what I want."

Harrigan laid out his demands. Simple and blunt: He wanted me to bring half the diamonds to him at my parents' home in New Jersey, instructions to follow. He surmised that I was in the care of the FBI and assured me if he saw a single agent or SWAT member approaching, he would kill my family.

I had forty-eight hours. Enough time to fly to Charlotte to pull off the operation and fly back to Newark Airport. It didn't sound like he knew I was in New York, or privy to the operation taking place in Charlotte. He was ready to hang up. Chaff handed me a small sheet of paper from the memo pad on the nightstand. Again, he motioned for me to read. I took the paper, confused. He waved the back of his hand to urge me on.

"Harrigan, wait."

"Time's a-wasting, Tobias," Harrigan said.

I picked up Chaff's note. "You're a detective for the Chicago PD. When you are caught, it won't go well for you in jail and you will be caught. Guaranteed."

"We'll see." Harrigan hung up.

"Why did you make me read this to him? Just to piss him off?"

"No, to make him nervous. People who are nervous make mistakes."

"What mistake would that be?"

"He doesn't know I'm alive. He'll never see me coming."

***

The sleep I was counting on never came. My outrage lasted for hours, pacing, making idle threats I could never fulfill, sitting, standing, and holding back tears. All the while, Chaff tried to comfort me, but I don't think I could remember a single word. My grief entered the stage of acceptance. I sat down in the only overstuffed chair in the room, verbalizing my thoughts, trying to stay in control.

The situation was what it was. Susan, my family, and I were helpless from the demands of a Chicago detective gone bad. Anything noteworthy about the man was stripped away by greed. Harrigan was right. The only way out of this was to make him happy. Give him what he wants. But how? Now that the FBI was involved.

Chaff was listening patiently to my ramblings. He could tell how distraught I was. "How am I going to put my hands on the diamonds? I no longer have the key to the deposit box since giving it to Special Agent Ryan on the helicopter."

"Are you done? None of this is going to help. We need a strategy," Chaff urged.

"Happen to have one?" I growled. I was annoyed with his comment—so calm and businesslike. "A strategy, my ass. What we need is a time machine to go back before any of this ever happens."

"No time machine, but I'm working on a way out of all this and your whining is not helping. Let's review the facts."

"Here's a fact for you. That bastard has my family and there's nothing I can do about it. I want to tear his heart out. They're not your family. Damn! Why'd you take those diamonds in the first place?"

Chaff's demeanor changed. He became sullen. "Not true," he said. "You are my family, Tobias; so is everyone connected to you. You've been my family for a long time. You and Father Romano and Moorefield—and now Susan. You're all I have.

"And as far as the diamonds go, they killed Jimmy and Blake in cold blood. I will be next if I give in to them, and you can be sure they will kill you if they get their hands on them, just because they can. Trust me."

It struck me how insensitive my statement was. Growing up, Chaff had no one except the street. Jimmy Scariff had become his mother and father, mentor and protector. Trevor Masters had taken that away. To any normal person, Chaff had nothing. Back then, the street was family and home. His father died in jail, and he never heard from his mother again. Where he was and what he became was a symptom of circumstance. The kiddy gang was his whole world.

His past could have easily fallen into a deep well of self-pity, but he survived. In fact, he did more than survive, he rose above. I admired his attitude. Chaff didn't want to stare at his wounds or conduct some melodrama about the scars. Until Johnny Willow was no longer a link to his past, he would not escape it entirely. That was why he agreed to help the FBI. That was why he was willing to give his life for me that day at the bank.

Chaff was not only my friend. He was family. I left my self-indulgent suffering behind and faced him.

"You're right. I'm sorry."

"Good. Sorry is good. For what it's worth, I'm sorry for getting you and Susan into this mess. I never give up control of my life to anyone, Tobias. It's how I made it through. I'm not going to give up now to some greedy megalomaniac. I promise you, Harrigan's power trip is an illusion. You're going to have your chance to cut his heart out right after I hand him his balls. Let's get started on a plan."

"What about the FBI?"

"What about them?"

CHAPTER 32

At five in the morning, my eye muscles gave in. I slept hard for an hour until Special Agent Ryan intruded with a wakeup call. She informed me that Conrad Smith's crew was onsite, ready when we arrived. Ryan explained that Conrad was on a case in Atlanta when he got the call and agreed to help. She painted it as a stroke of luck. His team had already assembled and just had to relocate to Charlotte, a three-and-a-half-hour drive—three if they used their flashing blues. Four Suburbans, four agents each, and set up by noon.

She said that Spriggs was on the way to the hotel to collect me and Chaff, but Chaff was not in the room. I hung up the phone and lifted myself gingerly from the bed and waited for my eyes to adjust to the darkness. My pupils expanded to their edge, trying to gather enough light to negotiate the obstacles in the room. A strong whiff of coffee squeezed under the door. I followed the aroma toward the thin slit of light beneath. Through the peephole, I found Chaff and Spriggs sitting in the hallway side by side with two cups of coffee, laughing about something. I opened the door, shielding my eyes from the bright lights.

"You guys look real chummy."

Spriggs glanced at me and covered her mouth with one of her hands, chuckled, then diverted her gaze.

"Dude, did you forget something?" Chaff raised his brows, snickering.

He looked at me waist-high, which made me look down. "Nuts! Sorry. Just woke up, smelled coffee." I backed into the room wearing boxers. The spring-loaded door stopped and a hand slid around the side with a steaming black cup of coffee dancing in the air.

"This might help. We're leaving for the office in five. Can you make it?"

I latched onto the cup and took several immediate sips with gradual effect. Chaff followed behind. He flipped the latch over and left the door ajar. He told Spriggs that I would be right out. I threw some water on my face, wet my hair, and brushed my teeth with the hotel's miniature complement of toiletries. "What did you tell her?" I asked, gargling, then spitting into the sink.

"When she came knocking, I stepped outside to tell her I was not going to make it. Told her that I was having some dizziness and difficulty breathing. She made me sit down. She checked me out and agreed that I should stay behind. We waited a little to give you more sleepy time."

"Good, so our plan might work. Also, you and Spriggs . . . more than patient-nurse stuff going on?"

"Well, Bucky, you'll have to wait for next week's episode to see what happens next. I told you that *sympathy thing* gets them every time."

"You're a regular Don Juan, my friend. Good luck with wooing the special FBI agent."

"I'm fun'n with ya. Don't worry, I'll be on an eleven thirty flight and should be in Charlotte at midafternoon, plenty of time to obtain what we need. Moorefield is en route to Jersey."

"Does Spriggs know?"

Yeah," he said with a sheepish grin.

"I knew it. You couldn't restrain yourself. I knew there was something going on with you two."

"I think she's solid, but yeah, now the weak link in our plan. If she spills to Ryan too soon, we're in deep doodoo. But I don't think she will—extreme empathy for you and your family. The details rocked her a bit, but in the end, she agreed. If our plan is to work, timing is important."

"Spriggs agreed just like that," I said as I slipped my shirt over my head. "Hard to believe."

"Believe it," Spriggs' voice came from the door. She pushed it open enough to poke her head in. "Are you two finished with your boy talk? We need to get going." She grinned from ear to ear, no doubt gleeful to have overheard our private chatter.

"How much do you think she heard?"

"It doesn't matter now. Let's go."

We came in with nothing, so there was nothing to gather up. Spriggs was still smiling when we walked out into the hall. "We good?"

"Yeah. Yeah, we're good. You?" We glared awkwardly at each other. A weird staring, spy-crafty kind of connect: eye squints, brow lifts, and facial contortions, but somehow it confirmed her loyalty to the plan, making us both laugh in understanding. I noticed a sparkle in her eyes as she looked at Chaff. The little flip of her ponytail confirmed my suspicions. I cracked a smile.

"Yeah. Good," Spriggs finally said.

We got to the lobby and Chaff asked the concierge to call a cab. Chaff extended a hand and a tight grip. "So, this is it," he said. "All ends today."

"I don't like the sound of that." For the final time, I asked, "You think Willow will show?

"Anyone's guess what Willow will do, but I guarantee he will be on the scene in some dark shadow or stinkin' manhole. Stick to the plan. It will all be okay, and, Tobias . . ."

"Yeah?"

"Susan will be okay too."

I offered a tilted wave and then Chaff was gone.

***

From 26 Federal, we cabbed to our helicopter, then a short lift to LaGuardia. Ryan, Spriggs, Lantz, a couple of bad-looking escorts, and I walked single file up the stairs into the fuselage of a private jet, the FBI letters printed large on the tail. These guys were not into stealth. When they arrive somewhere, they want everyone to know.

After we were all aboard and cruising at thirty thousand feet, Spriggs gave me the once-over, checking my pulse, blood pressure, and heartbeat. "You nervous?" she asked. "Your blood pressure is low, but your heart rate is elevated." She put her palm on my forehead. "Clammy too."

She deferred to Doctor Lantz. He laid his stethoscope on my chest, back and front. "Breathe in. Aha. Breathe out. Very good." He conferred with Spriggs.

"Could be a panic attack or stress reaction, but my thought is the air pressure."

I felt lightheaded and compelled to defend myself. "I'm not a girly-man, but I'm also not wearing a cape."

"Tobias, it's okay," Spriggs said.

"Any reasonable man would be nervous about taking down a violent group of men with guns and no conscience."

"We agree."

"I've had run-ins with them before. They're not the kind of men that threaten you and walk away."

Spriggs glanced at Doctor Lantz, amused. "We know," she said.

"You know what I mean? I'm not feeling panic, just concerned."

My mouth was running on. Internally, I was yelling, shut up, you talk too much.

"Tobias, stop. You talk too much. We aren't thinking that," Spriggs said, laughing at me. "We think the cabin pressure at this altitude may be having an adverse effect." She touched her comm and asked the pilot if he could descend to twenty thousand feet. The pilot called it in, seeking permission. A minute later, you could hear the whir of the engines throttling down a notch. "You'll feel a little better in a few moments." Spriggs tapped the back of my hand to reassure me.

Ryan spoke up. "You don't have to worry about any violence, Tobias. Once you are in the bank, you will be removed from the take-down scene. It'll all be over in seconds once they enter. Conrad Smith has twelve men in strategic positions, four on the rooftop, four on the ground, and four inside. He's efficient and knows what he's doing. I wouldn't worry."

"Of course not, you're Special Agent Ryan, saving all of us men."

Ryan grinned like she was pleased with the recognition. Empathy and humility nowhere in sight.

No doubt that Ryan believed there was no need to worry. How else could she get through her days walking in and out of dangerous situations without confidence in her survival skills? I wondered about what kind of childhood led her to this life. Where and when did her hard-ass nature take root? Blood oozed out of her arm, so I believed she's human, but the iceberg personality could chill whatever room she entered. Underneath it all, she was not all stiff and unbreakable from what I saw back at Federal Plaza.

"Doesn't the plan call for me to walk outside with the case if he isn't stupid enough to escort the others inside, or did you forget? That calls for a little worry."

"I guess so, since your friend, Mr. Lundergan, bailed on you."

I opened my mouth to respond and thought better of it. My stomach felt queasy enough. I didn't want to start sparring with the Very Special Agent Ryan. Instead, I turned my head toward the window. She didn't know the rest of the plan, the one Chaff and I devised—that Spriggs was privy to. Didn't know that the real case holding several million in rough diamonds was not at First Citizens Bank in downtown Charlotte and that the real ones would be on their way to New Jersey.

I went over the plan in my head: after taking down Willow and company with a case full of fake rocks, I would meet Chaff at Bradford Airfield, a small airport north of the city. Together we would take a chartered Cessna to New Jersey. God willing, we'd make the exchange with Harrigan, and Moorefield would take care of the rest. A simple plan with a blunt end to match Harrigan's single demand.

Special Agent Ryan didn't make conversation easy and no relationship brewed between us, but I felt some sympathy for her. She was unaware that her day was about to become long—very long. Her icy nature would soon be under extreme heat.

CHAPTER 33

Conrad Smith arranged a seven-seat Suburban to pick us up from Charlotte's Douglas International Airport and ferry us eight miles to downtown Charlotte. We arrived at two thirty in the afternoon. Smith set up a quasi-base camp at the Ritz-Carlton, city center, ten blocks south of the First Citizens Bank location.

When we arrived, Conrad explained to us that the general manager wasn't happy to have the FBI parading through the lobby with agents dressed in SWAT gear. He argued for a maintenance entrance in the back of the hotel and a small business suite with a conference table.

We pulled into the back of the hotel facing a block wall and a solid steel door. The door opened from inside. A nervous-looking man in his fifties stood there holding the metal lock bar. "This way," he said. His eyes scoured the surrounding area, anxious, worried like he was letting a gang of criminals in and didn't want the police to notice. The irony made me smile.

"You are not to tell anyone we are here. Understood?" Conrad said tersely. The man didn't answer. Just nodded, then scurried down a hall out of sight.

"What? No Ritz treatment? No oatmeal raisin cookie; no glass of champagne? I feel cheated."

Spriggs elbowed me and gave me a motherly look, communicating that my humor needed to be put in a lockbox for now. Everyone acted stone-cold. Maybe the pre-op jitters or a type of FBI pep rally before a big operation goes down, minus the pep or the rally.

Automatic lights flipped on when the door opened. I looked for windows. There were none. Pads of Ritz-Carlton memo papers and number two pencils were on the table at each of twelve chair positions. Conrad Smith's team had the split-screen TV set up so we could view the entrance to First Citizens Bank, the inside layout, front to back, and several rooftop locations with snipers posted. The fourth split showed a street view of traffic on S. Tryon Street and West 4th.

"It's all we need." He pointed to the street view. "There's only one remaining ingress, so we should see our targets entering the bank. Back entrances are sealed. This goes the way you laid it out, we won't be here long and I can hustle my team back to Atlanta."

"Your compromise is duly noted. Thank you," Ryan said.

They stood like two chieftains from different tribes, squared off and arms hanging like robotic limbs waiting to be clicked to the on position. Hard to tell if Conrad noticed Ryan was a woman with a stunning figure and flawless face. She had no effect on him. His eyes never moved away from hers. He was not a slacker in the looks department either: no more than an inch taller than Ryan, blond, blue-eyed German traits. His jaw was cut to a right angle and either his shirt was a size too small or his pecs were inflated in a weird male mating ritual. Conrad was all muscle.

Ryan asked, "Why so far away from our operational site?"

"Their leader may be acting in stealth, you said. That means we don't know where he is or where he will be. I didn't want to give away our presence until we are ready."

"Smart. Of course," Ryan concurred.

"Is this our man?" Conrad considered me an object to be measured and put in place.

"None other," I smiled, then held out my hand. He didn't budge. His stare moved from my feet to my head like an alien ray meant to probe what lurked behind my clothing. I unconsciously clasped my hands in front of my man parts.

Conrad barked out an order to one of his agents. "Get these people suited up and connected." Referring back to Ryan. "Questions?"

"No, your men, your op. I'll monitor from here. Doctor Lantz will stay with me. Special Agent Spriggs will enter the bank as a customer ahead of Tobias and remain infield for medical support. Strictly backup."

"Very well." Conrad nodded to Spriggs. "Everything is in motion in fifteen. Prepare the insertion of Mr. Wheat, and we wait for the mice to gather."

Prepare the insertion? What? I'm the cheese? I couldn't tell if it was just hubris or if the man lacked the basic knowledge that other human species inhabited planet Earth. The language of war and tactics made Ryan's cheeks swell with agency pride. I thought she was going to kiss Conrad goodbye, straighten his collar, and tell him to do good today.

Spriggs and I were escorted back outside where a SWAT vehicle had arrived, ushered inside where an agent fitted me with a bulletproof vest and a comm device. I understood why, but the idea of it brought the vertigo of danger back to reawaken my queasy stomach. I was about to put my shirt on top of the vest as instructed, but an agent stopped me.

"That won't work. Try this." He handed me a bulky sweatshirt to hide the effects of the vest. It felt awkward, like a home base umpire. Spriggs was instructed not to wear one. The agents inside the bank would give her a vest once she entered. Everyone was connected to the hive, ready to go.

"Frequency?" she asked one of the agents.

"Preset party line," one of the men answered. "No need to touch . . . new breed, voice-activated."

Spriggs let her hair down and put on a pair of glasses and a sport coat over a white blouse and jeans, instantly becoming a successful millennial. She did a comm check. "Good to go."

They separated us when the briefing finished and placed us in different cars. The plan was for Spriggs to drive herself to the bank several minutes ahead of me, enter and take cover.

I was put in another car, an SUV with a driver, an Uber pick up. A wheelchair in the back. We'd drive ourselves to the bank. She would park in their underground garage and I would be dropped by curbside while the ever-helpful FBI Uber-man would open my chair and help me get settled. The point was to make me appear vulnerable. Better bait.

Approaching the main entrance to the bank from S. Tryon Street, I recognized Spriggs walking brusquely along the sidewalk and through the doors. A voice popped into my ear—several voices:

"Agent Spriggs is in."

"Copy."

"Comm check."

"Copy one. All clear."

"Copy two. All clear."

"Copy three. All clear."

Four more voices entered the crowd of *copies*.

"Tobias, you're next. Take your time and remember you are alone. There are no police. Make it believable."

The voice sounded female, so I assumed it was Ryan.

"Am I supposed to say copy?"

No one said anything. "Hello? Anyone copying?"

"Stay off comm, Mr. Wheat, unless we direct you."

Must be Conrad.

"Roger, dodger," I said.

The car stopped. The driver pulled out the wheelchair and opened it near my door. I started to climb out of the car when the earpiece tingled online. "Let him help you. I repeat. Let Agent Marks help you."

I let him reach into the car and pull me toward him. He placed both of his hands under my arms and lifted me into place on the chair. I weighed one ninety. I didn't spot any veins popping on his neck. No sweat. No emotion. I flipped the metal foot pads down for my feet and rolled away three or four yards toward the bank's entrance, stopped and spun the wheel to turn me around.

"Pick me up in ten minutes, please." I spoke loudly so that if they were listening, they would know to come without delay. The driver gave me a thumbs up before driving away.

I was all alone, second-guessing my depth of courage. I had no delusions that Johnny Willow would show himself. I didn't know if one, two, or more would come, but someone other than him would be arriving shortly.

My heart was beating wildly again. Staring at the entrance, I thought of Susan and my parents. They were counting on me. I couldn't give a darn about Johnny Willow and whether the FBI caught him. I didn't care about the assholes that were about to find themselves trapped and incarcerated. I only cared about the asshole holding my family hostage. For that, I needed God, Chaff Lundergan, and luck, in that order.

CHAPTER 34

The automatic door opened and I rolled into the lobby of the bank. It was adorned with Old World charm, mahogany walls and marble accents. The agency personnel cleared the lobby of customers and employees. The place was hollow. Six teller windows, only two operational, so it seemed. Looked like six small jails waiting to incarcerate the bad guys. Special agents stood at the ready. One acted as a loan officer at a desk on the floor and still another was sitting in the big chair behind the bank manager's nameplate in the office: Mr. James Bertowski.

Where was Spriggs? She came in right before me.

A thick, round metal vault door hung open behind the teller's pit. Inside the vault were a series of safety deposit boxes: small, medium, and large. The latter had a twelve-inch width and eighteen-inch height. The vault door remained open during the day, intending to show confidence and a not-so-subtle invitation for customer deposits.

The atmosphere was stark, even spooky. The loan officer-agent approached me.

"Mr. Wheat?"

"Yes."

"I'm Special Agent Wilson. We need to secure you in an office on the second floor."

"Wait. Won't they want to see me when they enter the bank?"

"Once they're in, they belong to us."

"But, Agent Ryan gave me the key to the box."

"After everything is secure, we will come get you."

"Go with it, Tobias," my comm link instructed. I didn't respond and acquiesced.

Agent Wilson grabbed the handles of the wheelchair and we sped through the lobby to the elevator banks. He pushed me inside, reached in, and pressed the second-floor button. "Special Agent Spriggs will be there to receive you."

***

The elevator door opened and I rolled out to a walkway with a circular metal railing that overlooked the bank floor. I didn't see Agent Spriggs. The walkway curved around to a set of offices on the S. Tryon side of the bank. I leaned over the wood-and-iron railing and called down to Agent Wilson. His eyes focused on the front door and the loud screeching of tires on the pavement.

"Spriggs isn't here," I said. "Where is Spriggs?"

The agent looked up at me. A loud, thunderous explosion suddenly echoed into the expanse of the lobby. My eyes reflexively turned to the source, then back to see Agent Wilson's neck ripped open and blood splash out into the open space. His knees wobbled and his body dropped to the floor.

"My God!" I screamed, recoiling from the horrific scene. I rose from my wheelchair and hovered over the rail, eyes bulging. I turned toward the source of the sound and saw Trevor Masters standing inside the door holding two guns; one was a pistol-like machine gun. He was wearing army fatigues and a vest much larger, much thicker than mine. Another gun was clamped to a thigh holster. He was dressed for battle.

My ear vibrated. "What's happened? Report! Report, damn it!"

Voices came in waves. Frustrated, excited special agents jammed the comm line.

"Humvee . . . sidewalk."

"Blocking the door. No shot!"

"No shot!"

"The target is inside! Repeat. Target inside!"

"Taking fire! Man down! Man down!"

"Backup! Backup! We need . . ."

The voices crowded into my ear with vibration so penetrating that I thought my head would explode. I pulled the device from my ear.

Masters gave me a menacing glance, smiled, then raised his arm and began firing. The two agents behind the teller windows, stunned by the violent entry that took out Agent Wilson, tried to draw their weapons. Too late. They rocked back from their posts, taking multiple rounds before succumbing to the barrage and landing doll-like against the back wall.

I watched in horror as Trevor Masters unleashed hell. The agent in the manager's office flew out of the doorway, rolling on the floor, and came up shooting. I counted four rounds, direct hits to Masters's chest, knocking him backwards a few steps before Masters opened fire and put him down. The echoing gunshots subsided. Blue smoke rose into the lobby and the smell of sulfur soured the savage remains left behind.

Okay, Doctor Lantz. I believe I'm now having a panic attack. It was an odd thought to have at that very moment, but I had never been in this kind of moment before. I didn't know what to think. *Where the freaking hell is Spriggs*?

I put the comm device back in my ear. "Copy. Copy. Anyone there? Spriggs? Ryan? Anyone?" Ryan would have seen this on her screen back at the command base. Why was there no response?

I was alone again. I felt complete helplessness, caving in to my circumstances with the trembling knowledge that I might soon meet my end. My eyes were engaged like calculators trying to solve the formula for escape. Not forthcoming.

A cold jolt of fear pumped through my body. My heart hiccupped and my legs gave out for an instant. I fell on all fours, dizzy and nauseous, one hand holding the rail for support, my other pressing against my chest as daylight diminished.

***

"Tobias. Can you hear me? Tobias, wake up." A soft, anxious voice hovered over me. A hand stroked my hair. My chest was burning, aching. A horrible whiff of ammonia hit my senses with a sudden putrid awareness, making me come to, gasping, choking, peeling my eyelids back and raising my head to attention.

"Where . . . what . . .?"

"Tobias, it's me, Special Agent Spriggs. You passed out—possibly a mild heart attack."

Her pleasant smile and beautiful features were an antidote to the rotten smell that woke me. Then, as if some other-worldly shadow departed from her, Wallace appeared looking down at me from ten stories up. At least that's what it felt like. "Hello, Mr. Wheat. You gave us a bit of a scare. Are you okay?"

"I gave *you* a scare?" I said in disbelief. "You're standing holding a gun and your sociopath friend just wiped out an entire FBI team. Why the hell would you be scared?"

Spriggs helped me to my feet. Wallace brought the wheelchair close and Spriggs helped me sit down. "Tobias, they want the key. I think you should give it to them."

"We checked your pockets," Wallace said. "No key. That would make our little rendezvous today meaningless. Scary thought, don't you think? You want to make this easy and tell us where it is or do I need to start eliminating hostages, starting with this one?"

He pulled the hammer back and pointed his gun at Agent Spriggs's head.

"If I give it to you, then what? Are the others dead?" I leaned and motioned to the offices where the employees and a few stray customers could be seen through the open door, faces straining their necks as witnesses.

"They're fine, Tobias," Spriggs answered. "Their hands are tied, and they're frightened, but they'll be okay."

"Is that how you got in? As a customer?"

Wallace nodded. "Harrigan clued us in to FBI tactics. I thought something like this would happen, so I came to the party early. Very friendly people, the FBI. Put us up here. Gave us water. Didn't even collect our phones."

"How did Harrigan know?"

"He didn't. A guess. A damn good one. We waited at the airport for the friendly FBI skies to land and followed them to their little ritzy hideout. They made it so easy. Johnny is there now, having a nice chat with three of your colleagues. I take that back. Two of your colleagues. One of them got a little aggressive and needed a distemper shot." Wallace grinned with a smug delight at his play on words.

I peeked over the railing. Trevor Masters was standing near the door watching the action outside. I didn't hear Ryan's order, but she must have been forced to stand everyone down or else they would have already stormed this place. Our plans went so wrong, outsmarted by Johnny Willow and his two hired guns. Chaff would be waiting for me and Spriggs. He would try calling when we didn't show. Our plan to save Susan—all gone. "What the frig!"

There is one moment in life that I have experienced a few times when everything that can go wrong, goes wrong. Anticipating failure makes you fret all the way to the last possible saving outcome. But when you reach the ground, when you are about to crash, when things can't get any worse, you give in to it. You laugh at the expected trouble because, at that point, it can't hurt you anymore.

Anxiety and fear—and caution—are released to go their separate ways. I think of the men at the Alamo, screaming war cries, charging with bayonets through the hail of bullets all the way to the last piece of lead and the bite of death. I think of Wallace and Masters and how foolish they were, how unaware that I had reached my own crash site and that it was time to strike back.

"Agent Spriggs, do you still have some of that medicine from Doctor Lantz that raised my energy?"

She gave me an odd stare. I looked back at her without blinking, hoping to communicate my newfound warrior self. I knitted my brows, squeezing the muscles around my eyes until my head, neck, and shoulders began to vibrate, stirring up a new batch of adrenalin in my body. Spriggs opened her med bag and pulled out a needle and a small bottle of liquid.

"What's that?" Wallace pointed to the bottle with the tip of his gun.

"B12. It will help raise his energy and give his immune system a boost."

Wallace reached down and grabbed the bottle, read the label and returned it, giving his approval.

She faked sticking the needle into the bottle and instead drew air into the hypodermic tube. Spriggs came close. Wallace followed with a natural distrust. I rolled up my sleeve. Spriggs leaned in with the needle. I blinked once. The message was transmitted. I grabbed the needle as she spun away and in a lightning-fast maneuver, I shoved the needle into Wallace's thigh, aiming for his femoral artery, and depressed the syringe enough for the air to enter his veins before he jerked back in reflex.

"You bitch!" he yelled. He raised his gun to her head. Spriggs pulled her hand out of her med bag and whipped her stethoscope into his face. His pupils dilated. He fell backwards like a fallen tree. The air hit his heart. His eyes remained open.

There wasn't time to process what had happened. The adrenalin was still having its effect. Spriggs grabbed his gun and moved to the rail, aiming down at Trevor Masters—three shots to the head and Masters was no more. Spriggs remained standing with her arms outstretched holding the gun with both hands pointing down at his body. I saw a single tear take form on her cheek, then she let out a loud scream—a war cry—a victor's shriek, shouted into the heavens, thanking the gods for the defeat of her enemies. Her arms shook, unable to release the tense muscles holding aim. I don't think Spriggs ever fired her weapon at anything beyond a black-and-white target.

I managed to stand and removed the gun from her hands. "Special Agent Spriggs. It's over." She collapsed into my arms, trembling, and released a barrage of tears. We were both spent.

CHAPTER 35

"I'll be right back." Spriggs went to the office where the hostages were. She pushed the door open. A reflex of emotion released from inside the office as she entered. I was glad no one was hurt. She pulled a small knife from her sack and cut the plastic tics Wallace made her attach to each person's wrist. They applauded Spriggs, not really knowing what had happened. Mostly they clapped for their own lives.

I took a moment and tried to get some response on my comm device. I knew he would be listening.

"Mr. Willow, you must have been watching. Did you enjoy it?"

There was silence. Several seconds passed. My nerves were shot. If I didn't have a final heart attack after all this, I figured God wasn't finished with me on planet Earth. What was next? My confidence strengthened.

"Hello, Tobias," a controlled, even-tempered voice answered.

A subtle jolt of awareness rose the hair on my arms and neck, as if a metal detector had found its mark and underneath was buried a layer of hardened fear.

"You and your friend managed to make me a little richer. Wallace and Masters were necessary evils, but now that we are so close to the objects of my desire, I am grateful to you. I was planning to go to an island. I might now buy the island."

"Look, asshole. You're just supposed to say *copy that.*"

"You think this is funny, Tobias?"

"No, the opposite. I think it's sick. You're a freak of nature, Willow. A stinking weed waiting to be plucked and thrown away. What stupid idiot would wait ten years chasing a case of diamonds, killing people for them? Seriously?" Silence again. "You know you're on a party line. The agents you didn't kill are anxious to meet you; no doubt making plans. Make sure you smile at the snipers, Willow."

Suddenly, three gunshots violated my ear. "Ouch!" I pulled the comm from my ear. "What just happened?" I put the device in my other ear. "Ryan . . . Willow . . . Hey! What did you do?" I couldn't get enough oxygen in my lungs—hyperventilating—sucking in air as fast as I could. I spun out of control, looking everywhere, nowhere. "No, no, no . . ."

"Wheat!"

His voice plunged into my head like an ice pick. "What? What did you do?" I was tired, emotions spent, pacing, twice stepping over Wallace's body. I had no more adrenaline in my body, only fumes that gave me the will but not the means.

"One down, two to go. You want to try again?"

My eyes closed, anticipating the terror of someone shot, someone dead. Again, I felt helpless.

"Wheat. I just wanted your attention. He'll probably be okay, but it will hurt like a son of a bitch when he wakes up. Tough guy. Also, so you know, Special Agent Ryan isn't wearing a vest."

He sounded calm and monotone. "I didn't like your speech. You think I'm evil, but that depends upon your perspective; after all, you lied to me about coming alone. You manipulated me, and you intended to murder me. Who sinned first? The difference between us, Tobias, isn't evil. It's the exploitation of virtue. You anticipate honesty and I anticipate lies. My way was more effective than yours. That's what has you angry, suffering the anxiety of defeat.

"Take your wife, Susan, for example. She believes you are coming for her, that you will rescue her. She sees the virtue in you. I detect an evil plan; one that promises an exchange, but betrays in the end. Do you see it too, Tobias?"

"To hell with you!"

"You first," he said. His voice twitched up a notch. More taut, impatient. "Time to finish this. You . . . copy?"

There was a wickedness in the sarcasm. He didn't care what I said to him. I felt a repulsion at his voice, hating that I had to hear it, speak to it, and agree with it for the sake of Ryan and the others.

And what about Susan? Chaff's plan would fail since I was unable to make our planned connection. She was all alone. No one was coming for her and my parents.

I held my head in my hands, helpless to gather my thoughts coherently into a meaningful solution. I wanted to scream, to yell at God, and urge him to pay attention. Tears were held back only by the conviction of anger I had for Johnny Willow and Harrigan, and this diamond crap that was thrust upon my family by the madness that comes of greed.

"I copy. You're in contact with Harrigan?" I asked.

"Yes. He said to tell you your father will be okay. He needed to be taught a lesson. Men, always the heroes, huh? Sometimes they should be more like your wife. Docile. Pleading for her life because she knows her life does not belong to her. Not until things are settled. You should see her begging for your life too. She doesn't yet know that you are the killer. Harrigan doesn't know either, but it won't go well for your family when he finds out."

"Why? What do you mean?"

"Well, because Wallace and Harrigan were very good friends—verrrry good friends. You might say it was a touching relationship."

The revelation was jarring, but it explained a lot. At the very least, it explained why Detective Harrigan would jeopardize his career. There are many shades of love, some not so pretty or pure, but effective motivations nonetheless. *A rose by any other name would smell as sweet.*

Spriggs returned, hearing one side of the conversation. She pantomimed a question to figure out who I was talking to. I held out my hand and shook it to communicate that I couldn't be interrupted. I formed the letter W in the air.

"Wheat? Who's your FBI friend?"

I think she figured out what was going on because she ran to the exit door, bypassing the elevator. She must have flown down the stairs. She returned in an instant, then showed me her ear, indicating she was wired in. She no doubt took it from one of the downed agents. Both of us were now listening.

"Let them go and I'll give you what you want."

"Sure, I'll send them over." A door opened and closed. "There. How's that? Now bring the damn case to me, Wheat! I'm bored with this game. You'll bring me what I want or you will be responsible for dead hostages. I assure you, Harrigan will not be happy with the news."

I didn't know what to say and deferred to Agent Spriggs for some agency insight, some protocol they had figured out for situations like this.

"I take your silence as a token of our new relationship," Willow said. "Tell your FBI friend the only advice she should give you is to comply. It's FBI protocol. She knows that."

"I need time to think," I said, and pulled the comm from my ear. I didn't know how to turn off the transmission on my end and fumbled with the device before putting it in my pocket.

"You don't need to put it in your pocket," Spriggs said. "Once out of your ear, it's silent."

"Good. Does he still see us?"

Spriggs looked around for cameras and saw one mounted near the ceiling at both ends of the catwalk between the elevator and the offices at the other end. "I think so."

She motioned with a nod for us to move into the office where the employees and customers were waiting. "That was an open line. Every agent within a half mile would have heard your conversation. The FBI will be here at any moment and I'm sure they are working on an interdiction at the Ritz, assuming he's still there."

"You need to wave them off! Spriggs! My family! If something happens to Willow at this point, Harrigan will kill my family and go into hiding. Call them off! Now!"

"Tobias, it'll be okay. Trust me. But he's right about one thing."

"What?"

"It is protocol to comply with his demands. We would hope to catch them after the fact, but saving the hostages is always the number one objective in these situations. Agents will not go in unless Ryan and the others are freed."

Her explanation lessened my fear by a fraction, but not enough to keep from worrying about Susan and my parents. If Harrigan found out I killed his lover, he may take his retribution out on them. Willow would save the information to use later to manipulate me. I knew that. The question now remained about what was more important to Harrigan, the diamonds or Wallace? I couldn't believe I was thinking this, but I prayed it was the diamonds.

A loud noise emanating from the front of the building drew our attention, a tractor or diesel truck, then a sudden engine rev before a slam of metal on metal and tires screeching. Spriggs looked out one of the office windows. "They're moving the Humvee—pushing it away from the bank doors. Agents will breech the bank any minute . . . tear gas and smoke. Tobias, close the office door."

"Everyone's dead."

"They won't take any chances. Close the door!"

I did as told, immediately followed the loud percussion of tear gas canisters being fired through the plate glass windows. Seconds passed. Then loud voices yelling *all clear,* echoing through the lobby. Footsteps rushing up the stairs. More seconds and three men burst through the office door in tactical gear, guns raised. Several women screamed. Others put out their hands to hold back their fire. Spriggs moved forward, showing her badge. "Special Agent Spriggs! We're okay in here. No one's hurt, just frightened and shook up."

The men stood down and began to evacuate the hostages. Spriggs found the tactical team leader outside the door, Agent Kane, and explained the situation here and at the Ritz. "We have already breached the Ritz. They were gone, took Special Agent Ryan and left Doctor Lantz. He's shook up, but okay. We cut the camera feed, then put up a helicopter and alerted the local and state police. Sorry it took so long to get here, but when we heard the conversation between Mr. Wheat and Willow, we used it as a delay tactic till we could get to the hotel. Too late in the end."

"Conrad?" Spriggs questioned.

"He'll be okay. He took three shots to his vest, at close range. Knocked him pretty good. A couple of broken ribs. On his way to the hospital as we speak. Does your man here know where they might be going?"

I answered his question. "No idea. But we know he wants what he thinks is in that vault, so he can't be far."

Kane glanced at the body on the floor. “This your handiwork?” he said to Spriggs. Her eyes redirected their focus toward me, then nodded. “Meet our hero. Saved the lives of all the good guys today.”

Kane extended a hand. “Always glad to meet a hero, Mr. Wheat. By the way, there’s a man down the stairs waiting to speak with you. A Mr. Chaff Lundergan. You know him?”

CHAPTER 36

I didn't realize how shaky I was until I tried to stand. Spriggs insisted that I stay in the wheelchair and wheeled me to the elevator. The moment the doors opened, Chaff was standing there.

"Your surprises never end." He gave me that goofy, wide-mouth smile—all teeth.

"You okay, buddy? Kind of a shitstorm in here; bodies all over the place. What happened to Ryan's easy in, easy out?"

"Yeah, unreal, right? Good to be smart, bad if the perps are smarter."

Chaff put his hand on my shoulder and squeezed. "I'm glad it's not you. Damn if this isn't a FUBAR moment."

"How did you know to come?" Spriggs asked.

"For as long as I have known Tobias, he always does exactly what he says he will do. Always on time. Always follows directions." Chaff chuckled. "He was always the perfect student at the academy. So shiny back then, I could have used him for a flashlight. When he didn't show up, I knew something was wrong. Pissing off Agent Ryan is the least of my worries, so I took an Uber here. Found the SWAT team with their skirts all aflutter and figured things didn't go down the way we all planned. Fill me in."

***

I gave him the short version. How Willow outsmarted us and how his man had come to the party early. The carnage was obvious. Explained that we now had a second hostage situation. Brought him up to speed on Harrigan's propensities and my new enhanced fear for Susan's safety. Chaff couldn't believe what had happened, but he was not surprised by Johnny Willow's cleverness. Having spent two years with Willow and his crew, he knew how hard it was to corner him.

We were escorted from the scene by Agent Kane and ushered into a command vehicle. For the first several minutes, it felt like an interrogation. Kane tried to figure out what the hell happened and was considering his next move. He made a call, conversing with someone higher up the chain, who I could only believe was Executive Director Garrity. He listened to the person at the other end of the phone, his head tilted up. Glaring at Chaff, then me, he ended the call.

"What do you think we should do?" he asked Chaff, a surprising deferment.

"Me?"

"Deputy Chief finds your insights worthwhile." Kane crossed one arm across his chest and raised the other to support his chin in thoughtful repose. "I don't know why he has faith in you, Mr. Lundergan, but the fact that you are here and not in a hotel room in New York City suggests to DC that you have an alternative plan. Please share?"

"Well . . . I would say that we should wait."

"Wait. That's your plan?"

"Willow's only means of communication now is my phone, which he believes Tobias has. Brazen enough to believe he can still capture his *objet du désir.*"

I lowered my head, smiling at the dimpled metal walls. The confused look on Kane's face was amusing. I couldn't let him hang. "Object of desire," I said. "The diamonds he came for. If he wants those badly enough, and trust me, he does, then he will contact me when he thinks he's safe."

"Right." Chaff followed. "That's when you will have your next chance. We trade the diamonds for the hostages."

"That's the plan." Kane was dumbfounded. "We just let him walk away?"

"For now, yes. Trust me." Chaff glanced over at me. "He won't get far, and he will be much easier to capture when he has no diamonds and no hostages to threaten."

"Trust you? I don't even know you, Mr. Lundergan. Why would he come back?"

"You're not listening. To get the diamonds."

Agent Kane showed no happiness at the obtuse nature of Chaff's explanations. Kane's instinct was more military—tactical, not strategic. He just wanted a straightforward attack plan where he could deploy his assets and catch the bad guy. His frustration showed in his narrowed eyes and the slight twitching of blood vessels at his temples.

"You want to bag all that bull and enlighten us stupid people?"

My phone—Chaff's phone—vibrated in my pocket. I pulled it out and looked at the screen wide-eyed. No ID. "It must be him. Are we doing this or not?"

The reflex response: not unanimous.

"Do it," Chaff said.

"Wait," Kane replied, still in hesitation mode.

Spriggs threw it back to me. "You decide."

"Hello?"

"Wheat. I'm sure you are not alone. Don't put this on the speaker or I will hang up." My ears were tuned to Johnny Willow's voice. My eyes were trained on Chaff for any hint of an idea. I nodded my head to let them know it was Willow.

"Time we meet."

"You're the boss. What do you want me to do?"

"I'm glad you had time to think things through. Meet me on the roof of The Green Garage, 435 S. Tryon, in thirty minutes. This time you will come alone, or I will relay a not-so-nice story to Detective Harrigan. The only thing I should see on you or near you is a flashy metal case full of diamonds. I don't want to be a babysitter. I get the case and you get Ryan. What condition you get her in is up to you. Now don't respond. Just end the call and don't tell them where you are going."

He had to know that I would replay the conversation for the FBI. That I wouldn't be alone. Not with four of their agents lying dead in Citizen's Bank. No way were Kane and his team going to walk away and let me simply hand off the case. He was planning something.

I was apprehensive, but as I stated earlier, he was the boss and I would do what he wanted, and as much as the FBI would let me do. Strangely, I had the feeling he not only knew they would be there, but wanted them there.

I pushed *End.* All eyes were fixed on me, waiting for an explanation.

"He wants me to come alone. This time, he means it."

"Not going to happen!" Kane said, furious. "We'll take him out at first sighting."

"Spriggs, tell him," I said.

Kane reflexively turned toward her, inviting the information.

"They have Tobias's family, his wife and parents," she said in her usual mild tone. "A Chicago detective, Jack Harrigan. He's at the other end of this. He's holding them at their New Jersey home. He's not on our side. And . . ."

"And what?" Kane asked in an ill-tempered tone.

I cut in. "And he might be unstable. The guy I killed in the bank was his lover. If and when he finds out, revenge will become a factor." I looked at Spriggs, then added, "Save the hostages, right? Protocol and all that. So, we need to send more troops?"

"So why aren't the police there? For God's sake, that's five hundred miles from here. What are we going to do about it? Our job is to get Special Agent Ryan back. That's our focus."

"With all due respect, sir, my focus is on my wife and parents. Civilians. I believe they take precedence over career agents, being aware of what they are getting into when they sign up."

Kane was noticeably hot under the collar and may have felt put in his place.

"I'm not trying to be callous about Ryan."

Chaff spoke up. "Harrigan said he would kill them if he saw any police or FBI. He's part of all this. Willow's in touch with him. I know you guys like to break down doors and breech the crap out of buildings, but these guys are driven. Their motivation is attached to ten long years desiring this single object. At least keep a distance if you won't let Tobias go alone. Dig in somewhere he can't see you. Take a sniper's shot if you must, but don't blow it. If Harrigan believes his partner has the diamonds, it will draw him out. It's our best way of saving Susan and taking them both down at the same time."

"Believes he has the diamonds?" Kane quizzed.

"Right," Chaff said. "We're going to give him what he thinks he wants."

"There you go again with that esoteric crap. Spriggs, can you interpret?"

I was sure Kane was more used to taking his orders from Conrad Smith. Now he was in command and a little resentful of being put in the seat of decision rather than at the end of a pointed finger.

“Agent Kane, the case we will be giving him is fake. No diamonds. Only rocks. Very convincing rocks. Our hope is that he will give up the hostages without a fight before he realizes what he does or doesn’t have.”

“What happens to Mrs. Wheat when he finds out?” Kane’s expression questioned whether I agreed with this plan.

“I don’t see that we have a choice. Our original plan was to take the diamonds directly to the source. We will reengage if necessary.” I looked at Chaff. “Right, partner?”

CHAPTER 37

The Green Street Garage was only four blocks away. The fact that four lives hung in the balance on what happened four blocks from now was a depressing and tortuous thought that was releasing an avalanche of stomach acid.

I'd learned from the previous encounter that nothing is straightforward with Johnny Willow. I didn't know how or when, but some twist, some double-crossing diversion, would precede our meeting with Willow. You could count on it. Everyone was waiting for it and on edge: Kane was walking around with his hand unconsciously on his pistol grip. Spriggs popped three pieces of gum in her mouth. She had to remove the ball just to talk. And I smelled of perspiration like I'd just left the gym.

Kane deployed four snipers no one would detect. Spriggs talked him out of putting up a helicopter as an obvious insertion of police presence. Others in his command were instructed to take up hidden positions to close off the city once Agent Ryan was confirmed safe. He contacted the CPD and asked for backup should it be necessary to cover a broader band around the city, as well as train stations and airports. I didn't believe any of it was secret or undetected by Johnny Willow.

Chaff was detained in the command vehicle watching the feed from helmet cams mounted on Kane's special sniper agents, since Willow still didn't know he was alive. I was carrying millions of fake unspecified rocks. I never felt so rich or scared. The command vehicle feed could only see me from a distance, from wherever snipers two and three were positioned. I was still wired or tagged or whatever they call these comm devices. Spriggs was whispering words of encouragement and repeating Chaff's words of caution spoken earlier.

I entered the S. Tryon Street side of the five-level garage. It's a squatty structure in the relative center of Charlotte's high-rise sky. As I ascended to the roof, I heard Kane say, "This is it. Look lively out there." I tried to imagine those words being shouted in front of a cavalry brigade with swords drawn, rushing headlong into exploding cannons as enemy fodder. "Look lively, men!" The thought was amusing and had its effect of calming me by one scintilla on the fear scale.

The elevator doors opened in a block-walled antechamber to the roof. I pushed open a glass door. The evening sun squeezed between buildings and reflected off windows, creating blinding light prisms. I raised my hand to my eyes, an unproductive shield. Squinting wasn't any better.

I held the door open and tried to get my bearings. Willow said rooftop but didn't specify a location. There were no cars on this level—unusual. Then I spotted the red cones near the ramp descending to the lower level. Construction equipment, a pile of wood under plastic, steel girders, five-gallon buckets of tar or paint and other supplies strewn across the cement roof assured no vehicles would interrupt our meeting.

The next moment brought an instant adrenalin rush; the kind that makes you run.

"Wheat, nice of you to come."

Johnny Willow's voice penetrated my comm. He was wearing Ryan's earpiece. His voice invaded my senses and I instinctively ducked as though he were pointing a gun at me. A shiver formed in waves from my neck to my ankles. I scanned in every direction. *He's not here. Where do you hide on a rooftop?* The entire tactical team had to hear the transmission. They had to have eyes on him. Right?

I was in awe of how brazen Willow had to be, keeping the FBI at bay while stealing millions in diamonds right under their noses. At least that was his plan.

"Did you come alone?"

"Yes," I said.

"There you go again, Tobias. Lies. Where's the virtue?"

I ignored his taunting. "Where's Agent Ryan?"

"Ah . . . yes, where is Agent Ryan? Do you think she's worth three or four million, Tobias?"

"I didn't come here for a chat. We had a deal. You want what I have. Let her go and I will leave the diamonds here." I tried to shut off my fear and tap into the strength that turns cowards into warriors, a conversion that takes place when there's nowhere left to run.

My ears perked up when I heard the elevator motors come to life. He must be on his way and I would be face-to-face with the murdering psychopath and the end of this horror story. Unwanted goose bumps rose along my arms and a nervous twitch had its way through my cheek.

The doors opened to lots of commotion; running, giggling, shoving, bursting through the door, seven or eight kids of various young ages streamed out on the roof with skateboards. Some in frayed, low-hanging jeans with no shirts and neckerchiefs hanging from back pockets. Others in shorts and tie-dye T-shirts. All at once, they laid down their skateboards and rolled past me to the construction area. They jumped over any object they could find, high-fiving each other when one outperformed another, cheering for the most dangerous leaps and tricks. They were surprisingly choreographed as each one took his turn displaying badass stunts, challenging the others to skate duels.

It was mesmerizing. For a moment, I forgot why I had come. I watched as they took shape in a single file train of rolling, thunderous wheels and wood, weaving around the entire roof from one end to the other, then leaping, one at a time, over the steel girders until only inches away from me. The last boy flew past me. With a giant grin, he reached out and grabbed the case out of my hand.

"Hey! No! NO!"

"What's going on?" Someone broke silence on the comm. Multiple voices crammed the circuit; so many I couldn't make out what was streaming into my ear.

I was running as hard as my broken body would allow toward the train of little thieves. This was Willow's diversion. His trick. It was also an exact replication of how Chaff Lundergan's friends had stolen the case when he was twelve and under the tutelage of Jimmy Scariff. The irony was not lost on me. The tactic was brilliant then and effective now.

In single file, they exchanged the case among them five or six times, having fun exploiting their paid-for adventure before heading around the cones and down the ramp into the darkness of the garage.

"They have it! They have it!" I screamed into my comm.

"Who has it?" Kane's voice punched through.

"Skateboarders. Kids. They're on the ramps. They grabbed the case!"

Kane's men hastened to the garage entrances to block their escape, but it was too late. The kids were down the ramps going at lightning speed. I leaned over the edge of the roof and watched as they exited out a side door and broke off in multiple directions down city streets and alleys on their way to rendezvous with Willow and their deserved payday.

I turned around, shocked to find Agent Ryan stumbling toward me. She called my name, pointed behind me and collapsed. I started for her. She was saying something. "Behind you . . . garage."

I looked back over my shoulder and saw someone—Willow—standing in the garage across the street. A reflection of the sunlight appeared in front of his face. An explosion. A piercing pain in my upper back a millisecond later. I fell to my knees and felt the hard, rough, sledge-hammer surface of cement slam on my forehead.

CHAPTER 38

There is no explicit rule that criminals follow, bar one: don't get caught. Johnny Willow followed that rule faithfully, with great success. There is a second rule about killing without cause. He failed the second rule. I lived.

Johnny Willow didn't know that. On that day, he waited until Special Agent Spriggs rushed to the scene, took my pulse, and declared me gone, even though she saw my eyes flutter. I couldn't speak through the pain, barely able to breathe, but my comm device still sent signals to my ear. His last communication was with Spriggs:

"He was a bothersome little shit. He made this much more difficult than it had to be. Keeping my diamonds was a big mistake."

"You're a murderer. Subterfuge, smuggling, and theft would put you away for life, but now, you're going to fry for the murder of Tobias Wheat."

"You're delusional. Goodbye, Special Agent Spriggs."

The day's sun had set and our little cabal of saviors reconvened inside the command vehicle. The plan was in motion. The FBI retrieved Special Agent Ryan, banged up, dehydrated, a possible concussion, with a deflated ego from the manhandling dealt out by Johnny Willow; otherwise, she'd live. An ambulance spirited her away.

They took me off the roof in a body bag for the most convincing sight and unzipped me inside the command. I was not feeling in the best of shape. Spriggs removed my bulletproof vest and checked me over. I heard her say to the others that my head injury was worse than the round I took to the back. “Thank God it wasn’t a head shot. He’ll definitely be sore, hard to breathe for a while.” She came close, held two fingers up and said, “How many?”

“All of them,” I said.

She took a small penlight from her pocket and moved it back and forth in front of my eyes, watching to see if my pupils dilated or constricted.

“I see a bright light. I’m not dead, am I?”

Chaff stood over Spriggs and looked down at me. “The lump is unattractive but you’re going to be okay.”

“Thanks a lot.” I tried to sit up.

“Whoa.” Spriggs pushed down on my shoulders. “You’re not going anywhere. Just relax. You can listen just as well from your back.” Spriggs brushed my hair, which made me think of Susan. “Take it easy. You might also have a concussion.”

Kane appeared satisfied, if not yelling at anyone indicated satisfaction. “Tell me again how the rest of your plan is supposed to work.” No sarcasm in the question. He was honest in deferring to Chaff.

“Well, Agent Kane, Tobias and I are dead; best friends in life and the afterlife. Spriggs, do you see dead people?”

She was in the middle of a swig of water and had to gulp down her laughter at the reference, then nodded. “I do.”

“Good.”

"Why is that good?" Kane asked.

I answered for Chaff. "Because they have no one to call now. No one to lead them to the diamonds. Greed converts to fear once the Africans figure it out."

"That's right," Chaff confirmed. "The gig is up. Shooting Tobias in the back in a fit of spite is Willow's undoing. He screwed himself and Harrigan too."

Kane let out a gleeful smile of understanding. "Okay, we wait. But how will we know when the Wheats are safe?"

I heard a soft buzzing near my head where Chaff was standing. He pulled a new phone from his pocket.

"You're dead. Who the hell could be calling you?"

"Moorefield. Besides Fanny, he's the only other one listed in my new contacts list." Chaff smiled, then answered the call. I could see his face straighten in concern.

"F—k! Okay, we're coming."

That wave of fear struck me. I closed my eyes as tight as I could, wishing this all to be over. Before Chaff could explain, I said, "He took Susan," grimacing through tight cheek muscles.

Chaff reached down and pressed his fingers onto my shoulder. No witticisms this time. "Yes. Moorefield couldn't get a shot. Harrigan is wearing a vest. Susan is not. Moorefield called in reinforcements from the Bureau. He still holds some sway over there."

"Are we talking about Jake Moorefield?" Kane asked, surprised.

Chaff responded, "Yeah, you know him?

"That guy is a legend. I thought he was retired."

"He's tried once or twice. Trust me. He's as anxious to close this out as we are. Moorefield was on the original task force back in '98 when the Africans were flooding us with blood diamonds. He has a singular desire to take Harrigan down—an ugly penchant for dirty cops."

"I don't blame him. How can we help?"

Kane had come around. The FBI doesn't like taking orders or suggestions from the outside, but in the last few hours, he grew into the job a little—saddled in, as they say—and realized we weren't telling him what to do. We were pointing the way and that brought some level of comfort.

"Any chance of getting a helicopter to take us back north and a small army when we get there?"

"You bet, and I'm coming with you with a couple of my own. Mind if I ask how you are going to find him?"

"Moorefield put a tracker on his car while surveilling the Wheat home. He would have taken Harrigan out by now, but Harrigan had the Wheats tied to chairs in front of each of the main windows."

CHAPTER 39

We lifted off at eight in the morning and headed north. The stop at Quantico added some minutes to the trek, but compared with the other alternatives of transportation, we still made great time.

The airports and train stations were being watched, so Willow's only reasonable transit would be by car. Highway patrols in North Carolina, Pennsylvania, and New Jersey were informed and standing by. They had specific instructions not to intercede, only to mark and report Willow's progress north or a Harrigan sighting.

Moorefield kept us informed. Without actionable data, identification of the suspect was beyond difficult. No one knew what they were looking for. Special Agent Ryan, maybe, but she was in bad shape, sedated, having been pistol-whipped and kicked multiple times.

Chaff spent two years with him. If anyone knew what Willow looked like, it was Chaff. He gave us the best description he could: sandy-blond hair with roots showing in streaks, brown eyes, guessing five eight in height, medium build. Without a picture, it wouldn't be a lot for the troopers to go on. His hair color description could identify half the men in the country.

Chaff spent more time describing his personality than his physical traits. He called him sadistic. "Torture for pleasure," he said. "One moment he could be your best friend and the next, he could cut off your ear and hand it to you. He kept Wallace by his side and Masters on a leash. Never went clubbing, no solid female relationships—all business, all the time."

It would be an interesting description if we were writing a book, but it would be hard to put that all on a bulletin for the State Police—*Sandy-blond megalomaniac.* That would cover most of it. A sketch artist was suggested, but we didn't have the time.

The last time I took this ride, it was daylight, and I was forced to tough it out with Agent Ryan's holier-than-thou attitude. This time I was silently praying for her to get better. She'd been through a lot. Once she recovered from her physical wounds, it would be a long time trying to recoup her ego, having been caught flat-footed at the Ritz.

It was a different mix this time. Kane and his two hand-picked agents, Spriggs, me, and Chaff, the dead and the living. We discussed numerous plans and approaches should we find our expected targets.

For me, there was no *should* about it. I would find them with or without help; a broken heart, bruised lung, a small, golf ball-size lump sticking out of my forehead; none of that would stop me. My inner rage and strength filled all my terrified spaces. Being shot once? That made me a panicked mess, paranoid about my shadow. Shot twice, only days in between? Hell, yeah! I was ready to slay the dragon.

Chaff took his headset off while talking to Spriggs. He was pointing at them. There was negligible distance between her lips and Chaff's ear as she spoke to him. He nodded and put his headphones back on.

"Tobias, you read me?"

"Yeah, I read you. The sweaty, red cheeks tell me you have a thing for Spriggs. Either you're afraid of falling out of the nice helicopter or she's holding your hand for other reasons. Whatever it is, it makes for sweaty, red cheeks."

"A nuance of interpretation, Wheat. I claim nurse-patient confidentiality."

"No sweat, my friend. Pun intended. So, what are you thinking?"

"We're on a private channel. Spriggs showed me how. I wanted to tell you how sorry I am for getting you and Susan tied into all of this. It started out to be a genuine intention. I wanted to give you guys a wedding present, then it all went south. I'm sorry we met at the academy too. None of this would've happened had you never met me."

"Chaff, take your self-pity and go screw yourself. First off, Father Romano started this, not you. The academy years are some of my best memories. I'll hang onto them forever. As far as Susan is concerned, a bullet traveled through you and into me. I'm no Indian, but I'm pretty sure that makes us blood brothers. Inseparable. Tighter than ham on rye."

"Darn."

"Now what?"

"You made me hungry."

I gave him the finger and laughed. It made Spriggs raise her eyebrows a bit, not knowing what we were saying, and ease back when she saw us laughing.

I felt a little guilty about the humor we shared considering Susan's situation. She must be terrified and anticipating the worst. I had an image of her in my mind:

eyes red and dark circles forming below. There isn't a fighting bone in her whole beautiful body. Harrigan was right. She would be docile, defenseless, and submissive.

In my helpless state, unable to save her at this very moment or hours ago, I found humor to be a healthy distraction. The more a person thinks about negative outcomes, the weaker they become. I didn't want to be weak for her. I needed Chaff's confidence and Kane's man-at-arms instincts and combative nature. I needed to control and use the adrenalin instead of letting it control me.

Before we left Charlotte, we switched out our comms to make sure Willow couldn't hear us when we came close. Kane had a contingent of twenty agents standing by waiting for instructions.

Like before, we arrived at Quantico to refuel and check in with Moorefield. It was dark. Flashing, red lights poked into the sky from other craft and the towers controlling them. We would never find our adversaries in the dark, but we could get close; ready to pounce.

Chaff and I had become ghosts, and we couldn't wait to haunt the crap out of Willow and Harrigan.

We all ponied up to a table in the mess while our bird was refueled. Until we received a direction, we sat with long faces, poked at cold sandwiches, and sipped on lukewarm coffee.

Spriggs noticed the sullen look on my face. She reached over and touched the back of my hand. "Tobias, stay hopeful. Harrigan wouldn't take Susan just to hurt her. He intends on using her to get what he wants. That keeps her alive. And don't forget, your parents are safe."

"Yeah, that's something, thanks. I was just thinking. Susan and I have only been married for six months. I hardly know her yet. You know, *married know*. Our honeymoon period has turned into a dark, depraved excursion into hell . . . for both of us. Instead of thinking about each other, we've been worrying about survival. Love isn't in the back seat; it's not even along for the ride."

Chaff's phone went off. Moorefield called in a location. Harrigan was headed due west on the PA turnpike. He made it as far as Harrisburg and stopped west of the city in the small town of Carlisle. The tracker was still pinging on Moorefield's laptop but not moving for the last hour. His guess was Harrigan either stopped for food or a hotel. He concluded a hotel, since taking a hostage out to dinner might scare the diners. I don't know why, but it raised my spirits to know where they were.

Kane was gung-ho. "We could end it there; call in the state police to surround the place until I deploy my team." He already had them in transit. "Suburbans on the trail like a midnight train," he said proudly.

Chaff and Spriggs didn't think it a worthy idea, since that would put Willow in the wind. Knowing Susan's safety hung in the balance, they deferred to me.

"I'm no sleuth. No experience chasing or catching bad guys. But it seems to me, as smart as these two guys have shown, they wouldn't meet out in the open like that."

"So, what are you saying?" Kane asked.

"I'm saying I think they have some preplanned meeting place. A hole-up. Somewhere they are both headed towards, not a random connection on the PA turnpike."

"Sounds plausible," Chaff surmised. "Any ideas?"

"Not one."

Agent Kane took a phone call. He listened while connecting with the eyes of everyone around the table. "Excellent," he said. "Send it to my phone and get it out to the state police in a five-state radius." He hung up and stared at the display on his phone. "Well, people, we received our first break. Special Agent Ryan came to and had a nice chat with a sketch artist. We now have a picture of our nemesis." Kane held the phone up and waved it through the air in front of our faces. "Ryan told the artist his hair was brown-rooted under bleached-blond patches. She guessed a height of five eight, about one eighty-five for weight."

"Exactly what I said," Chaff commented.

"There's more," Kane went on. "She said he has a twitch; he would often jerk his head to one side and sometimes bark out some unpleasant curse words that didn't match circumstances."

"Tourette's Syndrome?" Spriggs said.

"Yeah, what she called it," Kane confirmed.

"What is it?" Chaff asked. "And I did notice his jerky movements. I thought he was just trying to act tough or something. I never thought of describing him that way."

Spriggs jumped in. "It's a tic disorder. Doctors don't know what causes it and it's not treatable. It might be stress-induced. Tourette's is harmless to the afflicted, but quite noticeable to people around them. It's not unusual for them to also manifest attention deficit issues."

Chaff looked away, considering what Spriggs said. "That explains a lot."

"In any case, a person with Tourette's is very noticeable. It would be almost as good as having a photo."

It came through as a sketch on Kane's and Spriggs's phones, but the artist added color. Shadowing. A beard stubble. A small diamond in his right earlobe. *Figures*. A cleft chin but no other hardcore discernible facial feature. Still, it put us ahead of where we were moments ago. Adding Spriggs's description of Willow's syndrome would "spotlight our target," as Kane described it.

Chaff heard from Moorefield again. He arrived twenty minutes after Harrigan and took up a position to stake out our *villain de jour*, as he put it. He confirmed Harrigan took a room in a small Home Suites motel.

Chaff asked if he saw any openings to rescue Susan. Moorefield said they made it to a room before he arrived. He used binoculars to surveil the room until he could ID Harrigan through his second-floor window, but never got the least glimpse of Susan. His guess was she was restrained and on the floor, possibly in the bathroom. Susan was Harrigan's last ace. I was sure he wasn't going to make it easy to rescue her. Moorefield said he would get back to us if anything changed.

Then, the strangest thing happened. Kane took a call from a Maryland state trooper. His perplexed look was contagious. We were all mildly mystified watching his facial gyrations and listening to him repeat, several times, the words, "No way! Is that so?"

When he ended the call, we all gave him the zombie stare. I was the first to use words. "Those were some engaging facial maneuvers. Is there an explanation or do we need an interpreter?"

Kane stood there in an oaf-like trance, then shook out of it. "That was Officer Adams from Maryland's State Police post in Cumberland, Maryland. He claimed a man calling himself Johnny Willow, fitting our description, just walked up to him at a rest stop off I-68 and turned himself in. They're holding him and trying to confirm his identity. The guy had an arsenal in his trunk and five grand in his glove box, and an empty briefcase in the back seat. Said he was heading north, as in Canada, and changed his mind."

"That is some incredible mind-changing," Chaff said, stunned like the rest of us at the revelation.

"Nah . . . I don't believe it. There's got to be an angle. A dangerous angle," I said.

"I agree with Tobias," Spriggs added. "Unless something scared him . . . something big."

Kane spoke to the maintenance crew on his phone while the rest of us argued over the meaning of this new development. "Find a comfortable spot, folks, and get some rest. The bird is fueled but there's work to do on the rotors. We will head out at daybreak."

CHAPTER 40

I saw two birds: one very small, and one two or three times its size. They were fighting in mid-flight, the small one pecking at the opponent's underbelly over and over. The larger one flew in, evading erratic swoops and high dives with a blue-and-white egg held in its beak, a prize for its daring theft. Other small birds arrived. Pecking . . . pecking . . . pecking . . .

"Tobias. Tobias, wake up. We're ready to go." Spriggs was squatting in front of me when my eyes opened. "You're dreaming. Nightmare?"

"No. Not a nightmare. Hopefully, a premonition."

"You haven't complained. How is your heart, and your chest . . . and your back . . . and your head?" Making fun as she announced each of my newly acquired scars. "I'm sorry for laughing, but it is a little funny, don't you think?"

"I'm gonna go with not funny. Help me up. Where is everyone?"

"On board the helicopter, waiting for us."

I darted—hobbled—into the bathroom to take care of business and throw some water on my face. Someone made coffee. I grabbed a cup, then trotted—limped—to the helicopter with Spriggs as my crutch.

"So, where are we going?" I asked. "Out to the rest stop where they found him?"

Kane answered, "No. The state will take him to the Allegheny County Jail. He'll face a magistrate by eight or so. I put in a request to hold. An hour and a half flight."

"Moorefield?" I nodded to Chaff.

"No movement."

We took off at a severe right turn and moved at high speed with nose down.

"Tobias, we have Johnny Willow," Chaff said.

"Yeah?"

"He can no longer hurt us. I believe it's time to let the FBI take Harrigan down."

"That doesn't sound like a question."

"It's not," Kane said. "My team is there and in place. They'll take him when he exits the hotel for his car. That will put an end to all of this."

"Before you give the go-ahead, hear me out. I didn't sleep any better than the rest of you, so I'm tired and a little grouchy. *But*, I thought about the situation for hours. I have never been an FBI agent, so I don't think like Kane, or Ryan, or even Chaff. I've never been a criminal. I don't think like they do."

"Get to your point." You never had to lean in to hear Kane's voice.

"My point is, why would Willow turn himself in? He's not afraid of Harrigan. He certainly didn't seem to be afraid of us with his move back in Charlotte. Something scared him this time. Spriggs made the point a while back. It could be the only reason he turned himself over.

Something or someone. I'm betting on someone—someone who knows and works for Tejan Cole, possibly Tejan himself."

"So, you think he has come back into the picture?"

"I think he has never left the picture. Chaff once told me that the man keeps track of things all the way down the line. I think theft, which equals betrayal, which equals elimination. What if this whole time Harrigan and Willow were not after the diamonds for themselves? What if they're retrieving them and returning them to their African connections, and I don't mean partners."

"You're saying an African Mafia-like syndicate who hired them way back when to be nothing but a cog in the blood diamond wheel, but the cog doesn't do the job, gets greedy and the Africans are here to fire the cog?" Kane was summarizing Tobias's suspicions.

"Precisely." Three pairs of eyes stared at me. "What? You all think I'm way off base?"

Chaff was the first to react to my speculation. "He chose to turn himself in for protection. Man that makes a lot of sense." Chaff turned to the others for their thoughts.

"What about Harrigan? What's his angle?" Spriggs asked. "It doesn't make sense. He should be as nervous as Willow."

"Maybe he is. Maybe he didn't take Susan hostage to trade her for the diamonds."

"Then what?"

"A deal of some sort to save his ass." I thought about my own assessment; my spine tingled, temples pulsing. Susan doesn't know. She doesn't know anything. "Oh God! Either way, she'll be sacrificed."

"What?" they all said at the same time.

"His trade isn't going to be with us . . . with the FBI. He intends to trade her to the Africans. Blame the missing diamonds on Willow. In fact, why not tell them that Willow has them and never intended to turn them over?"

"Hold on, Tobias. Now you're getting out there in the weeds letting your mind make up stuff. Your theory made a lot of sense, but assumptions are a crap shoot. Don't go there. Besides, if all real, he never needed Susan in the first place."

I think Chaff knew I was right but was trying to lessen the pain of knowing Susan's fate.

"Think about it. The last thing Willow told Harrigan was that he got the case. But he got played by us. Finds fake diamonds, tells Harrigan what happened, who does or does not believe him. It doesn't matter what he believes though, because all Harrigan cares about is the Africans; either saving his ass or leaving the line open for future business. And Susan? His shield until he can get his plan together . . . then she's history." My eyes watered over as I came to that conclusion. I threw my head back in my seat and stared at the thin metal roof of the helicopter. I prayed a hopeless prayer would find its way to a merciful God. I prayed that his all-powerful hand would reach down through the clouds and pluck her from danger.

“All right. I’ve heard enough,” Kane said with a commanding tone. “I’m giving the green light. This will all end in ten minutes.”

We flew in silence. A half hour since we took off. Waiting for the results of Kane’s assault team was the most excruciating ten minutes of my life. I poked my head out the door and saw farmland in patches of green and brown, checkered in meaningless patterns. Peaceful. Far from the madness of greed and power. That’s what I would give Susan when this was all over.

I noticed Chaff opening his phone, staring at the display. Probably a text message from Moorefield. Then, Kane got the call. Their faces said something went wrong.

Spriggs looked over at me, reading my mind, my worry, then back to Kane. “Well, what happened? Is Susan okay? Do they have Harrigan in custody?”

“They weren’t there,” Chaff said bluntly. He deferred to Kane.

Kane’s jaw tightened like he wanted to punch something or throw something. “They had the place surrounded, made their assault, and there was no one in the room. No evidence that they were even there. The car Moorefield saw them arrive in is still sitting in the parking lot. Harrigan switched out and left Moorefield to babysit an empty nest.”

I felt gut-punched. “Bullshit! The FBI got played again. Damn it! They could be anywhere now.” My face felt flush. Sitting inside the small space of the helicopter, strapped to my seat and with hopeless thoughts, imagining the worst outcome, the stress took its toll again. Darkness invaded my senses.

CHAPTER 41

I found Spriggs by my side when I came to. Familiar beeping and chirping sounds filled the surrounding spaces. Oxygen fed into my nose again. Another tube full of liquid dripped into my arm, the room lighting a notch below dim.

"Spriggs, where am I?"

She smiled. "Cumberland Memorial. How do you feel?"

"Like I entered the land of déjà vu. What happened? Did we crash or something?"

"No, we're all fine. Your heart gave out. Your cardiovascular system couldn't handle the stress. I had to use the onboard defibrillator to bring you back."

"How many times can a guy die? I can't say I'm glad. I died back there in more ways than one. He got away, didn't he?"

Spriggs ignored my question. "Don't be so glum. I have some news. Kane and Chaff interrogated Johnny Willow several hours ago."

"Several hours! Crap! How long have I been in here sucking air into my nose?"

Spriggs took note of the time. "About four hours. It's noon. And before you freak out, just listen. At first, Willow refused to talk, but they made it clear the list of crimes he is wanted for would put him away for life. I think he knew murdering you would give him the death penalty, since it occurred in the act of a federal crime. He didn't know that. He doesn't know you are alive. The FBI took Old Sparky off the table in exchange for information leading to the arrest of Jack Harrigan and Susan's rescue."

"Did he take it?"

"Hell yeah. That's the good news. We know where Harrigan is going."

"And the bad?"

"I didn't say there was bad news."

I groaned through a tortured face. "C'mon, Spriggs, there's always bad news."

"The bad news is that you're staying here. No more stress. No more blackouts. If I have to cuff you to this hospital bed, I will."

"Did my kidnapped wife give you those instructions?"

"Of course not."

"Then I'm coming. Where are we going?"

"Do you always get your way?"

It was a stare-down for a few uncomfortable moments. "So?"

Her face straightened and she gave in. "Harrigan is in the air. Literally. They realized he had never stayed in the hotel; entered, turned the lights on, and made sure he was seen through the window, then left, taking a different car. He chartered a flight from a local airfield, taking Susan with him. Moorefield never knew."

"Son of a bitch! Will this never end?" I pulled the oxygen from my nose and reached for the needle taped to my upper forearm.

"Tobias! No." Spriggs stopped me. "You could hurt yourself doing that."

"I need to get out of here. I need to be out there looking for my wife. Get this thing out of me or I will do it."

Spriggs surrendered and with gentle hands, removed the IV. "Your clothes are there," she said, pointing to a chair near the window. "Tobias, your heart is weak. It can't take the level of stress it's been under. Please reconsider. They're doing everything they can. I know they will find her."

"Not true. You know nothing. You're just trying to calm me down. Where did Willow say he was going, damn it?"

"Canada—Toronto."

It felt like someone opened all the windows and doors and let the cold air in. The revelation deflated me; sucked out all the hope and replaced it with despair, cold and debilitating. Spriggs waited until she thought I was listening again.

"It was their backup plan. Harrigan has a fishing lodge on Lake Ontario. According to Willow, it's accessible only by boat. Lots of stashed guns and ammo. None of that will stop us though. The FBI cooperates with Canada. Kane made contact with the Royal Canadian Mounted Police. Everyone is headed there now. Plans are in motion."

"Chaff's with them?" I asked.

"Yes."

I continued getting dressed, not caring Spriggs was in the room. After all, she's a nurse. My nurse. She saw a lot more; even helped bathe me back in Charlotte.

"There's something else I need to tell you," she said.

I stood and pulled my jeans up to my waist, bent my knees to tuck in, zipped and buckled. "It can't be worse than what you already told me," I grumbled, feeling disgust, not anger.

"Johnny Willow is dead."

I turned around and eyed her, my shirt only half on, dangling from my shoulder. "It isn't the worst news. Not like Toronto, but shocking to hear. What the hell happened?"

"They were moving him from the magistrate to the jail where he would be detained until the FBI could pick him up for transfer. We were all there. A sniper's round took off the back of his head. It was gruesome. It could have been any one of us."

"The Africans?"

"That's the current theory."

"No coming back from that," I said in repulsion with the ease with which these people took life. *How does money—carved out of the earth, stamped, and shoved into your pocket—outweigh the worth of a man*? "Metal against soul," I muttered.

"What?"

"Nothing, Agent Spriggs. At least now we know my intuition was correct. None of that matters anymore. I need to find a way to get to Toronto. Don't charters file a flight plan?"

"Yes, the same trail Kane is on."

"Well, we might be late, but we're going to the party. If Harrigan knows about what happened, he's going to be even more desperate."

"He's got a better chance with us than he does with his African friends. Maybe we should let him know and try to talk him down," Spriggs said.

"I think Harrigan is all in at this point."

CHAPTER 42

The Christian belief I grew up with and learned to love at Saint Joseph's Academy is to love the sinner. Pray for him. Love your enemies. Pray for them. I was never told there is a cutoff point where those rules no longer apply when the sinner and the enemy won't let up. I was never told because the Church's position has never changed. Refusing repentance is my personal contribution to the rule.

Jack Harrigan had long ago given up being a detective or being a human being. I think that is the key: humans are to be forgiven, but when you cease to be human, when you are inhumane, forgiveness is optional and replaced with pity. I do pity him for whatever judgment he will face, but he should be glad I'm not his god. There is no amount of forgiveness that will change my resolve to kill this man and turn him over to fate. I will beg for my own forgiveness when Susan is returned to me unharmed.

Spriggs agreed to help. Maybe it was sympathy, or maybe it was the anticipated proximity to Chaff Lundergan. I've seen that puppy gaze between a man and a woman before. You think you're being subtle, not advertising it, undecided, studying, sipping at the idea of a relationship from a distance. But the only people you are fooling are yourself and the person locked into your admiring gaze. The rest of us? All in the audience watching the performance. I'm glad for Chaff and Spriggs. That's worth praying for.

On the way, Spriggs told me she was in contact with Kane. He approved the excursion, probably at Chaff's urging. We headed for Ward Island, just off the harbor waters of Toronto, a small jughandle of land that jutted out into Lake Ontario. Kane talked to Spriggs about a landing strip on one side of the land form, then we'd ferry over to Ward.

Apparently, Harrigan had a place on the inner waterway slicing between Ward and Algonquin Island. Rows of cottages lined the channel, squeezed beside each other with identical docks and boat slips. In any other place, they would be considered a vacation getaway, but as Spriggs relayed, it's a permanent colony for Canadians, fished all four seasons, and ferried to the city when needed. A strange place for Harrigan to hole up, but he may have bought it years ago, before he lost his mind. *What would the neighbors think of his new female friend, tied and gagged, pushed along the dock before he slithered into his hideout?*

The day was verging on sunset as the charter pilot landed our small Piper Cub. I wondered why Chaff had not called me, so I questioned Spriggs. "Anything I should know?"

"No, I wondered the same thing. Chaff and I agreed to communicate upon arrival. Let's give it some time."

A police boat was waiting for us. We jumped on and motored out in seconds. The water was glassy, yielding a smooth, graceful drive at high speed.

"Here, we're in range now. We can use these." She handed me another comm device. The channel came alive and I heard constant chatter from checkpoints, and moment-by-moment commands.

"Where are you?" I recognized Kane's voice.

"A mile and a half out, coming to you by boat," Spriggs replied.

"Remain at the ferry, Agent. You copy?"

"Copy."

"Where is Chaff Lundergan?" I asked. "Anybody?"

Spriggs turned to me and ran her hand across her neck, then put her finger up to her mouth to indicate I was to listen, not speak.

Kane's voice came back. "He went rogue."

"Jeez!"

"My feelings exactly, Mr. Wheat," Kane said. "He's not armed."

"What is he thinking? Is he wearing one of these comm things?"

"Yes, he hears everything you hear," Kane replied. "But please stay off the—"

"Chaff, are you out there? Chaff, come in."

I detected a low voice. "Copy. I'm here. I can see them." It was Chaff, speaking in a whisper. The chatter on the comm went silent with everyone paying attention to Chaff's comments.

The FBI and the Canadians did not arrive in stealth. Harrigan would know he was surrounded. Police helicopters flew above, red-and-blue police cars parked in haphazard lines fifty yards from the cottage. The police were busy getting curious and scared civilians out of the way or telling them via bullhorn to stay indoors. The FBI team was busy developing tactical strategies and hostage rescue scenarios.

So it appeared that Chaff had taken matters into his own hands. Most likely from guilt. He felt responsible for Susan being kidnapped and tortured and now, accountable for bringing it all to an end, to save her life, even if it meant giving up his own life, again.

Jack Harrigan was in a boatload of trouble. There must have been a hundred law enforcers surrounding him. With that kind of force, I should feel confident, but I didn't. "What the hell is Harrigan's plan?" I said to Spriggs. "He's finished, damn it. Shouldn't someone be telling him to come out with his hands up?"

"I don't know, but as long as he has your wife, he has power."

"You can see them? That doesn't make sense. You would think he would know we had snipers perched," Kane said to himself. "Does anyone have a shot?" He didn't wait for an answer and gave a general order, "If so, take it; report after."

There was a pause on the comm system, an eerie silence punctuated by static interruptions like someone was about to speak but chose not to.

"Is anyone seeing this?" Chaff's voice came. This time not whispering.

Multiple voices came through in flat, defeated tones.

"Copy."

"Sun of a bitch."

"Damn."

"Now what?"

My voice was anything but defeated or flat. I screamed into the comm, "What the frig is going on! What do you all see?"

Chaff came back. "She's wearing a suicide vest. Just sitting there, hands tied behind her back, legs tied to the chair and gagged. I don't see Harrigan anymore."

With his comm wide open, we heard a double-click. "I thought you were dead." Harrigan's voice. "Willow said you might switch sides. Nice trick coming back to life. Come inside where I can make your death more permanent."

"We have to get to them!" I said in panicked breaths. I started forward.

"Tobias, no," Spriggs said. She grabbed my wrist and held me back.

"Spriggs, control him, damn it. Put cuffs on him if you must. I can't let anyone else become a hostage," Kane demanded.

I felt the cold metal ring snap around my wrist. I looked down at a pair of handcuffs. I eyed Spriggs with a menacing threat in my eyes before I heard the click of the other cuff around her wrist.

Several tortuous minutes passed. No news. No explosions. No voices. Then I heard the familiar voice of Jack Harrigan.

"Hello, boys and girls. I guess you can see the predicament everyone is in."

Harrigan took Chaff's comm device for his own use.

"You can all see that Mrs. Wheat and the previously dead Mr. Lundergan share the same fate. Kind of him to let me see him die twice. A rare opportunity." He laughed vindictively. "It's not the way the Bible describes it: the Chaff and the Wheat gathered together, or should I say, Mrs. Wheat."

Spriggs held her finger to her mouth again, mouthing the word *please* for me to not respond, imagining what was swarming in my head. She had to hold me back, latching onto my belt from behind and pulling with all her might. My rage might drag us both into the fight.

Leading up to this moment, Harrigan's grip on my wife and parents was taut, but the threat was healed by the promise of a trade. The distance between us gave me hope for an ending far off, but coming. That possibility was gone. Only an escape now. One that cared not who paid the price.

The proximity of being this close to the reality of Harrigan's desperate plan created a frantic now-or-never response, tensioning every muscle and nerve in my body. My mind was in revolt, wanting to stampede into the center of the menace. Kill his strategy—kill him. Save the world.

"What do you want?" Kane asked. I knew him by now. He tried hard to be creative in his strategic thinking, but failed too many times.

"Who is this?"

"Special Agent Jim Kane."

"Special Agent . . . I love how you guys use that term. What exactly makes you so special?" He laughed like a corrupt idiot. "I was once special, but now I'm exceptional."

If only I could get my hands around his throat, I would explain it to him.

"The full force of the United States government with prejudice. WHAT do you want?"

"We'll see, Jim. Full force or not, by now, you have called in your bomb experts. They used a scope to see the pretty, flashing red light on Mrs. Wheat's chest and the phone sitting on the nightstand near the couch. My phone is set to speed dial that phone and when I do . . . poof! So, I want your very nice helicopter to set down on the street outside. Only the pilot onboard. I fly away, never to bother you again, and they live. That's my deal. Anyone, anything follows us, I make the call.

"What about my pilot?" Kane asked.

"Tell him to be a good boy, and he'll live. But your chopper dies along with its radio. The only thing he will suffer is separation anxiety. He can tell you later—much later—where we landed, but it won't do you any good. Wait for the green light on the vest."

My eyes craned to see, but I was too far away.

"Okay," Kane said.

CHAPTER 43

Harrigan's end run was magnificent, brilliant by his own standards, but also dangerous and risky. If we took him at his word, we'd get my wife and friend back unharmed, at least to the extent they were not blown up. Harrigan would get away to somewhere unharmed. Not a single drop of his blood would be spilled. I was assuming he had a stash of cash going with him.

They haven't invented a curse word to describe what I was feeling at that exact moment. No pejorative would be useful to pin on him. Creeps would find him creepy. Jack Harrigan was a study in the complete conversion of a man's soul darkened and anxious to meet its new owner. Yes, I damn him to hell. Forgiveness is out of the question, putting that thought to bed for good.

Spriggs and I craned our necks to focus on a helicopter arcing across the sky above our heads.

"Okay, Agent Spriggs, I'm mad as hell at you. You can take this thing off me now. It's over. He won. I want to be with my wife when he leaves."

"Don't be mad at me, Tobias. Kane is right. You would have walked right into a bad situation. Getting yourself killed doesn't save anybody." She took out a small key and unlocked my cuff.

"May I?"

I held out my hand for the key, indicating I would unlock her cuff. She looked into my eyes and smiled, dropping the key in the palm of my hand. We were standing at the ferry dock. I dropped the key as if it were an accident. We both bent down to retrieve it. That's when I attached my end to the metal railing running along the dock, leaving her cuff in place.

"You didn't just do that," Spriggs said, mouth agape. "Tobias, stop. Give me the key!"

I reached for the gun in her thigh holster.

"Don't do it, Tobias. There's no walking back from that."

I walked off the dock to the road that lifted into the colony. The sign said Fifth Avenue. Cute. Spriggs's voice shouting at me from the pier, squealing. Her displeasure trailed behind me. The disturbing echo made me pull the device out of my ear and let it dangle.

I headed for the helicopter. Watched it land; walked to it as I listened to the surprised voices of FBI agents and mounted police. "Stay back! Do not approach!" Nothing was going to make me stop. I kept walking, ducked beneath the rotors, and leaned against the nose, waiting for Harrigan to approach.

He came out the front door confident, carrying a duffle bag and holding his right hand high in the air to show he had a phone. His index finger less than a millimeter away from the screen. The sun glared off the chopper's front window and made Harrigan squint and use the phone as a sun protector in front of his eyes.

"Are you the pilot?" he asked.

"No, I'm the navigator. I'm here to tell you where to go."

"I don't need a navigator," he said, coming closer.

"The hell you don't." I pulled Spriggs's nine-millimeter up and pointed it at his head. "Today, you are going to the only place you deserve."

The angle of the sun shifted low in the sky. He got closer and focused on my face. "Well, if it isn't Tobias Wheat. Another would-be corpse come back to life. Well done. I must say, you both scared me a little," he said with grim sarcasm. "Now get out of my way."

"You're insane, Harrigan!"

I stood my ground and cocked the hammer on Spriggs's gun. I'm not sure if that was how it worked. I didn't check for a safety switch. I hoped the intimidation made him change his mind. Harrigan was a hardened police detective. I was sure he was able to assess danger in a person's eyes. He looked at me seriously for a moment, shrugged a laugh as though he weighed nothing but fear and desperation. He was right.

"You don't understand how this works, do you?" he said. "I push this little button on my phone and your wife and friend are no more. There's enough Centrex in the vest to take out the entire house and the one on either side." He glanced to his right and left to add impact. "Is there someone inside those cottages too? That would be bad," he said with a mocking pout.

I wanted to rip at his face.

"We couldn't be fifty feet away. You go with it when that happens."

"And you."

"I've been dead before. Just like you, all I have to do is pull this trigger and you die."

"A Mexican stand-off. Hmm. Who will blink first, Mr. Wheat? I personally have nothing else to lose. No family. No business venture, thanks to you. No home. Nothing. I might as well just push the button. You, on the other hand, have lots to lose, but I'm only guessing."

My hand trembled. I tried to stop it, but Harrigan took notice. My muscles were in mutiny with my mind and my intention to kill him. My hand dropped. The gun swung on my index finger at my side and I stepped away. Defeated. I did have too much to lose.

"Good boy, Tobias. You made a smart decision." Harrigan climbed into the cabin and commanded the pilot, "Let's go."

The chopper spun up over the water, turned northwest, and faded into a soft Canadian blue sky. So, I waited. We all waited for the vest to be deactivated; for the little red light to go out indicating Susan and Chaff were safe. I entered the cottage. Susan sat in terror, back-to-back with Chaff. Both were held in place with plastic ties, leaving deep cuts on wrists and ankles. Susan's eyes had washed out her mascara, which dripped in channels down her cheeks. Her forehead was bruised, her knees red and scraped, clothing torn in several places surrounding the vest that hung heavy on her torso.

"My God, Susan!"

She struggled to speak, but the gag made it impossible. All she could do was make muffled sounds. Her eyes widened as she shook her head hard and fast, grunting, attempting to stop me. *Was she trying to save me?* My spirit was crushed under the thought of her torment. A single FBI bomb technician came in behind me in a heavy suit and helmet. He motioned for me to leave.

I remember a moment when I was very young and I fell through the ice where the older kids played pond hockey. I held my breath and looked up. I tried to see through the blur, waiting to rise through the frozen crust into the exposure of light, wind, and fire. I heard the scraping of ice skates and the knocking of the wooden hockey sticks crashing against each other, kids screaming.

And then a much larger crashing sound exploded the water around me and released bubbles of oxygen that rose around me like a sudden snow squall. It was all beautiful and surreal. Two large hands grabbed my coat near my shoulders and dragged me up to the surface, launching me into the hands of others who were waiting to drag me to shore.

At the first wisp of wind the cold released harshly upon my senses. I shook and shivered violently. Days passed before I could feel the warmth passing within my body.

Now, standing helpless in front of my wife, all I could do was shake and shiver and wait for the hands of God to save her—*please*!

The technician took off his helmet and stepped back. He turned away and spoke into his comm. "Nothing I can do without setting this thing off; motion sensors and booby traps built into it. It's a very sophisticated job."

The tech guy turned to leave, insisting I go with him. I wasn't going anywhere. No way. Kane's voice infiltrated my ear. "Tobias, there's nothing you can do. Vacate, now. I don't want to go in there and rescue you."

"Stay back. I'm staying till the end. Thank you and your men for everything you tried to do. This is where I belong."

"I call bullshit. No one belongs there. Everyone out."

"What . . . who is this?" The voice was familiar. "Ryan? Is that you?" I said in disbelief.

"The one and only. I heard you guys needed help up here, so I took a late flight. Got here in time for the big helicopter ride."

"Agent Ryan," Kane cut in.

"Sir."

"Where the hell are you?"

"Flying a helicopter. I was giving a free ride to a bad guy. But he didn't hold on real well, dropped his phone and fell out during one of my hard right turns. Disappointed. No tip for the effort. You can let the Canadians know I'm sorry for polluting Lake Ontario."

"You're okay?" Kane asked.

"I might have a flesh wound from our little dance in the cabin, but nothing to worry about. See you on the ground."

I heard a click and turned back towards Susan. The light on her vest went green. "Holy! Green light!"

"I love saving men," Ryan said before setting her bird down near the Ward Island pier.

***

Susan and Chaff were untied and relieved of the explosive vest. The reunion brought tears to all three of us. I couldn't believe it was over. Susan put her arms around Chaff and said, "Thank you for coming to save me."

It was beautiful. A medical team arrived to take care of Susan. I found it hard to let go of her hand. I held it for just a short time before they wheeled her out on a gurney on the way to a hospital.

Another voice came through on our comms. "This is Special Agent Spriggs. Will someone please come and release me? Tobias Wheat may yet die."

Chaff slapped me on the back. "You always did have trouble making friends."

We made our way to the pier and found Special Agent Ryan talking with Kane and several of his team members, all smiles and laughter.

"It was you flying the chopper?" I asked.

"Yep. One of my many skills, Mr. Wheat." She winked at me. "I couldn't let you guys have all the fun."

"What happened up there? How did you—?"

"I would love to tell you I have superhuman powers, but it was luck, actually. He wanted me to take him to Hamilton International. I'm assuming he was leaving the country. As you all know, phones don't work in water. My original plan was to ditch the two of us, but I noticed he wasn't strapped in. We had a discussion about meeting God, then a gun battle, then an Olympic event. I would give his high dive a one, maybe a two, but the screaming was priceless."

***

Anticlimactic doesn't begin to describe the moments following. A breeze kicked up. I looked up into the sky. A storm moved in off the lake. Not threatening, rather promising that it would wash away the evil staleness of air and the dread I felt only moments before. My heart beat softly, rhythmically in my chest. The stress was all gone. My wife would be okay. Chaff would be okay. I would be okay. What a day.

The FBI changed hats and became a cleanup crew. Kane shook hands with his Canadian counterpart. The red and blue continued to flash for a while, no longer blinking at a crime scene, but flashing like a Christmas light show foreshadowing some goodness to come.

I spent the following few days in the hospital with Susan. She did great. Amazingly, she didn't let the horrible experience sour her. No doubt a smudge that would remain in her memory, but not a debilitating one.

My mother and father were frantic at first. I spent an hour on the phone explaining all that happened and why. Chaff visited us both in the hospital. I think he was now officially accepted as one of the family. He informed us that he was taking a vacation for a couple of weeks to release all the bad vibes and rejoin the world. He didn't say, but I suspected he wasn't going alone, since Agent Spriggs told me she, too, was taking a few days.

The briefcase? Yeah, still there in the deposit box. The fake case of rocks was a sleight of hand that had its effect on all parties. But for now, no one asked about the real one. No one wanted to open Pandora's box. I hope when white whiskers break out on my face, it will still be there. Contained. Unable to infect anyone. A deadly sin choked off from the world. But, I know in reality, the FBI will eventually come for it and Chaff will be glad to give it up.

Moorefield retired—again. His intelligence, his muscle, and his fidelity to two kids who should never have met will be remembered in a forever embrace of appreciation.

Yep, the Chaff and the Wheat grew together and were never to be separated.

EPILOGUE

The heavy oak door creaked open. The sound was not unexpected or bothersome, since no one bothered to notice me walking in. The light came with me and collapsed into a streak, made to wait just outside. My steps echoed along the marble. I tried to lift my heels to glide on the balls of my feet to reduce the noise. I don't know why I was self-conscious about making noise. *It didn't belong*, I told myself.

The small, round red light above the door I was to enter held me back. I had to wait. I had to prepare myself; remember all of it. Form it into an understandable language, thoughts becoming words, like osmosis: sun and water becoming oxygen. A process invisible, and spiritual, a gloom that is expelled inside a closet of darkness.

The name plaque on the door to the right said Father Romano. A person, a woman with tears, exited the small room, a tissue squeezed into her hand, held to her nose, sniffling but smiling. The door shut and the light turned green, indicating it was okay to enter.

The little room was dark as hell and the walls empty, with only a small crucifix barely visible above the screened window. I knelt on the thin, red plastic meant to be padding. My knees followed the impressions left by the previous penitent. The inner door to the window slid back.

"Bless me, Father, for I have sinned."

Excerpt Blurb

Read Excerpt

The phrase, blinded by love wasn't made up for no reason. Ethan Cross was the perpetrator who blinded me at the ripe old age of seventeen, then left me to walk right into hell. I'll kill him if I find him…

Please enjoy an excerpt from

Crimes of a Secret Nature

Available May 2023

Excerpt: Crimes of a Secret Nature

CRIMES OF A SECRET NATURE

CHAPTER 1

JAIL

1.

At nine in the morning, the bank's doors opened to an empty lobby. Ethan and I were the only customers. Not me. Him. He brought me here to show me he had money. Turns out, he didn't have money. The bank had money, and he was going to take it.

I remember the moment like chimes ringing in my head.

"Ethan, you need a withdrawal slip," I told him.

"Not this time. Alana knows me."

"The teller?"

"Yeah, we're old friends."

I laid the slip down on the counter in front of him. "Well, just in case. Here's the slip."

"I told you I don't need it."

She looked at me—Alana—like I hadn't been read into the play. I felt embarrassed, so I stepped back and paced, waiting for Ethan to finish the transaction.

Alana was the only teller. It was odd, but it was also early.

Ethan and I were going off to see the world…so romantic. I looked out the windows. Studied the cameras hung in the corners of the lobby. Twiddled my thumbs. I was never good with waiting.

I can't get those chimes to stop ringing. I laid back on my cot and squeezed my pillow into my face, trying to smother the memories. It didn't work, so I sat up and tried to arouse my cellmate.

"Marcie. Hey, Marc…you awake?" She replied with a snore; the moving bump of the mattress above me, proof that she rolled over—down for the count.

I got up and made my one-thousand and ninety-fifth mark on the wall. A little more than twenty-five-hundred days to go.

Gosh! Isn't there anything else to remember other than that day? I put the black marker under my mattress—the only contraband they would ever find during a cell check.

There are three walls, one with a toilet hanging off of it, and a barred front door to choose from. Today, I thought I would mix things up and just stare into thin air. Blot out the memory of why I'm here.

***

My mother named me Edith Marie Jewell. What was she thinking? A name for an eighty-year-old spinster. Thanks to my dad, a nickname was assigned. By age five there wasn't a soul that didn't call me Eddie. By age seventeen, I was in jail and famous among the convicts.

The twelve years between were lessons in humility, but that last year was a lesson in stupidity.

The phrase, blinded by love wasn't made up for no reason. Ethan Cross was the perpetrator who blinded me at the ripe old age of seventeen, then left me to walk right into hell. I'll kill him if I find him—an unlikely wish.

For now, I'm just pissing in the wind thinking about him. Can't do anything about it. I'm not sure I can piss in the wind, anyway.

"You got's that mean look on you's face again. What's got you?" Marcie asked, waking up.

"Aha, you're awake. I'm thinking about all the secrets that are in the world—who's holding them and what they are." I hazarded a jail-house smile.

"That's funny, Eddie. That's what is mak'n you mad? If'n all the secrets in the world is told, there'd be a lot a hush'n an ear whisper'n. It'd explode all the brains in the world."

I turned and looked up at Marcie hanging over the edge of her bunk above me. "Thanks for warning me, Marc. I think you just saved my brain."

We laughed for a good ten minutes over that exchange. That girl keeps me entertained.

The days after my name change, I thought I was special. A six-year-old wonder who didn't have any special talents or knowledge, but knew my thoughts belonged solely to myself. No one else knew what I was thinking; no one could invade my mind; and no one knew my secrets—oblivious to the other human wonders. All I knew then was that my mother always referred to me as her special little girl.

Silly that I would think of such things sitting here in my cell, but what else is there to think about? In jail, you get the past and the present—no future.

That's not entirely true. I'm here because I harbor one major mother of all secrets that resides way off in my future. Ethan Cross and the FBI want to uncover it.

Fat chance! I'll never tell them. They won't get my brain to explode.

As secrets go, their essence is a perfume that rises above the skeletons in the closet. Everyone wants to open the closet and look inside. People can smell a good secret. And secrets cannot be esteemed unless others know you have one. Most are benign: harmless caged bits of gossip, trinkets of knowledge or hidden desires attempting to avoid embarrassment, often just secrets of the heart.

Other secrets are whole mysteries, clandestine particles of knowledge that have the power to change lives, change functions, change the status quo, and even put people in prison.

I spend hours with Marcie, my cellmate—I have lots of hours—poring over my memories and giving up the secrets of my childhood. But the biggest one is still secret. The last time we spoke about secrets, it went like this:

'I've not told anyone, Marcie. Going to my grave with this one.'

'We's all got secrets, Eddie,' Marcie said. 'And we's all special. That's how God made us.'

'I suppose'

'Ain't no suppos'n. It's the truf.'

'You make my point, Marcie. I'm not any more special than you. We're both living the good life here in this luxurious cell.'

It was amusing to watch Marcie laugh. Her tummy jiggled like a bowl of jelly.

'Yeah, we's got a two bedroom, one-bath mega-home. We's rich and famous, too.'

She jiggled some more.

'How do you figure rich?'

'We don't owe no one nothing,' Marcie said. 'And in here, you is famous with the ladies for what you did.'

'Fame I could do without.'

'Tell me more about you as a little girl, Eddie.'

'Not proud of those days, Marcie. I wasn't nice.'

'Mean girls,' Marcie said. 'You one of them?'

'I was a pretender.'

'What does that mean?'

'It means that from grade to grade, the scenarios were the same, if not more intense.'

I got up and paced in a tight circle.

'Ninth grade produced shocks to the system pounding away at the force field of innocence.' I stopped to stare at the bars. 'Insults were flung into dark emotional corners that produced tears and embarrassments.'

'I don't know what any of that means,' Marcie said. 'Those words went whizz'n right by.'

Her doe eyes blinked with an innocent request for explanation.

'It means we were no longer little girls playing with dolls. We played with torturing other girls.'

'Not you, Eddie!'

I pulled my legs up to my chest and held them in place with my arms, resting my chin between my knees. My eyes strained for something through the cell bars.

'I can’t tell you more right now, Marcie. My past haunts me when I think of it.'

'Secrets of da past can haunt you good,' Marcie said. “Depends on what part of da past you dig’n up.”

Marcie was right. The past definitely haunts me. Particular parts more than others. Tears formed over the stark view between steel bars, provoking the mind to shame. In my school years, I had surrendered my pride and sense of common decency to avoid being a target of mean girls. Being a player in both teams was my internal struggle and one of my secrets.

By the time my fourteenth birthday rolled around, I realized so many others, like me, were special, which meant none of us were special. We gossiped. Competed. Whispered our secrets. Formed alliances, and sneered at anyone who was smarter, and laughed at anyone who wasn’t exactly like us—the special ones. If you were pretty, we made you the leader. If you were clever, you were the lieutenant leader. Popularity grew out of these two characteristics.

Not pretty, nor clever; afraid of shrinking into invisibility? The solution was simple: keep cheering on the leader and sneer and laugh on their behalf.

Thus, pretender.

Marcie reached down from her perch and stroked my hair. “Don’t you be all sad, girl. Nobody go’n to judge no more.”

“I know, Marcie. Thank you for that. It’s just that being here makes you think about how you got here.”

“You knows how you got here, girl. You robbed that bank.”

“It’s not as simple as that. I was referring to my whole life. Don’t you think about your past life before you got sent off to jail?”

“Well, I is a bunch of years ahead of you, being here nearly ten years and all. You here only three of them. I’ve had lots of time to forget most everything and everyone before they gave me this pretty orange suit I’m wear’n.”

“They didn’t spend much time shopping for us, did they? I have one just like it. We look like motorcycle chicks.”

“They got a whole prison of motorcycle chicks,” she said. "Uh-huh...that's right."

Marcie’s laugh sounded like she had the hiccups. When we stopped laughing, I told her that she looked pretty in orange.

“No one in here as pretty as you, Eddie. You got’s that nice brown hair with that natural streak of white, and you’s got that pretty face, and under that orange suit, you got's a body curved in the most pleas'n way. Too bad they're no men 'round to admire it. You's perfect far's I can see."

"Oh, I got admired alright. And that didn't work out too well. Look where I am now."

"That man's admiration ain't worf noth'n. Forget him."

Marcie was a genuine beauty as far as I was concerned. Everything on the inside was pure and honest. Outside, she was a plump cutie with sparkly eyes and soft flawless brown skin that made me jealous.

Prison sanity is a fragile mental state. Marcie's friendship kept my mind balanced and protected from faltering over the edge of loneliness. The odd truth about Marcie is her hidden intelligence. One of the guards told me her file says she has an IQ north of one-twenty, but she speaks like she's never seen the inside of a book. She's a genuine riddle I haven't been able to solve. Her secret I guess.

About the Author

Michael A. Durney lives with his wife, Linda, in North Carolina where he enjoys the glorious mountains, lakes and streams, old towns, and city life where his characters reside.

The Murder of Tobias Wheat is his fifth published work. Although, not a *# 1 New York Times best* seller—yet, he is hopeful that readers enjoy these stories, tell their friends, and help launch a new writing career. Please consider leaving a review.

He and his wife wait happily for the frequent visits from their four adult children and their seven grandchildren. Until then, a glass of wine, a little music, and another story in the making. Cheers!

Made in the USA
Columbia, SC
29 March 2023